"VIVA GRIMES!"

"Comrades!" she cried in her deep contralto. "Comrades! I present to you our new Governor, John Grimes. The Federation, this time, has made a wise choice. John Grimes is a man of action. John Grimes is a man of the world, of many worlds, who knows that each and every planet has its own character. He knows that we, here on Liberia, have our own character. He knows that we have opened our world and our hearts to the poor, the distressed and the oppressed of many planets. There are people here, our guests, who, were it not for us, would be living lives of deepest misery—or who would not be living at all.

"Governor John Grimes will appreciate what we have done, what we are doing. . . ."

Grimes' punishment for space piracy was to be made governor of a planet of anarchists . . . and punishment it was!

DBM

THE ANARCH LORDS

A. Bertram Chandler

DAW BOOKS, INC.
DONALD A. WOLLHEIM, PUBLISHER
1633 Broadway, New York, N.Y. 10019

Cover art and frontispiece by David B. Mattingly.

DEDICATION

For Vice-Admiral William Bligh R.N., one-time commanding Officer of the H.M.S. *Bounty*, one-time Governor of New South Wales, with belated apologies for the participation of an ancestral Grimes in the Rum Rebellion of 1808 A.D.

FIRST PRINTING, SEPTEMBER 1981

1 2 3 4 5 6 7 8 9

PRINTED IN U.S.A

Chapter 1

"You got off lightly, Grimes," said Rear Admiral Damien.

Grimes's prominent ears flushed angrily as he scowled at the older man across the vast, gleaming surface of the desk, uncluttered save for telephone, read-out screen and the thick folder that must contain, among other documents relating to himself, a transcript of the proceedings of the recent Court of Inquiry.

"You got off lightly, Grimes," Damien repeated.

His elbows on the desk, the tips of his steepled, skeletal fingers propping his great beak of a nose, he stared severely at the owner and erstwhile master of the star tramp (the privateer, the pirate) *Sister Sue*. Grimes thought irreverently, *If it weren't for that schnozzle his face would look just like a skull . . . Come to that, his uniform tailor must use a skeleton for his dummy . . .*

Briefly he entertained the ludicrous vision of a spidery tailorbot, fussily measuring and recording, scuttling around and over an assemblage of dry, articulated bones.

He grinned.

"What are you thinking, Grimes?" demanded Damien sharply.

"Nothing, sir."

"Ha. Of course. Nothing that you'd dare to tell me, you mean. May I remind you that the crime of Dumb Insolence, with its penalties, is still listed in Survey Service Regulations despite all the efforts of the Human Rights League to have it removed? And even though your Master Astronaut's Certificate of Competency was suspended by the court you still hold your Survey Service Reserve commission. And you have not yet been released from Active Duty."

"I was under the impression, sir," said Grimes stiffly, "that my Reserve Officer's commission was a secret."

"Was—and is. But *I* know your status. I can still throw the book at you if I feel like it." Then Damien allowed himself a grin and, briefly, looked almost genial. "But I didn't send for you so that I could haul you over the coals, although it has been like old times, hasn't it?" (That grin, Grimes decided, had become wolfish.) "Officially I'm supposed to be conducting a little inquiry of my own. The safe passage of merchant shipping is among my responsibilities—so, quite naturally, I'm interested in such activities as privateering. And piracy. But I already have your confidential report. And Mayhew's. I know what really happened—which is more than can be said for Lord Justice Kirby and his assessors, or for the boarding party that brought your ship in under arrest. That ex-girlfriend of yours—or not so 'ex'—did a good job of brainwashing your officers. My people thought that the apparatus she brought aboard *Sister Sue* was just an aid to interrogation, not for the implantation of false memories."

Damien laughed. "And it was a good story that the witnesses told the court, wasn't it? The wicked Kate Connellan and the even wickeder Countess of Walshingham seizing the ship at gunpoint and forcing you to embark upon a career of piracy . . . But somebody had to carry the can back. They didn't survive—and you did."

He opened the thick folder, found the right page. "And what did that old fogey Kirby say? Ah, here we are. 'Nonetheless I am of the strong opinion that the master, John Grimes, was not entirely blameless. He deliberately set his feet onto the downward path into violent crime when he placed his ship, his people and himself at the service of the notorious Commodore Baron Kane, as he is now known. John Grimes should have pondered the truth of the old adage, *He who sups with the devil needs a long spoon.* But John Grimes was like too many in this decadent day and age, money hungry. Had his avarice put only himself at risk I should not think so hardly of him—but all of his crew, merchant spacemen and women, ignorant of the arts—if they may so be called—of war, were compelled, willy nilly, to share the perils to which their captain had deliberatly exposed himself, persuaded by him that privateering is no risk and all profit . . .' Sanctimonious old swine, isn't he? 'And some of his crew whom he deluded were not even experienced spacemen. His engineering officers, for example, young men recruited from industry and the Halls of Academe on the world of Austral, true innocents abroad . . .' "

"Those bastards!" exploded Grimes. "*They* were with the Green Hornet and Wally!"

"I know, I know. But they don't, not now. They have that fine set of false memories. They're little, woolly, innocent lambs, all of them, in their own minds, and in old Kirby's mind." He switched to his imitation of the judge's voice. " 'It is obvious to me that John Grimes is unfit to hold command. I have considered the cancellation of his qualifications but have decided to temper justice with mercy, hoping that in the fullness of time he may come to see the error of his ways. Therefore I order that his Certificate of Competency be suspended for a period of ten Standard Years.' "

"And what am I supposed to be doing with myself for all that time?" asked Grimes.

"You still have your ship. We released her to you. We'll see that she finds employment. I've no doubt that your mate—your ex-mate, rather—will make quite a good master . . ."

"While I sit and sulk in the owner's suite when I'm not getting into his hair. No, sir. That wouldn't be fair to Billy Williams. Come to that, it wouldn't be fair to me. It'd be worse than just being an ordinary passenger." He got to his feet, began to pace up and down. He pulled his pipe from a pocket of his civilian slacks, filled and lit it. He said, speaking through an eruption of acrid fumes, "I think that the Service should do something for me in the way of employment."

"I didn't give you permission to smoke, Grimes. Oh, all right, all right. Carry on asphyxiating yourself. As far as the universe knows you're a civilian shipmaster—ex-shipmaster, rather—and I have no jurisdiction over you. *But* you're still on pay, captain's salary. We'll not let you starve even if *Sister Sue*'s running at a loss."

"Thank you, sir. I'll not hurt your feelings by refusing my pay. I've earned it. But I want to be *doing* something."

"Why don't you write a book, Grimes? Your autobiography should make fascinating reading."

"And would the Survey Service provide legal defense if I were sued for libel? And if such a case were heard by Lord Justice Kirby the best lawyers in the universe couldn't save me."

Damien laughed. "All right, all right. If you wrote the book I'd probably be among those screaming libel. Now, Grimes, sit down and listen. I sent for you so that I could sound you out. I've an offer to make that I'd not be making if you'd indicated that you'd be quite happy bumbling around in that rustbucket of yours even if not in command of her.

"Have you ever heard of Liberia?"

"In Africa?"

"No. Not the province. The planet. The colony."

"Oh. *That* Liberia. Founded by a bunch of freedom-loving anarchists during the days of the gaussjammers. I've heard about it but I've never been there."

"How would you like to go?"

"Doing what? Or as what?"

"As Governor."

Chapter 2

"You have to be joking," said Grimes at last.

"I'm serious," Damien told him.

"Then this is another piece of dirty work for you."

"On the contrary, Grimes. If you take the job it will be in the nature of a clean-up operation."

"That sounds even worse. Sir."

"Grimes, Grimes, you have a suspicious mind."

"With very good reason."

"Do you want the job, or don't you?"

"Tell me about it first," Grimes said.

"Very well. Liberia is a Federated Planet but not now fully

autonomous. I'll not bore you with a detailed history; you'll be able to read it up before you are installed in the Governor's Lodge. Suffice it to say that the original colonists, the idealistic Anarchists, after a bad start during which their settlement almost perished, became devotees of the goddess Laura Norder . . ." (*I'd better laugh*, thought Grimes, *to keep the old bastard in a good mood.*) "Their numbers increased and eventually they were able to exercise control over their environment. There was a resurgence of Anarchism and armed revolt against the authorities. The president—he was more of a dictator, actually—appealed for help to the Federation. After the mess had been more or less cleaned up it was decided that the Liberians would be far happier if governed by an outsider, somebody whom everybody, right, left and center, could hate. So now there's an elected president who, in effect, just does what the Earth-appointed governor tells him.

"Liberia is an agricultural planet. When it was first settled it was little more than a mudball crawling with primitive yet motile plant life. Now it is all, or almost all, wheatfields and beanfields and orchards. It has been called the granary of the Shaula Sector. There is only light, very light industry. In the past all heavy agricultural machinery has had to be imported. Now, as such equipment wears out it is not replaced."

"So they have their own factories?" asked Grimes.

"No. They're getting away from the use of machinery. They're using manpower."

"They must be gluttons for hard work."

"They're not. They import their labor."

"But who would ever emigrate to such a world, to sweat in the fields?"

"Quite a few, Grimes. Quite a few—although I doubt if they were expecting what they got. Have you ever wondered what happens to all the refugees? There was the so-called Holy War on Iranda, sect against sect. The losers—those of them who had not been slaughtered—were evicted. They were evacuated by Survey Service transports. Liberia, very nobly, offered to give a new home to those hapless people. And do you remember when the New Canton sun went nova?"

"Before my time," said Grimes. "But I've read about it."

"A large number of the New Cantonese finished up on Liberia," Damien said. "Wars, revolutions, natural disasters—all have contributed to the build-up of Liberia's vast pool of slave labor."

"Slave labor?"

"It's not called that, of course. It's indentured labor. It's got to the stage where the Liberians need no longer import expensive machines. It's got to the stage where they're pampered aristocrats, waited on hand and foot. (I wonder what their anarchistic ancestors would have thought!) The real ruler of the planet is not the governor, or the president, but the commanding officer of the peace-keeping force, Colonel Bardon, Terran Army. He's got the president eating out of his hand."

"And the governor?"

"The last governor—your predecessor?—met with an accident. It seems that he tried to put a stop to many of the abuses. The military didn't like it. His aircraft crashed when he was on the way to investigate conditions at one of the orchards. The Board of Inquiry decided that the disaster—killing the governor, his wife and his personal pilot—was attributable to pilot error."

"A not uncommon cause of such disasters, sir."

"The Board of Inquiry, Grimes, consisted of Major Timms, Captain Vinor and Lieutenant Delaney, all of them Bardon's officers. And there were witnesses who saw the aircraft—a helium-filled blimp with electric motors—explode and come down in flaming fragments."

"Oh. I'm surprised that they, too, didn't meet with accidents."

"Most of them did. The one who didn't managed to stow away aboard a bulk carrier and make it to New Maine. He told his story to our Sub-Base Commander there, who passed it on to Survey Service Intelligence."

"Then why isn't this Colonel Bardon relieved of his command?"

"Politics, Grimes. Politics. For quite some time now the Army has been the Lord Protector's pet. For some reason he despises the Survey Service. And Field Marshal von Tempsky refuses to believe anything bad about any of his people, especially when the complaint is laid by us. Nonetheless, it's a known fact that the Army sweeps all its misfits and bad bastards under the mat by shipping them off to outworld garrison duties."

"And the Survey Service is doing the same, sir?"

Damien chuckled. "You're a misfit, Grimes, but even I wouldn't call you a bad bastard. Your forte has always been giving bad bastards what they deserve. People like Colonel Bardon, for example. . . ."

"So you want me to become governor of Liberia so that I can put a spoke in Bardon's wheel?"

"You could put it that way."

"But since when, sir, has the Survey Service been appointing colonial governors?"

"A good question, Grimes. We never have done so. But the Protector of the Colonies—Bendeen—is a friend of mine. We were midshipmen together. He got as high as lieutenant commander, then married into a political family. Not long after he resigned his commission and went into politics himself. His wife's family found a safe seat for him and he was elected to the Assembly. Surprisingly, despite his idealism and an honesty more typical of spacemen than politicians, he attained ministerial rank. He has his sights set on the Lord Protectorship but I don't think he'll make it. He tramples on too many corns."

"And he wants to trample on Field Marshal von Tempsky's corns?"

"Yes. And those of the Cereal Consortium. He hasn't forgiven them for the engineered famine on Damboon, which resulted in the downfall of the Free Democrat regime."

"Mphm." Grimes knocked out his pipe in Damien's wastepaper disposer, refilled and lit it. "Mphm. So I'm supposed to be Protector Bendeen's cat's paw. If I take the job, that is. . . ."

"You could put it that way, Grimes."

"Mphm. But won't it look fishy? A Survey Service dropout, a master astronaut who's lost his ticket after a widely publicized inquiry, appointed to a governorship. . . . Won't there be questions asked, in the World Assembly, by the media, on every streetcorner?"

"Our rumor factory will be working overtime, Grimes. The El Dorado Corporation has its tentacles everywhere. It will be hinted that El Dorado is behind the appointment, that highly placed people on that world are pulling strings to find a soft, highly paid job for a man who was one of their officers, a Company Commodore, and who served them to the best of his ability. Bendeen will try to convey the impression that your appointment is not one that he would have made of his own free will."

"You should have become a politician yourself, sir."

"Whatever makes you think that I didn't?" asked the Rear Admiral.

Chapter 3

Grimes watched *Sister Sue* lift off from Port Woomera.

He stood there, on the stained and scarred concrete of the commercial spaceport apron, staring up at the dull-gleaming spindle that was the ship—*his* ship—climbing steadily until it was no more than a speck in the cloudless blue sky, listening to the cacaphony of the inertial drive until it was no more than a faint, irritable mutter. And then the sky was empty and the only noises were those normal to a working spaceport at ground level—the whining of motors, the occasional clank and rattle from conveyor belts and gantries, now and again a shouted order.

Williams would do all right, he thought, despite his initial diffidence, even though the ex-Mate had made it plain that he had hoped that Grimes would be along in an advisory capacity.

("The old ship won't be the same without you, skipper," he had said. Then, "I'll look after her for you. You'll be back. I know you will." And Grimes had thought, *But ten years is a long time*.)

And now *Sister Sue* was up and away, outbound for Caribbea with a cargo of manufactured goods, everything from robotutors to robutterflies, the beautiful little devices that had been developed to deal, lethally and expeditiously, with flying insect pests. (They would sell well enough, Grimes thought, while the craze lasted.) Her discharge completed she would go on Time Charter to the Interstellar Transport Commission, carrying anything and everything anywhere and everywhere.

At least, thought Grimes, Williams had a good crew. Magda Granadu was still Catering Officer/Purser and the two old-timers, Crumley and Stewart, were still Reaction Drive Chief and Radio Officer respectively. The other engineers, Reaction Drive and Mannschenn Drive, were *real* space engineers, not refugees from universities and bicycle shops. (Their predecessors, together with their false memories, had been given passage back to Austral.) The Chief, Second and Third Officers were all young, properly qualified and actually employees of the Commission which, by the terms of the charter party, was required to supply necessary personnel.

So that was that.

Ex-Captain Grimes, ex-Company Commodore Grimes, soon-to-be-Governor Grimes climbed into the ground car that had been waiting to take him to the airport from where he would fly to Alice Springs to spend a few days with his parents before leaving for Liberia.

They met him in the waiting room at the base of the mooring mast.

Grimes senior, a tall, white-haired old man, greeted his son with enthusiasm. "I envy you, John," he said. "I really do. I just write about adventures; you have them!"

Matilda Grimes—also tall, red-haired and pleasantly horse-faced—frowned disapprovingly. "Don't encourage him, George. Ever since he left the Survey Service he's been doing nothing but getting into trouble. I hoped to see him become an admiral one day. I never dreamed that he'd become a pirate." She turned on her son. "And what do you intend to do now, John? You've had your Certificate taken from you . . ."

"Only suspended," said her husband.

She ignored this. "You'll never command a ship again, not even a merchant vessel. And after that trial. . . ."

"Court of Inquiry, my dear."

". . . nobody will ever employ you."

"As a matter of fact, Matilda," Grimes said, "I shall shortly be going out to take up a new appointment."

"*What*!"

"What as?" asked Grimes's father.

"Governor, as a matter of fact. Of Liberia."

"I've always thought," said his mother, "that the standard of intelligence in the World Assembly is appallingly low. Now I am sure of it. And I've never trusted Bendeen. Any man who would give up a career in the Survey Service for one in politics must have something wrong with him. Appointing a pirate as governor. . . ."

"There are precedents," said George Whitley Grimes. "Sir Henry Morgan, for example." He realized that the other people in the lounge were looking curiously at the small family party and said, "I suggest that we continue this discussion at home."

The robutler brought in drinks. *The Old Man must be doing well*, thought Grimes. The machine was one of the very latest models, a beautifully proportioned and softly gleaming cylinder moving on silent treads rather than something unconvincingly humanoid. From a circular port midway up the thing's body a sinuous tentacle produced the drinks ordered—dry sherry, chilled, for Matilda Grimes, a pink gin for Grimes and beer for his father. A dish of assorted nuts, placed on the coffee table, followed.

"Here's to crime," toasted George Whitley Grimes, raising his glass.

"I'll not drink to that!" snapped his wife. Nonetheless she gulped rather than sipped from hers.

Grimes sampled his pink gin. He could not have mixed a better one himself.

He said, "You seem very prosperous, George."

"Yes. It was that *If Of History* novel."

"The Ned Kelly idea that you were telling me about the last time that I was here?"

"No. The one after that, based on the Australian Constitutional Crisis. *If* Gough Whitlam, the Prime Minister, had refused to relinquish office after the Governor General fired him. . . ."

"Don't go putting ideas into his head," admonished Matilda.

"The last time that he was here the pair of you talked about privateering and piracy—and look what happened! The next thing we hear will be that he's fired the President of Liberia!"

"Perhaps I shall," murmured Grimes. "Perhaps I shall. . . ."

His father looked at him intently over the rim of his condensation-beaded glass. He said softly, "Tell me, John, did you really leave the Survey Service?"

"I did."

"Did they call you back?"

"Did they?" pressed his mother, suddenly alert.

It was useless, he knew, to try to lie to her.

He said, "No comment."

"And isn't it true," his father went on, "that after your piratical antics a bill was pushed through the Assembly making privateering illegal anywhere in the Federation of Worlds?"

"You read, watch and listen to the media, George."

"I do. And there have been some nasty rumors recently about Liberia. But you can't tell us anything, can you?"

"I can't. And I think that you'd both be wise to keep your suspicions to yourself."

"We shall," promised his father. "But I shall be tempted, mind you, to give them an airing in a novel."

"Please don't. The El Dorado Corporation might add two and two to make five and then be after my blood."

"All right." The older man finished his beer and, ignoring his wife's frown, demanded a refill from the robutler. "And now, young John, I am going to put an idea into your head—one that even Matilda will approve of. You're really a spaceman, aren't you? That's all you want to be, ever will want to be. And you don't want to wait ten years to get your Certificate back—especially when you've a ship of your own of which you should be the captain. You'll be governor, of a world called Liberia. When in Liberia do as the original Liberians did. . . ."

He talked, drawing upon his historical knowledge.

Grimes listened intently, as did his mother.

When his father was finished Grimes grinned happily. "It could work," he said. "By all the Odd Gods, I'll make it work!"

"But you will have to finish the job that you're being sent out to do," said his mother, frowning worriedly. "You'll have to finish that job first."

"Of course," Grimes assured her. "Of course."

Chapter 4

Grimes took one of the regular airships to Sydney and then a ramjet to New York. The World Assembly was housed in the old UN Building which, miraculously, had survived all the troubles that had plagued the city since the United Nations had taken up residence there. Staring down at Manhattan as the jet descended to the airport Grimes wondered what it had looked like during the days of its glory. He had seen photographs, of course, but would have liked to have been able to recognize, in actuality, such fabled towers as the Empire State and World Trade Buildings; the ornamental lakes that occupied their sites were all very well but, from the air, were no more than irregular puddles of blue water. But there was Brooklyn Bridge, rebuilt only recently to the old design. And that must be the Chrysler Building. . . . It was too bad that this was to be a brief business visit only.

An official World Assembly car was waiting for him and whisked him swiftly to the Assembly's headquarters. He was expected there; a young officer in a smart, sky-blue uniform escorted him along moving ways and up escalators, delivered him to the office of the Protector of the Colonies.

Bendeen—a slim man, not overly tall, gray-haired and with a heavily lined face—came from behind his littered desk to greet Grimes. The WA lieutenant withdrew and the door automatically closed behind him.

"So you're the famous—or notorious—Grimes," said Bendeen. "All right. You can admit it. This office is bugproof—or so the experts loaned to me by Rear Admiral Damien assure me. We can talk. Officially, as you may have learned, I was pressured into finding you a job. In actuality you were strongly recommended to me by the Rear Admiral. Drink?" What Grimes had taken for just another filing cabinet detached itself from the wall, rolled up to them on silent casters. A tray was extruded from it; on it were two glasses of what looked like pink gin. "As you see, Governor, I share your taste in tipples. Your very good health."

"And yours, Protector," Grimes replied.

(His father's robutler, Grimes thought, was much better at mixing drinks than this thing of Bendeen's.)

"You're booked out, Grimes, on *Sobraon*. The VIP suite, of course. She lifts from Port Woomera tomorrow so that means another ramjet flight for you. Can't say that I envy you. I hate those things. If God had meant us to fly He'd have given us an ample supply of non-flammable, lighter-than-air gas. Which, of course, He did. But where was I? Oh, yes. Your commission as Governor. It's on the desk somewhere. Ah, here it is. A splendid example of the engraver's art with eagles and dragons and hammers and sickles and lions and unicorns and hammers and sickles and rising suns and . . . oh, yes, emus and kangaroos all over it. And the Grand Seal of the Assembly. No not a *seal*, but a seal. Red wax, you know. And your name, in Gothic script. It'll look fine when you have it framed on the wall of your gubernatorial office. . . ."

"Isn't there any sort of swearing in ceremony?" asked Grimes, at last getting a word in edgewise.

"You'll have to wait until Libertad—that's the capital of Liberia—for that. I'm told that the president likes to put on shows to impress the oppressed masses. And they are oppressed, you know. Not only is there the hard, manual work for precious little pay but there're all the lucrative rackets indulged in by Bardon's boys. I don't know what Bardon's got on von Tempsky but, as far as VT is concerned, the colonel can do no wrong. I've tried to have him replaced but the Field Marshal piles on more Gs with the Lord Protector than I do. So I'm relying on you to catch Bardon with his hand in the till—or in the pocket of one of the indentured laborers. From what Damien has told me about you you're used to playing by ear. And you're a sort of catalyst. Things sort of happen all around you and, more often than not, you turn them to your advantage.

"There's a case waiting for you at the airport with plenty of light reading for your voyage—spools and spools of it. The VIP suite, of course, has a playmaster. You'll get a good idea of the world you're going to—history from the first settlement to the present. And now, finish your drink. The car's waiting to take us out to Kennedy. Don't forget the commission—there's a case for it somewhere. Ah, here . . ."

They emerged from the Protector's office into the corridor. Bendeen's manner changed, became stiff, hostile even. He said, as they passed through the door, ". . . this appointment was none of my choosing. But you are now the Governor—until such time as you are relieved."

Which will not be soon enough, implied the Protector's expression.

Grimes took the hint. This corridor must be well covered by audio-visual bugs. He kept his distance from the Protector, set his face into sullen lines. The two men maintained their charade until they shook hands, with a marked lack of enthusiasm, at the airport and Grimes boarded the ramjet for Woomera.

Chapter 5

The master of the Trans-Galactic Clipper *Sobraon* was well-accustomed to the carriage of Very Important Passengers and to playing the urbane and courteous host. VIPs who were also ex-pirates were, however, outside his normal experience. He had heard of Grimes—who among the spacefaring community had not?—and had never been among his admirers. Even as a small boy he had not considered pirates and privateers glamorous; as a shipmaster he regarded them as vicious and dangerous criminals. When he had been shown his passenger list for the forthcoming voyage, with the names of those worthy of special attention marked with a star, he had stared at it incredulously.

"Not *the* Grimes?" he had demanded of his purser.

"I'm afraid so, sir," she had replied.

"But . . . A *governor* . . . Can't you be mistaken, Liz? Surely there must be more than one John Grimes in this universe."

"Not with jug handle ears. His photograph was among all the others in the Security parcel."

"But he was on trial for piracy."

"A Court of Inquiry, sir, not a trial."

"Even so, he had his Certificate dealt with. The judge and the assessors must have thought that he was guilty of something. And with good reason. And am I supposed to have him at my table?"

"With all the other VIPs." She grinned. "At least he'll be less boring than the others."

He scowled at her. "The man's a pirate, with blood on his hands. Get this straight, Liz, I don't want you and your tabbies fawning on him as though he were the latest tridi heart-throb. All that concerns us is that we're to deliver him from Port Woomera to Port Libertad with celerity and enjoying a far greater standard of luxury than he deserves. If I had *my* way I'd put him in one of the J Deck dogboxes!"

"You still could, sir. You're the master."

"Ha! And how long should I stay in one of the Line's senior ships if I did that? He must be treated correctly, Liz—with *icy* correctness. Convey subtly that any respect accorded to him is to his rank, not to himself. But subtly, Liz, subtly. Perfect service—but without the personal touch. The liquid hydrogen hand in the velvet glove . . ."

"Is velvet a good insulator, sir?"

"How the hell should I know? That will do, Liz; you've plenty to look after."

When the girl was gone he rang for his chief officer and then issued to that gentleman instructions as to how the VIP was to be treated.

Sobraon lifted from Port Woomera, slowly at first and then with increasing velocity as the thrust of her inertial drive built up. Grimes was a guest in the liner's control room, such courtesy often being extended to senior astronauts traveling as passengers and to civilian VIPs. He strongly suspected that the invitation had been extended to him in the second capacity. He looked out through the viewports at the fast receding scenery—to one side the semi-desert with its green rectangles of irrigated land, crisscrossed with silvery canals, to the other the dark sea with, far to the southward, the white glimmer of the Antarctic ice barrier. Twice recently he had been on Earth, he thought, and on neither occasion had he paid a visit to the Space Academy in Antarctica. The first time he might have done so, as a graduate who, despite the circumstances of his resignation from the Survey Service, was now a successful shipowner. On the second occasion it might not have been politic. A privateer-turned-pirate would hardly have been regarded by the Commandant as an Old Boy whose career should be emulated by the cadets.

He heard one of the officers whispering to another, "I wonder what he's thinking about? Is he working out how he could skyjack the ship?"

He looked around to see who it was.

It must have been Kelner, the liner's chief officer, who flushed and turned away hastily as Grimes's eye caught his. The ponderously portly Captain Harringby must, too, have heard that whisper—but the expression on his heavy face was approving rather than otherwise. Then the shipmaster looked at Grimes who, although no telepath, could tell what he was thinking. *I invited you up here only because Company Regulations require that I give you the VIP treatment. But I don't have to like you.*

Grimes shrugged. So he was *persona non grata*. So what? It was not for the first time in his life, almost certainly would not be for the last. He would stick it out, seated stolidly in the spare chair. He would, after trajectory had been set, graciously accept the invitation, no matter how grudgingly offered, to partake of the ritual drink with the captain and his senior officers. Throughout the voyage to Liberia he would be the very model of a modern Governor General. (*All right, all right*, he told himself irritably, *I know that it should be Major General and, in any case, I'm only a Governor*. He looked at Harringby, smugly omnipotent in his command chair, and thought, *And I'd sooner be a shipmaster again*.)

* * *

Trajectory was set (competently enough, Grimes admitted) and *Sobraon* was falling down the warped continuum on the first leg of her passage, Earth to Liberia. (This was, actually, no more than a deviation; Trans-Galactic Clippers specialized in carrying rich passengers around the truly glamorous worlds of the Galaxy—to Caribbea, with its warm seas and lush, tropical islands, to Atlantia for the big game fishing and the ocean yacht races, to Morrowvia, with its exotic cat people, to New Venusberg, with its entertainments to suit all warped tastes, to Waverley, with its reconstruction of a Scottish culture that owed more to myth than to actual history, to Electra, where those of a scientific bent could feast their eyes on the latest marvels.)

Trajectory was set, the powerful gyroscopes pulling the ship around her axes until the target star was ahead, then making the necessary adjustment for galactic drift. (Grimes flexed his idle hands on the arm rests of his chair; for so long he had been doing what Captain Harringby was doing now; it seemed—it was!—all wrong that he was no longer doing it.) The Mannschenn Drive was actuated. Deep in the bowels of the great ship the rotors began to turn, to spin, to precess, to tumble down and through the warped dimensions as the temporal precession field built up.

There was the usual brief disorientation, the transient nausea and, for Grimes at least, a flash of prevision.

He saw, as plainly as if she had been standing there in person, one of his fellow privateers, Captain Agatha Prinn of the star tramp *Agatha's Ark*. She was dressed—how else?—in her uniform of severely cut, short-skirted business suit, gray, with minimal trimmings of gold braid. She was holding a paper bag. She dropped it. It burst when it hit the ground, releasing a cloud of fine, white powder. . . .

Colors, perspective and sounds snapped back to normal.

Grimes blinked, found that he was staring out of a viewport to an interstellar night in which the stars were no longer bright points of unwinking light but were amorphous nebulae.

Agatha Prinn and a flour bomb? he wondered. *What the hell was all* that *about?*

He realized that Captain Harringby was addressing him.

"Your Excellency," (but that's *me*! thought Grimes) "we

are now on trajectory. Would you care to join me for liquid refreshment before lunch?''

It would make the old bastard's day if I said no, Grimes told himself.

''Thank you, Captain,'' he said as he unbuckled himself from his seat.

Chapter 6

It was a peculiar voyage, not altogether unpleasant, with its mixture of ostracism and adulation and downright pampering. Governor Grimes took his meals at the captain's table—and Captain Harringby, presiding over this lavish board, accorded the governor the respect due to him while making it plain that he did not approve of Commodore Grimes, the pirate chief. Now and again he permitted himself a flash of unkind humor, such as when the wine stewardess was dispensing a vintage Burgundy to accompany the roast beef. ''I suppose, Your Excellency, that you must, now and again, have acquired some very fine wines among your other . . . er . . . loot?''

''The Hallichecki,'' Grimes had replied stiffly, ''do not use alcohol.'' He added, after sipping from his glass, ''My privateering operations were against the shipping of the Hegemony.''

''But didn't you seize a Terran ship? One of the Commission's liners?''

''That happened after a mutiny, Captain. It all came out at the Court of Inquiry.'' He added, ''And, in any case, the attempted piracy was unsuccessful.''

The others at the table were looking at him, some with disapproval and contempt, others with what was almost admiration. There was the fat Joachim Levy, one of the Dog Star Line's managers taking his Long Service Leave and bound for New Venusberg. He pursed his thick lips, then said, ''*Our* ships are used to coping with piracy. When necessary they are armed—and their crews know how to use their weapons."

"I know," Grimes told him. "My Mate was ex-Dog Star Line. He was a very good gunnery officer."

Levy scowled and the plump, artificially blonde Mrs. Levy laughed. "So all the drills that the Dog Star Line officers have to go through are some use after all!" She smiled quite prettily at Grimes. "But wasn't it *fun*, Your Excellency? Sailing the seas of space with the Jolly Roger at the masthead and a cutlass clenched between your teeth?"

"Mphm," grunted Grimes.

"In the *good* old days," said Ivor Sandorsen, who was a Lloyd's underwriter, "you would have been hanged from your own yardarm, Your Excellency."

"As a matter of fact," said Grimes, "one of my ancestors was."

"Thus establishing a precedent."

"Another, better known, pirate," said Grimes, "established another precedent. Sir Henry Morgan. He became a governor."

"Had Lloyd's been in existence in those days, sir, he would have paid the just penalty for his crimes."

"In any case," said Harringby with a superior smile, "I think that His Excellency will admit that the governorship of Liberia is hardly a plum as such appointments go. More of a rotten apple, perhaps."

"Have you been there, Captain?" asked Mrs. Levy, who seemed to have appointed herself Grimes's champion.

"No, madam. Nor do I want to. I shall place my ship in orbit about that world and a tender will rendezvous to pick up His Excellency. Then I shall be on my way."

"Rejoicing?" asked Grimes.

"I shall most certainly not be weeping."

"And you, Your Excellency," asked Dorothea Taine, tall, dark, intense, author of a best seller which Grimes's father had scornfully dismissed as *Womens' Weekly* rubbish, "will you be weeping or rejoicing?"

"That remains to be seen," Grimes told her.

"Sir—Your Excellency, I mean—what's it really like being a pirate? Sorry. A privateer. . . ."

The young Fifth Officer made his diffident approach to

Grimes as he was just dismounting from one of the exercise bicycles in the liner's gymnasium.

"There are better and safer ways of earning a living," Grimes said.

"Safer, perhaps, sir. But . . . Would you know if Commodore Kane is still trying to find volunteers for his privateer fleet?"

"Drongo Kane is better stayed away from. In any case, as you must have heard, the Survey Service is smacking down on all privateering operations."

"Mr. Barray!" The Chief Officer had just come into the gymnasium for his own exercise session. "Here you are. I thought that you were supposed to be checking the equipment in your lifeboat."

"I . . . I've finished that, sir. It's all in order."

"Then find Mr. McGurr and lend him a hand in hydroponics. This is his tank cleaning day."

Crestfallen, the young man left the gym. Shedding his robe and, clad only in trunks, the Chief Officer mounted the bicycle that Grimes had vacated. As he started to pedal he said, "Even you, Your Excellency, must know that young men often evince enthusiasm for the most unworthy people and causes."

"Are you implying that I'm unworthy, Mr. Kelner?"

"I never said so, Your Excellency."

"I can *use* you, Your Excellency. Or may I call you John? After all, I know your father; I've met him at Australian Society of Authors meetings . . ."

Grimes looked at Dorothea Taine over his coffee cup. He was taking this midmorning refreshment in the lounge; he did not see why he should be confined to his quarters, luxurious though they were, even though he was something of a social leper.

"Use me?" he asked.

The writer smiled. Her teeth were too large for her small mouth. The heavy-rimmed spectacles that she affected made her big, black eyes look even bigger in her sallow face.

"I want to use you . . . John."

"How, Ms. Taine?" asked Grimes dubiously.

"Dorothea, please. Or you may call me Dot. I'm starting a

new novel. One of those If stories. *If* Dampier, the buccaneer and privateer, had established a settlement on the West Coast of Australia, long before the one was established at Botany Bay. After all, he was there. . . ."

"And he didn't think much of it."

"But something could, just could, have made him change his mind. He could have fallen madly in love with a beautiful Aboriginal girl. Perhaps she could have saved his life, just as the Princess Pocahontas saved the life of Captain John Smith in Virginia . . ."

Grimes entertained a fleeting vision of a naked black girl getting in the way of a boomerang flung at the piratical Captain Dampier by her irate father.

"Mphm," he grunted around the stem of his pipe.

"You see, John, I want to make Dampier a *real* character. I can't go back in time to meet him. But there's one real life character, aboard this very ship, who could serve as a model. You. Dampier wasn't only a pirate and privateer, he was also an officer, a captain, in the Royal Navy. You've been a privateer and a pirate—and also an officer, commanding ships, in the Survey Service . . . If I could only get *inside* you . . ."

I don't want to get inside you, thought Grimes unkindly. *You're too skinny, for a start. And you gush.*

"Perhaps some evening, or evenings, after dinner . . . We could get away by ourselves somewhere and you could tell me all about yourself . . ."

"It would be very boring for you," said Grimes.

"It would not, John. It couldn't possibly be."

"I'm sorry," he told her, "but all my evenings are fully taken up. I've all the spools on Liberia to study. After all, I'm being paid to be governor of the damn place so I'd better know something about it before I get there. . . ."

"Do you mind if I join you, Your Excellency? Joe's gotten himself involved in a non-stop poker game and I'm just a bit lonesome."

"Please do, Mrs. Levy. What are you drinking? A Black Angel?" Then, to the bar stewardess, "Another pink gin, please, and a B.A."

"I *like* this little bar. . . . Your very good health, Excellency."

"And yours, Mrs. Levy."

"That sounds dreadfully formal."

"Vee, then."

"Only Joe calls me that. I prefer Vera."

"Your very good health, Vera."

"I only found this little bar a couple of days ago, John. (Do you mind?) It's so . . . private. Not like the main bars, always crowded and always that so-called music so that you can't hear yourself think. I guess that there're still parts of this big ship that I haven't seen. We—the Dog Star Line, that is—don't have anything in this class."

"But you are getting into the passenger trades."

"Glorified cattle boats," she sneered. "Nothing like *this*. But I don't suppose that Joe will ever be important enough to qualify for the VIP suite. I would so like to see how the VIPs live. . . ."

"I must throw an official cocktail party before we get to Liberia," said Grimes. "You're invited, of course. . . ."

After all, he thought, *I might want a job in the Dog Star Line some day. Mr. Levy, for all his apparent inattention to his wife, looked as though he might prove to be a very jealous husband. . . .*

"Never mind," she said with sudden coldness. "I'll just take my place in the queue. Goodnight, Your Excellency."

She finished her drink and left—and Grimes knew that he would never be employed by the Dog Star Line as long as she was the wife of one of that company's managers.

"Satisfied?" he asked sleepily.

"Yes . . . and no, darling. But we've several hours before Jane brings in your morning tea."

"You'd better be out of here before then, Liz."

"It's not important really. We tabbies stick together, even though some of us have gold braid on our shoulders and some haven't. Jane would never run screaming to old Herring."

"Herring?"

"Captain Harringby. Haven't you ever noticed the fishlike look he has sometimes?"

"What if he did find out? What would he do?"

"Nothing, darling. Nothing. He's all show and no blow. Like practically every other passenger ship master he's scared shitless of the Space Catering Officers and Stewardesses' Guild. We have the power to make any voyage a hell for all concerned."

"Mphm."

No matter how successful I am, he thought, *I shall never be fool enough to buy a big passenger ship*.

He persisted, "But you didn't answer my question properly . . ."

"About being satisfied? Well, you aren't exactly bad in bed, although you could be better. But I'll educate you, darling. What satisfies me is that I've won the sweep."

"The sweep?"

"Yes. We all put in twenty credits and the prize goes to the first member of *Sobraon's* female staff to go to bed with the notorious pirate. You. And I get the prize."

"So that's why the purser brought up my supper tray in person tonight instead of entrusting the task to one of her underlings! All right, Liz. You've won. But it's been touch and go." He laughed. "I wondered why my personal needs were being attended to by different stewardesses every day and night. A fair go for all, I suppose. I almost succumbed this morning when that little carroty cat . . ."

"Sue . . ."

". . . intimated that she'd just love to wash my back while I was taking my shower."

"And now I'll rub your front and hope that you'll rise to the occasion."

Chapter 7

Sobraon was in orbit about Liberia.

Alongside her was one of that planet's meteorological satellite tenders, airlock to airlock and with the short gangway tube sealed in place, a means of transfer of personnel from spaceship to spaceship with which Grimes was unfamiliar. In the Survey Service spacesuits and lifelines were good enough for anybody, from admirals down. But now he was no longer a spaceman. He was a first class passenger. And he was a governor.

He was dressed as such, in the archaic finery that must always have seemed absurd to any intelligent human being, a rig neither functional nor aesthetically pleasing. Starched white shirt, stiff collar and gray silk cravat . . . Black tail coat over a gray waistcoat . . . Gray, sharply creased trousers . . . Highly polished black boots . . . And—horror of horrors!—a gray silk top hat.

He stood in the vestibule of the liner's airlock; at least Harringby had put the inertial drive back into operation so that Grimes was spared the indignity of floundering about clumsily in his hampering clothing. Nonetheless he was sweating, his shirt damp on his chest, sides and back. He derived some small pleasure from the observation that Captain Harringby was far from comfortable in his own dress uniform; obviously it had been tailored for him before he started to put on weight. The Chief Officer's black and gold finery fitted him well enough but his expression made it plain that he hated having to wear it. Liz, the Purser, carried her full dress far better than did the Captain and the Mate. She looked cool and elegant in her long, black skirt, her white blouse with the floppy black tie, her short, gold-trimmed jacket.

Also present were the Third Officer, who would be looking

after the airlock, and two Cadets. The young men were comfortable in normal shirt-and-shorts rig. Grimes envied them.

Harringby saluted stiffly. Grimes raised his top hat. Harringby extended his hand. Grimes took it with deliberate and (he hoped) infuriating graciousness.

"Good-bye, Your Excellency," said the shipmaster. "It's been both an honor and a pleasure to have you aboard."

Bloody liar, thought Grimes. He said, "Thank you, Captain."

The Chief Officer saluted, waited until Grimes extended his hand before offering his own.

"The best of luck, Your Excellency."

Do you mean it? wondered Grimes.

Liz brought her slim hand up to the brim of her tricorne hat, then held it out to Grimes who, gallantly, raised it to his lips while bowing slightly. Harringby scowled and the Chief Officer smirked dirtily. Grimes straightened up, still holding the girl's hand, looking into her eyes. He would have liked to have kissed those full lips—and to hell with Harringby!—but he and Liz had said their proper (improper?) good-byes during the night and early morning ship's time.

"Good-bye, Your Excellency," she murmured. "And—look after yourself."

"I'll try to," he promised.

Harringby coughed loudly to attract attention, then said, "Your Excellency, I shall be vastly obliged if you will board the tender. It is time that I was getting back to my control room."

"Very well, Captain."

Grimes gave one last squeeze to Liz's hand, relinquished it reluctantly and turned to walk into the airlock chamber and then through the short connecting tube. The tender's airlock door was smaller than that of the liner and had not been designed to admit anybody wearing a top hat. That ceremonial headgear was knocked off its insecure perch. As Grimes stooped to retrieve it he heard the Chief Officer laugh and an even louder guffaw from one of the tender's crew. He carried his hat before him as he completed his journey to the small spacecraft's cabin. His prominent ears were burning furiously.

* * *

The crew of the tender—Liberia possessed only orbital spacecraft—were young, reasonably efficient and (to Grimes's great envy) sensibly uniformed in shorts and T-shirts and badges of rank pinned to the left breast. The Captain asked Grimes to join him in the control cab. He did so, after removing his tail coat and waistcoat, sat down in the co-pilot's chair. He looked out from the viewport at the great bulk of the liner, already fast diminishing against the backdrop of abysmal night and stars, saw it flicker and fade and vanish as the Mannschenn Drive was actuated. He transferred his attention to the mottled sphere toward which the tender was dropping—pearly cloud systems and blue seas, brown and green continents and islands.

"It's a good world, Your Excellency," said the young pilot. He grinned wrily. "It *was* a good world. It could be one again."

Grimes looked at him with some curiosity. The accent had been Standard English, overlaid with an oddly musical quality. The face was olive-skinned, hawklike. Native-born, he thought. The original colonists—those romantic Anarchists—had been largely of Latin-American stock.

"Could be?" he asked.

"That is the opinion of some of us, Your Excellency. And we've heard of you, of course. You're something of an Anarchist yourself . . ."

"Mphm?"

"I mean. . . . You're not the usual Survey Service stuffed shirt."

"A stuffed shirt is just what I feel like at the moment."

"But you've a reputation, sir, for doing things your own way."

"And where has it got me?" asked Grimes, addressing the question to himself rather than to the tender's pilot.

"You've commanded ships, sir. Real ships, deep space ships, not . . . *tenders*."

"Don't speak ill of your own command," Grimes admonished.

The young man grinned whitely. "Oh, I like her. She'll do almost anything I ask of her—but if I asked her to make a deep space voyage I know what her answer would be!"

"Fit her out with Mannschenn Drive and a life support system," said Grimes, "and you could take her anywhere."

"If I were qualified—which I am not. Master Astronaut, Orbital Only—that's me."

"But you're still a spaceman, Captain. I'd like to have a talk, spaceman to spaceman. But . . ."

"Don't worry about Pedro and Miguel, sir. They're like me, members of the OAP, the Original Anarchist Party. We're allowed by our gracious President to blow off steam as long as we don't *do* anything. . . ."

"What could we do, Raoul?" came a voice from behind Grimes.

He turned to see that the other two crew members had taken seats at the rear of the control cab.

He said softly, "What could you do? I don't know. Yet. I spent the voyage from Earth running through all the official spools on Liberia . . ." (He remembered guiltily that there had been times when instead of watching and listening to the playmaster in his suite he had been doing other things.) "Before I left I was given a briefing of sorts. I still don't know nearly as much as I should. You have the first-hand knowledge. I don't."

"All right, sir," said Raoul. "I'll start at the top. There's our revered President, Estrelita O'Higgins. . . ."

"Mphm," grunted Grimes. He remembered how she had looked in the screen of the playmaster. Tall, splendidly bosomed, black-haired and with rather too much jaw to be pretty. But she was undeniably handsome. In the right circumstances she might be beautiful.

"Then there's your boy, Colonel Bardon. . . ."

"Not *my* boy," said Grimes.

"He's Earth-appointed, isn't he? Just as you are, sir. Most people say that he's got Estrelita eating out of his hand—but it could well be the other way around."

"Or mutual," said Grimes.

They made a good pair, Estrelita and the Colonel, he had thought when he saw them in one of the sequences presented by the data spools. The tall, handsome woman in a superbly tailored blue denim suit, the tall, handsome man in his glittering full dress. Like her, he had too much jaw. In his case it was framed by black, mutton chop whiskers.

"Whoever is eating out of whose hand," Raoul went on, "it's the Terran Garrison that really runs Liberia. They get first pick of everything. Then the Secret Police get their pickings. Then the ordinary police. The real Liberians don't get picked on much. There's some grumbling, of course, but we aren't badly off. It's the slaves who suffer. . . ."

"The indentured labor," corrected Grimes.

"You're hair-splitting, sir. When an indenture runs out the only way that a laborer can obtain further employment is to sign up again. All his wages, such as they are, have gone to the purchase of the little luxuries that make life bearable. And not only luxuries. There are habit-forming drugs, like Dassan dreamsticks. . . ."

"They're illegal," said Grimes, "on all federated worlds."

The pilot laughed harshly. "Of course they are. But that doesn't worry Bardon's Bullies." He returned his attention to his instruments and made minor adjustments; the beat of the tender's inertial drive changed tempo. "I've time to tell you a story, sir, before we come in to Port Libertad. There was a girl, a refugee, from New Dallas. You must have heard about what happened there. An independent colony that thought that it could thumb its nose at the Federation and at everybody else. Then the Duchy of Waldegren wanted the planet—and took it. We took a few thousand refugees. A lot of the prettier girls finished up in the houses owned—not all that secretly—by Bardon. Mary Lou was one of them. That's where I met her, in a dive called the Pink Pussy Cat. And—don't laugh, please!—we . . . fell in love. I was going to buy her out of that place. But some bastard got her hooked on dreamsticks and. . . ."

"She withered away to nothing," said Miguel.

Grimes said nothing. What could he say?

Raoul broke the silence, speaking in a deliberately brisk voice. "There's Port Libertad, sir. That statue you can see, just to the north of the spaceport, is Lady Liberty. She was copied from the old Statue of Liberty in New York harbor, on Earth. Those two big ships are bulkies, here to load grain. Some worlds, though, prefer to import the flour that's been milled here, on Liberia. Don't ask me why; I'm a spaceman, not an economist. Do you see that smaller ship? She's a fairly regular visitor. *Willy Willy*, owned by Able Enterprises. The master's Captain Aloysius Dreeble. A nasty little bastard on a nasty trade. He comes here to recruit entertainers—so called—for the brothels on quite a few of the frontier worlds."

"And New Venusberg," said Grimes. "That's where I last met him."

"You know him, sir?"

"All right, all right. I don't like him. And he doesn't like me."

Looking out and down Grimes could see the triangle of winking, bright, scarlet lights that marked the tender's berth. He picked up a pair of binoculars and stared through them. He could make out a body of men drawn up in military formation, flags streaming from portable standards, the burnished metal of musical instruments from which the afternoon sun was brightly reflected. A guard of honor and a band. . . .

From the speaker of the transceiver, through which the tender had been in communication from Aerospace Control, came a sudden blast of music, the drums almost drowning out the trumpets.

"They're warming up," said Raoul sardonically. "Be prepared to be deafened by our glorious planetary anthem as soon as you set foot on Liberian soil."

"And a twenty-gun salute?" Grimes asked, half seriously.

"No. I did hear some of the Terran Army officers discussing it before I boarded to lift off for the rendezvous with *Sobraon*. It seems that if you'd been landing in a Terran warship the Captain would have been able to accord the courtesy of a salute, in reply, to Madam President. But as you've no guns to fire you get none fired in your honor."

"This protocol," said Grimes, "is a complicated business."

"Isn't it, sir? We should never have strayed from the simple ways of our ancestors. They'd have given a gun salute to an Earth-appointed governor—and not with blanks, either!"

Looking at Raoul's face Grimes saw that the words had been spoken only in jest—but Miguel, when he spoke, was serious enough.

"If all that we've heard of Governor Grimes is true, Raoul, Bardon's Bullies would love to give him his twenty guns, each one loaded with H.E.!"

"There are more subtle ways of getting rid of unpopular governors than that," Raoul Sanchez said with sudden bitterness. Then, to Grimes, "My brother was the late Governor Wibberley's personal pilot."

A man with motive, thought Grimes. A double motive. His girlfriend and his brother, both . . . murdered.

He asked, "Are you qualified for atmosphere flight, Captain?"

"Yes, sir. Both LTA and HTA." He grinned. "Are you offering me a job, Your Excellency? I already have one, you know."

"I'm offering you a job. I warn you that it mightn't be good for your health."

"It wasn't good for my brother's health, either. All right, I receive your signal, loud and clear. You think that I might be interested in . . . revenge?"

"That thought had flickered across my mind."

"I am so interested. And now, sir, if you'll excuse me, I'll try to get this crate down in one piece."

And had he fallen into a trap? Grimes wondered. Wasn't it too much of a coincidence that these young men in the shuttle should all be OAP members, opposed to the present regime on Liberia? Were Raoul's stories, about his girl and his brother, true? (That could be checked.)

But he would have to employ some personal staff and he would prefer, whenever possible, to make his own choices. Any made for him by Colonel Bardon would be suspect from the start. And, thought Grimes, if Captain Sanchez were Bardon's man air travel, at least, would be safer for him than it had been for Governor Wibberley. Raoul didn't look the type to commit suicide just to help somebody else commit murder.

Chapter 8

A blast of sound assailed Grimes's ears as he stepped out of the tender's airlock, onto the top platform of the bunting-bedecked set of steps that had been wheeled into position. With an effort he identified it as music—the brass too strident and the drums too insistent—and with a further effort as the Terran Planetary Anthem, one of those forgettable songs with words and music composed to order by an untalented committee of lyricists and musicians. He stood to attention, his right hand holding his gray silk topper over his breast, his left hand grasping the cylindrical, gold-trimmed leather case in which was his Commission. It must look, he thought wryly, like a Field Marshal's baton. But would Bardon give him the respect that he would accord to a Field Marshal?

Sons of Terra, strong and free came to its blaring conclusion. Thankfully Grimes relaxed, put his hat back on to his head. Then there was a roll of drums, followed by more music—*Liberia's sons, let us rejoice . . .* He whipped off his hat, came again to attention. That anthem was over at last and he took a step towards the edge of the platform—and again froze. This time it was *Waltzing Matilda.*

The familiar words ran through his mind as he listened to the band.

Up came the squatter, riding on his thoroughbred,

Down came the troopers, one, two, three. . .

And there were the troopers, and there were more than three of them. There were Bardon's Bullies, drawn up for his inspection, resplendent in their dress uniforms of blue and gold and scarlet.

Up jumped the swagman, sprang into the billabong . . .

Grimes thought, *And this is one helluva billabong that I've sprung into this time . . .*

After *Matilda* there were no more anthems but Grimes was

in no hurry to descend the steps to the ground but made a slow survey of his immediate surroundings. That must be Bardon down there, waiting to receive him, even more splendidly attired than his soldiers, his finery topped by a plumed helmet. And the tall woman with him, in a superbly tailored suit of faded blue denim, had to be Madam President.

There was a crowd, but only a small one. There was a group of men and women, attired as was their President. There were the inevitable school children waving their little flags—the Federation star cluster on a black field, the Terran opalescent sphere on dark blue, the Australian national ensign with the British union flag in the upper canton and the Southern Cross constellation in the fly. There were spaceport workers in shabby, dirty, white overalls, small statured men and women, dark skinned and with Mongoloid features. There were officers from the ships in port. Grimes recognized one of these men—the weedy, ferret-faced Aloysius Dreeble, master of *Willy Willy*. Dreeble recognized him, grinned and raised two fingers in a gesture that would have been, had his palm been outward, V for Victory.

Grimes looked coldly at his old enemy and then turned away. He descended the steps with dignity. At the foot of them stood Bardon. The Colonel saluted smartly. Grimes raised his hat. The Colonel said, "Glad to have you aboard, Your Excellency." Grimes said, swapping lie for lie, "I'm happy to be here, Colonel Bardon."

"Your Excellency, may I introduce you to Madam President?"

Grimes removed his hat, put it to his chest and bowed. She inclined her head graciously. When they had both resumed normal posture they stood facing each other. Her eyes, gleaming black under heavy black brows, were level with his and looking at him appraisingly. The skin of her face was smooth and pale, her lips wide, full and very red. Her jaw was too heavy for a woman. But her smile, revealing strong white teeth, was quite pleasant.

She said, "I never dreamed that I should one day welcome a famous pirate as Governor of Liberia."

"Not a pirate, Madam President. A privateer."

"Pirate or privateer, Captain Grimes, you are bound to be an improvement over your predecessor."

"Indeed?"

"Yes. He was a psalm-singing do-gooder. You must know the type."

"I have met such people."

"Your Excellency," interrupted Bardon, "may I suggest that we inspect the Guard of Honor?"

The President shrugged and, with that well-fitting jacket of soft denim, the effect was spectacular.

She said with a smile that was not altogether malicious, "The Colonel wants us to help him play with his toy soldiers, Captain Grimes."

Bardon scowled, but not fiercely, and said, "My men are not toys, Madam."

It was, thought Grimes, very like an essentially light-hearted exchange of insults between husband and wife. But sometimes such apparently friendly gibes are symptomatic of well-hidden hostilities.

He walked with the President and the Colonel along the ranks of the Honor Guard, preceded by a Lieutenant with a drawn sword, with other officers bringing up the rear. At close quarters the men were not so impressive as they had seemed from a distance. Even so, Grimes could not fault the uniforms, well-tailored from spotlessly clean and sharply pressed cloth, with gleaming natural leather and brightly burnished metal. The archaic rifles, weapons brought out only for ceremonial occasions, held now at Present Arms, were beautifully maintained. On the features of each man the facial hair, a down-sweeping moustache, was brushed and trimmed into exact uniformity with the whiskers to right and to left. But even those tailored scarlet jackets could not hide the paunches or the wide, gleaming, cross-straps and belts hold them in. And there were the sagging jowls and the shifty eyes, some of them bloodshot.

Bardon's Bullies, thought Grimes. *They look it*.

He said, "Thank you, Colonel. A fine body of men."

"I am pleased that you found them so, Your Excellency. You can rely upon them for loyal service."

"Thank you, Colonel."

"I prefer soldiers in undress uniform," said the President, turning her sultry gaze on to Bardon. And then, to his rather embarrassed surprise, Grimes was treated to a similar, lingering glance. "And I am sure, Your Excellency, that you would feel far happier in something less formal."

"Too right," said Grimes.

She said, "You may dismiss your troops, Colonel Bardon."

Bardon turned to Grimes and asked, "Permission to dismiss the Guard, Your Excellency?"

Who gives orders to whom on this bloody planet? Grimes asked himself.

He said, "Dismiss the Guard, Colonel."

Orders were barked, Colonel to Lieutenant, Lieutenant to Sergeant, Sergeant to the enlisted men. Smartly, with a jingle of accoutrements, the detachment formed fours and, behind the band, stepping in time to the thud and rattle of the drums, marched toward the spaceport's boundary fence. Chattering shrilly, the schoolchildren followed their teachers in the wake of the departing military. The ground staff drifted back to their jobs. The spacemen strolled toward their ships.

Vehicles drove up—a huge, scarlet-enameled limousine for the President with the symbol of a clenched fist, holding a torch, in black, on each of its doors, an olive-drab-painted armored car for the Colonel and one of the Lieutenants, a superb RR Whispering Ghost, gleaming black and shining silver with the forward-leaning nymph on its bonnet holding a staff from which flew a Terran ensign, for Grimes. There was a civilian chauffeur, a young man with a full beard, denim-clad and with a scarlet neckerchief. Beside him, on the front seat, were two soldiers in drab battle dress.

Bardon said to Grimes, "Your ADC will look after you, Your Excellency, and will . . . er . . . show you the ropes at the Governor's Residence. Lieutenant Smith, please see that His Excellency is at the President's Reception, at 2000 hrs. this evening."

Smith saluted. He was old for his rank, his face both pudgy and sulky. The decorations on the left breast of his tunic were of the variety that Grimes referred to as Good Attendance Medals. If he had ever been in a war, even a police action, he had failed to distinguish himself.

"Until this evening, Your Excellency," said Estrelita O'Higgins.

"Until this evening, Madam President," said Grimes.

"Until this evening, Your Excellency," said Bardon, saluting.

"Until this evening, Colonel," said Grimes, raising his hat.

He had to take it off again when he climbed into the car, through the door which the ADC had opened for him. Smith followed him into the vehicle.

Chapter 9

Rather to Grimes's disappointment the drive out to the Residence did not take him through the city of Libertad but through countryside that, in a natural state, could have been beautiful but, with its too orderly orchards, was rather boring. He remembered that although cereals were Liberia's main exports here was also a considerable trade in various processed fruit products. Working in the aisles between the trees were the laborers, small, dark-skinned people, clad only in loincloths, picking the golden fruit and filling baskets with the gleaming globes. It was not the first orange plantation that Grimes had seen—but it was the first one in which machines had not been doing the harvesting.

Then there were terraced rice paddies, and more orchards and, eventually, a low hill on which stood the Governor's Residence. It was a low, rambling building, white-walled, its shallowly pitched roofs red-tiled. The main entrance was an imposing portico, with white pillars and a proliferation of intricately patterned iron lace. There was a wide, velvety lawn fringed with flowering bushes—plants indigenous to Liberia, thought Grimes, who was no botanist. There was a tall flagstaff at the peak of which the starry banner of the Federation stirred lazily in the light, uncertain breeze.

A small detachment of Terran Army troops—a Sergeant and six men—was drawn up before the portico. Unlike the Honor Guard at the spaceport they were wearing khaki, not full dress uniform, and were armed not with archaic but aesthetically pleasing rifles but with modern, ugly and viciously effective sprayguns. Like the Honor Guard, however, they looked far better from a distance.

Behind the soldiers were the liveried civilians, men and women in long, white trousers or skirts under high-necked, royal blue jackets. Some of these jackets were absolutely plain, others were decorated with silver buttons and varying quantities of silver braid. One man was wearing a chef's high, white hat. There was a civilian who was not in uniform, a short man, stocky, bald-headed, wearing a plain gray suit.

Grimes stared.

These, obviously, were the servants—but a mob like this to look after one man, even though he was a governor!

He voiced his disapproving surprise.

It was the chauffeur who made reply. He said smugly, "The Residence is a large building, Your Excellency. Even though there is only one level above ground there are three sub-surface ones.There is all the cleaning to do, and the cooking, and. . . ."

"And machines to do such work," said Grimes.

"Not here," said the chauffeur. "Not on Liberia. Not now. In order to create employment for the refugees whom we have accepted from all over the galaxy we have reverted to the use of human labor wherever possible."

"I thought," Grimes said, "that this principle applied only to large-scale enterprises, such as agriculture. Not to menial work."

"Are you calling *me* a menial?" demanded the man.

"Of course not," said Grimes hastily. The driver already seemed more interested in the conversation than the handling of the car; if he got involved in a real argument he might forget to stop and plough into and through the reception committee.

He did stop; only just in time, it seemed to Grimes. The doors opened. The ADC was first out. Grimes followed, putting on his top hat. He raised it in response to the Sergeant's smart salute. The short, stocky civilian came forward and bowed, presenting his shiny, bald pate to the Governor's inspection. He straightened up and said, "Jaconelli, Your Excellency. David Jaconelli. Your secretary."

Grimes took his clammy hand, pressed it briefly.

He said, "I am pleased to meet you, Mr. Jaconelli."

One of the servants, the one with the most lavish display of braid and buttons on his tunic, presented himself and bowed far more deeply than had the secretary. His sparse gray hair, Grimes noted, was scraped back and plaited into a neat queue, a pigtail. He came erect and regarded Grimes from black, slanted eyes. His face was thin, the skin tightly stretched over the bone structure, his complexion ivory yellow. A wispy beard decorated his far from prominent chin.

He said, in a high-pitched voice that was not quite a twitter, "Welcome, Your Excellency, from myself and from all of your servants."

"Thank you," replied Grimes. Then, "You are . . .?"

"My name is Wong Lee, Your Excellency. I have the honor to be Your Excellency's majordomo."

"I am pleased to meet you, Mr. Lee." (Or should that have been Mr. Wong?) "You may tell the other servants to return to their duties." Orders were given in a high-pitched voice in a language that Grimes thought was Chinese. "And now, if you will be so good as to escort me to my quarters. . . ."

Led by Wong Lee, accompanied by Lieutenant Smith and Mr. Jaconelli, Grimes walked into what would be his happy home until such time as his gubernatorial employment was terminated. Would he be able to resign before he got fired? he wondered.

The four men marched through what seemed, to Grimes, like miles of corridors, over long reaches of gleaming parquetry, past a never-ending display, on either side, of works of art, copies—but excellent ones—of paintings of all periods, representative of every school since some inspired Cromagnard daubed his crude but enduring pigments onto a cave wall. There was a Turner—*Spaceship out of sight in a gas nebula*, thought Grimes irreverently—and a Picasso—*Portrait of a lady after a Mannschenn Drive malfunction*. And a Rubens . . . Grimes had no objection to naked blondes but preferred them less fat. A Norman Lindsay. . . . None of his undressed ladies could be classed as skinny but they were far more to Grimes's taste than the models of the old Dutch master. Inevitably there was that famous woman who daren't smile properly—thought Grimes, cultural barbarian that he was—for fear of exposing her carious teeth. Then there were more Australian artists. There was Nolan, with his weirdly compelling perpetuation of a myth, the giant in his fantastic armor astride a horse that could have been borrowed (or stolen!) from Don Quixote. A myth? But there had been a Ned Kelly, whose name and fame had survived while those of countless far worthier citizens were long forgotten. And if the cards had fallen only a little differently at Glenrowan what might have happened? The course of Australian history, of Terran history, even, could have been changed.

Wong Lee noticed Grimes's interest in the Nolan paintings.

"A folk hero, Your Excellency?" he asked.

"Mphm. Yes, I suppose."

"Perhaps an honorable ancestor . . ."

"Not as far as I know."

They came to the Governor's suite.

There was a large, comfortable sitting room with, off it, an office—big enough, thought Grimes, for a full meeting of the entire Board of Admiralty. While the others watched respectfully he took his seat behind the vast, gleaming desk, enjoying the feeling of power. He had commanded ships and, recently, a flotilla—but this was different. Now he was boss cocky of an entire planet—on paper, at least. *De jure*. But *de facto*? That remained to be seen. He looked down to his reflection in the highly polished surface of the desk, saw behind his face the crossed flags, the banners of Terra and of the Interstellar Federation. He saw too, with something of a shock, that he was still wearing the absurd top hat. But he was the Governor, wasn't he? This was his Residence, wasn't it? If he couldn't make his own rules of etiquette, who could? Nonetheless he removed the head covering, skimmed it across the desk top to Wong Lee.

He got up then and, followed by the others, made a tour of his living quarters. There was a luxurious bedroom. He saw that his baggage had already been deposited there; it must have been offloaded and transported while he was inspecting the Guard of Honor at the spaceport. Somebody had begun to unpack and had laid out his civilian full evening dress on the bed. That somebody was a girl—tall, with glossy black hair swinging in a pageboy bob about her face, wearing a royal blue tunic and a long, white skirt that was slit to hip level, revealing a delectable length of smooth, ivory-skinned leg. She straightened up from what she was doing, turned to Grimes and bowed. Like the other servants she was of Mongoloid stock—a descendant, Grimes supposed, of those New Cantonese refugees. But there was some mixed blood—that wide mouth, the almost—but no more than almost—harsh angularity of the facial bone structure.

"This is Su Lin, Your Excellency," said Wong Lee. "She is to be your . . . handmaiden. I decided that you, as a space gentleman, accustomed to the ministrations of stewardesses aboard your ships, would prefer a personal attendant of the female sex."

"I like to make my own decisions," said Grimes.

"Then, Your Excellency, I will see to it that Peng Yuan, who was valet to your late, revered predecessor, performs the same duties for your honored self."

"I've already told you, Mr. Wong," said Grimes stiffly, "that I like to make my own decisions. I am sure that Miss Su will be quite satisfactory."

"It is not customary, Your Excellency, to use an honorific when addressing or referring to under servants."

Jaconelli and Smith exchanged glances, each permitting himself as much of a sneer as he dared.

Grimes restrained himself from saying that he was the Governor and that he made the rules. It would not do at all to cut the old man down to size in the presence of a subordinate and of the ADC and the secretary. As he knew from experience a wise captain does not unnecessarily antagonize his chief steward.

He looked at his wrist companion, the chronological function of which had been set to local time.

He said, "I think, now, that I'd like to get cleaned up and all the rest of it. What time should I leave the Residence for the Palace, Lieutenant?"

"1900 hours, sir."

"Thank you. And Mr. Jaconelli. . . ."

"Sir?"

"I take it that all of the late Governor Wibberley's papers will be accessible to me? In the office, perhaps. . . ."

"No, sir."

"No? Why not?"

"After the accident all documents were taken by Colonel Bardon. He said he was shipping them back to Earth."

"But there must have been copies."

"Yes, Your Excellency. But. . . ."

"But what?"

"He took them too."

"Why didn't you . . .?"

"Sir, I am only the Governor's secretary. Until your arrival the Colonel was the senior Terran officer on this planet."

"Mphm." Grimes glared at Smith, who had been listening to the exchange with interest and enjoyment. "You may go, Lieutenant. Be waiting for me in the car at 1900 hours."

"Very good, Your Excellency."

"And Mr. Jaconelli. . . . Please arrange with the Bureau of Meteorology for the release of Captain Raoul Sanchez, the shuttle pilot who brought me down from *Sobraon*, to serve as my atmosphere pilot."

"It was my understanding, Your Excellency, that Colonel Bardon was to second one of his officers to your service."

"Then tell the Colonel that I am making my own arrangements. Oh, and I'd like a crew list."

"A *crew list*?"

"A list of all the Residence staff. Age, sex, birthplace, national and/or planetary origin, qualifications, if any, etc. etc. and etc."

"Very good, Your Excellency. Will that be all?"

"Yes, thank you."

When the ADC and the secretary were gone the majordomo asked, "Will you require my services any further, Your Excellency?"

"No, thank you, Mr. Wong. You may leave. And you, Su Lin."

She objected. "But, Your Excellency, I am your body servant. I am to serve you in all ways."

"It is customary among our people, sir," said Wong Lee. "There is the help to be given to a great man in the removal of his formal attire and the donning of other ceremonial clothing. There is the bringing of refreshment when he so desires it. There is. . . ."

Meanwhile Grimes had succeeded in getting his pipe out of a pocket in his too-tight-fitting trousers and, after another little struggle, his tobacco pouch. He filled the vile brier and was patting his coat pockets in a vain search for a box of the old-fashioned matches that he preferred to other means of ignition.

And then Su Lin was holding a golden lighter, a miniature flame thrower from which issued a jet of incandescence. Grimes hated having his pipe lit for him but submitted to her ministrations. If he refused to submit to other, more intimate ones he would be likely to hurt her feelings. He would just have to see to it that the ministrations were not too intimate. During his Survey Service career he had always despised commanding officers who had engaged in liaisons with their personal stewardesses. (He was, in some ways, a snob; he had never shied away from the occasional affair with female shipmates who held commissioned rank.)

Wong Lee bowed deeply and glided away.

Grimes said to the girl, "Lin—or should it be Su?"

"Whichever pleases Your Excellency."

"All right. Su. Please wait in the sitting room while I get undressed and showered."

"But I am your body servant, Your Excellency."

Already she was helping him out of his tail coat and was loosening the cravat about his neck. He let her go ahead with it. After all, he thought, this was the girl's job, one for which she had been trained. And, he admitted, he liked being pampered, especially by attractive women. Her nimble fingers coped expeditiously with studs and buttons. (Why could not the items of formal dress be secured by sealseams?)

Surprisingly soon he was naked, unembarrassed but determined that things would go no further. He walked to the open door of the bathroom, into the shower cubicle. Before he could put a hand to the controls a slim, bare arm slid past his shoulder and a long, scarlet-nailed finger pushed the WARM button. He felt smooth, soft nudity against his back. He turned to face the girl and said, "I am quite capable of washing myself, Su Lin. Please wait for me in the bedroom."

Then, lest the order be miscontrued, he added, "And get dressed."

She stepped away from him and bowed, saying, her voice expressionless, "As Your Excellency pleases."

She turned gracefully and glided away from him; her smoothly working buttocks were like peaches poised on the long, slender (but not too slender) stems of her legs.

Feeling excessively virtuous Grimes continued with his shower. The water temperature was just right. He pushed the DETERGENT button, then the one labeled SCRUBBERS. The soft brushes worked up a scented lather all over his body. He thought that her hands would have made an even better job of it. Although the feeling of virtue persisted he was beginning to feel something of a bloody fool. But one of his own rules, which he was determined not to break, was NEVER PLAY AROUND WITH THE HIRED HELP.

"You stinking snob!" he muttered.

And, talking of stinks, he would have to get the detergent dispenser charged with something less redolent of a whore's garret.

The blowers soon dried him and he returned to the bedroom. The girl was waiting for him, once again respectably attired. Her face, utterly devoid of expression, could have been carved from old ivory. Expertly she helped him into his full evening dress, the archaic white tie and tails, with decorations. When he was fully clad he surveyed himself in the full length mirror of the wardrobe. The effect would have been better, he thought, had he been taller and slimmer, less stocky, but . . . *Not bad*, he thought. *Not bad*. He allowed Su Lin to make the final adjustments to the snowy white butterfly nestling on his Adam's apple.

"Thank you," he told her and walked through to the sitting room.

Lieutenant Smith, in his uniform mess full dress, was waiting for him.

He said, "The car is waiting for us, Your Excellency."

"Thank you," said Grimes.

He followed the ADC to the doorway. Before he could pass through it Su Lin came out of the bedroom carrying his hat, another topper, black this time. Grimes had deliberately forgotten the thing; he took it from her with a brief word of thanks that he hoped she sensed was insincere.

He let Smith pilot him through the labyrinth of corridors.

He thought, *I must tell Jaconelli to get me a chart of this bloody warren.*

Chapter 10

The gubernatorial car was waiting in the portico, the civilian chauffeur, in his livery of faded, frayed denim and red neckerchief, in the front seat and, beside him, two soldiers in khaki uniform. The rear doors of the vehicle opened. Grimes took off his top hat, climbed in. The ADC followed him. Wong Lee and Su Lin bowed deferentially as the Whispering Ghost purred away from the portico.

Grimes tried to make conversation.

"I'm not used to having an ADC," he remarked pleasantly to the Lieutenant.

"ADC, Officer Commanding the Governor's Guard, liaison with the Officer Commanding the Garrison. . . ." The officer's voice was surly. "I hope that you don't think up any other jobs for me. Your Excellency. If ever there was a penny-pinching operation, this is it. I'm surprised that they don't have me doing the cooking. . . ."

"Talking of cooking," said Grimes, hoping to switch the conversation to a topic dear to his heart, "what's the chef like?"

"Oh, all right, I suppose, if you don't mind mucked-up food. He's New Cantonese, of course. Like all the rest of the Residence mob, with the exception of my men and Jaconelli and myself." He laughed. "I'm surprised that they didn't appoint a New Cantonese as Governor. They'd be paying him much less than they're paying you, Your Excellency."

"Mphm." Grimes managed to make it sound like a reprimand. He didn't like and never had liked moaners. "Some people would think that being appointed ADC to a Governor was an honor."

"I . . . I suppose so, Your Excellency."

They sat in silence while the car sped down the winding road toward the city, taking a different route, Grimes noted, from that which had been taken during the journey from the spaceport. The dusk was falling fast but still work was continuing in the fields to either side of the highway. The last of the daylight was caught and reflected by metal implements, by sickles (sickles! in this day and age!) and the blades of hand-wielded hoes. A few of the laborers paused and straightened up to stare at the passing vehicle but most of them took no respite from their back-breaking toil.

Then there were no more fields but, to either side of the wide avenue, there were houses, each in its own garden. All of these buildings were low and rambling, the architectural style vaguely Spanish. Some—but only a few—of the gardens were well-kept; most of them were miniature jungles. The street lights were coming on but not all of them were working.

There was some traffic in the avenue. There was the very occasional solar-electric car. There was a sudden swarm of cyclists, skimming silently through the dusk. Motorized machines, thought Grimes at first, then saw that all the riders' legs were pumping vigorously. Workers, he decided, domestic servants possibly, returning to their compounds outside the city. And there were trishaws, tricycles with the passengers seated forward, flanked by the pair of leading wheels, with the operator on his saddle astern of them, pedaling hard. Most of the passengers were of Caucasian stock—and all the drivers Mongoloid. Grimes grunted disapprovingly. The use of such transport was justified only during periods of energy crisis—and such days were long past on all of man's worlds.

Ahead, now, was the President's Palace, a blaze of illumination, with its profusion of white pillars more Grecian than Spanish. The vast expanse of lawn surrounding the building was like dark green velvet, the drive along which the car made its approach was surfaced with well-raked yellow gravel. A flock of sheep drifted slowly across the headlight beams; the vehicle slowed to a crawl until the animals were past and clear. The driver turned his head to address Grimes.

"What do you think of our lawn mowers, Your Excellency? They're sort of cobbers of yours, Australian Merinos. Their ancestors came out with the First Fleet."

The ADC snapped, "Do not address His Excellency without permission, Garcia."

"*Mr.* Garcia to you, Mister. And, anyhow, this is *my* world, not yours."

Grimes shoved his oar in, hoping thereby to avert an acrimonious argument. He asked, "And do you have any other Australian animals here, Mr. Garcia?"

"Only yourself, Your Excellency."

Grimes laughed and the ADC growled wordlessly.

"Our beef cattle are Argentine stock," went on the driver, "and our dairy herds are from some little island back on Earth, Jersey. The pigs and the hens? From anywhere and everywhere, I guess."

The sheep were finally past and the car increased speed, passing a huge statue, a bronze giantess whose heroic proportions were revealed rather than hidden by her flowing draperies. She was holding aloft, in her right hand, a flaming torch. Clouds of flying insects—or insectlike creatures—attracted by the fatal lure of the flaring gas were immolating themselves by the thousand.

"I have often wondered," said the driver philosophically, "why the bastards, since they like the light so much, don't come out during the day. . . ."

An interesting problem, thought Grimes.

The vehicle pulled up in the wide portico. Waiting to receive Grimes was Colonel Bardon, in all the splendor of his mess full dress. With him was a group of local dignitaries—heavily bearded men in black velvet suits, in white, floppy-collared shirts with flowing, scarlet neckties, women in low-cut, black velvet dresses with scarlet scarves about their throats.

The ADC got out of the car first and stood to rigid attention. Grimes got out, putting on his hat. He raised it as Bardon saluted with a flourish, raised it again as the male Liberians swept off their own headgear—black, broad-brimmed and with scarlet bands—and as the ladies curtseyed. Then the party, Bardon and Grimes in the lead, passed through the huge double doors, held open by white-liveried servitors (more New Cantonese, thought Grimes) into an anteroom large enough to serve as a hangar for a fair-sized dirigible. The vast expanse of floor was local marble, highly polished, in which the multicolored veins were brightly scintillant. The high walls were covered with crimson, gold-embroidered silk. Overhead the huge electroliers glittered prismatically.

Attentive servants took hats, carried them away somewhere. Others swung open the enormous doors affording admission to the Reception Hall. This had a floor area that would have been ample for the apron of a minor spaceport. The decor was similar to that of the vestibule but on a much greater scale. Awaiting Grimes was the cream of Liberian society, the black-and-scarlet-clad Anarchist grandees and their ladies. At the far end of the vast hall were two platforms, red draped. On the lower but wider dais was a band, drums and gleaming brass. On the higher one Madam President was sitting in state; her chair was not quite a throne and the tiara adorning her glossy, black hair was not quite a crown. Behind her was a huge, gold-framed portrait of a heavily bearded worthy.

"Who's that?" whispered Grimes to Bardon. "Karl Marx?"

"Better not let anybody hear you say that, Your Excellency. That's Bakunin."

"Oh."

The music started. Grimes stiffened to attention, as did Bardon and the ADC. The Liberians also stood, but without rigidity. Nonetheless it was a mark of respect. Many of them sang. Grimes was both surprised and pleased that so many knew the words.

Once a jolly swagman camped by a billabong
Under the shade of a coolibah tree,
And he sang as he watched and waited till his billy boiled,
'Who'll come a-waltzing Matilda with me?'

Grimes wondered if those jumbuks, grazing on the wide lawns outside the Palace, could hear the national song of their long ago and far away homeland. And did they have an ancestral memory of the sheep-stealing swagman, a man who had been far more of an anarchist than these Liberians who attached that label to themselves.

Then it was the turn of the Terran anthem. Hardly anybody knew the words and the tune was not one to stick in the memory.

Sons of Terra, strong and free,
Faring forth through Time and Space,
As far as human eye can see
We run our sacred, fateful race . . .

Grimes wondered which was worse, the words or the music.

Finally Liberia had its innings. Almost everybody sang.

Liberia's sons let us rejoice
For we are strong and free . . .

"Mphm," grunted Grimes. Who was free these days?

We sing our song with heart and voice
In praise of Liberty!
And praise we, too, our homeworld, so free from want and care,
Stronghold of all the freedoms—
Advance, Liberia fair!

There was a final flourish of drums, then relative silence.

Bardon said, "And now, Your Excellency, I have to present you to Madam President."

"Lead on, MacDuff," said Grimes. He knew that he had misquoted but did not think that the Colonel would be aware of this.

"The name is Bardon, Your Excellency. Colonel Bardon."

The black and scarlet crowd parted like the Red Sea before the Israelites, opening clear passage toward the presidential dais along which Grimes, Bardon and the ADC marched, their heels ringing on the marble floor, keeping time to the rhythmic mutter of a single drum. The new Governor was acutely conscious that he was being observed, that he was being curiously regarded by all these bearded men and handsome women. (There may have been some ladies who could not be so categorized but he did not notice any.) He saw that Estrelita O'Higgins had risen from her thronelike chair, was making a stately descent of the short flight of red-carpeted stairs. If only she were holding a torch, thought Grimes, she would look just like one of those statues of Miss Liberty.

She stood there, at the foot of the stairs, waiting for him.

And who bowed to whom? Grimes wondered. Why had he not made a proper study of the protocol for such occasions? She was the (allegedly) elected ruler of a planet—but he was the appointed viceroy of Imperial Earth. Would she extend a gracious hand for him to kiss? At the spaceport they had bowed to each other, practically simultaneously, but this was the official reception, the state occasion.

She knew the drill (surely for this planet only!) even if he did not. She extended her long, smooth, pale arms and flung them around him, engulfing him in a powerful embrace. She must have been eating something with garlic in it, thought Grimes. But he returned her hearty kiss.

She released him, turning him around so that they were both facing the people.

"Comrades!" she cried in her deep contralto. "Comrades! I present to you our new Governor, John Grimes. The Federation, this time, has made a wise choice. John Grimes is a man of action. John Grimes is a man of the world, of many worlds, who knows that each and every planet has its own character. He knows that we, here on Liberia, have our own character. He knows that we have opened our world and our hearts to the poor, the distressed and the oppressed of many planets. There are people here, our guests, who, were it not for us, would be living lives of deepest misery—or who would not be living at all.

"Governor John Grimes, I am sure, will appreciate what we have done, what we are doing.

"I ask you, comrades, to welcome John Grimes and to take him to your hearts, just as you have taken so very many less fortunate outworlders."

A New Cantonese servant was bowing before them, extending a golden tray upon which were three tall goblets, each filled with a red wine. The President and the Colonel waited until Grimes had taken his before picking up theirs. Other servants had circulated through the hall. Soon everybody was holding a charged glass.

"Viva Grimes!" cried Estrelita O'Higgins, raising her goblet. (She was more than ever like those statues.)

"Viva Grimes!" sounded loudly from the body of the hall. "Viva Grimes!"

And everybody has had a drink but me, thought Grimes wryly.

He waited until the toast had been drunk, then made his own.

"Long live Liberty!"

He was probably more sincere, he hoped, than those who, so noisily, had drunk to his health.

The wine wasn't bad, although a mite too sweet.

Chapter 11

Guided by Estrelita O'Higgins, accompanied by Colonel Bardon, Grimes made the rounds of the great reception hall. The ADC trailed behind for a while, then lost himself in the crowd. The new Governor was introduced to the people who—in theory—were now his subjects. He made and listened to small talk. Now and again he was able to initiate a discussion on more serious matters. He sampled snacks from the buffet tables and enjoyed the savory, highly-spiced morsels. An attentive servant continually replenished his glass, even after only a couple of sips. On any other world but this, Grimes thought, a Governor would remain in one place and the people would be brought to meet him. Possibly this Liberian way of doing things was better. At least the newly installed dignitary did not go hungry or thirsty.

He met ministers of state and media personalities. He fended off searching questions about his recent experiences as a commodore of privateers. He asked questions himself, some of which were answered frankly while others were not. Politicians, he thought, were much of a muchness no matter what labels they had attached to themselves.

His conversation with Eduardo Lopez, Minister of Immigration, was interesting.

"You must realize, Your Excellency, that I have little choice regarding the ethnicity of our immigrants. To deny any distressed person or persons sanctuary on racial grounds would be altogether contrary to our . . . constitution? Yes. Constitution. . . ."

"I thought," said Grimes, "that a society founded on the

principles of Anarchism wasn't supposed to have such a thing."

"Contrary to our principles," said the President firmly.

"You are right as always, Estrelita," said the fat politician gallantly. "Principles. Of course, if I received a request for permission to enter from, say, an El Doradan, a representative of a society notorious for its devotion to capitalism, I should be obliged to refuse. But the poor, distressed and homeless, of whatever race or color, I must welcome with open arms."

"*We* must welcome," said the President.

"As I was saying—we must welcome."

"And can these immigrants become full citizens?" asked Grimes, although he already knew the answer to that question.

"Of course, provided that they show proof that they are fit and proper persons to become Liberians."

Grimes looked around him. Apart from the servants all those present seemed to be of Terran Anglo-Saxon or Latin stock. There were no Orientals, no Negroes.

"Have any outworlders yet achieved citizenship?" he asked.

"Er . . . no. You see, Your Excellency, the major qualification is freedom. As long as a person is in debt to the State he is not free. Once he has earned enough money to repay the debt he is free . . ."

"Debt?" asked Grimes.

"Resettlement is a costly business, Your Excellency, as you as a shipowner must know. Transportation between worlds . . ."

"The responsibility, I understand, of the Federation."

"Even so, there are costs, heavy costs. People come here. They must be fed, housed, found employment. . . ."

"Employment," echoed Grimes. "Menial work. Manual labor, for not very high wages. . . ."

"And would you pay a field hand, Your Excellency, the salary that you, highly trained and qualified, would expect as a shipmaster?"

"The laborer, in any field, is worthy of his hire," said the President.

Her hand firmly on Grimes's elbow she steered him away from Lopez, toward the flamboyantly red-haired Kitty O'Halloran, Director of TriVi Liberia. She was a large woman, fat rather than plump, and she gushed.

"Your Excellency. Commodore. I'm dying to get you on to one of our programs. Just an interview, but in *depth*. Just the story, told by yourself, of some of your *outrageous* adventures. . . ."

"Outrageous?" parried Grimes. "I'm a respectable Governor."

"But you weren't always. You've been a pirate. . . ."

"A privateer," he corrected her.

"Who knows the difference?" She tittered. "From what I've heard, you didn't know yourself. . . ."

Again there was the guiding pressure on his elbow. This time he was to meet Luigi Venito, Minister of Interstellar Trade, a tall, distinguished man with steely gray hair and—unusual in this company—a neatly trimmed beard.

"I thought, Your Excellency," said Venito, "that I might one day deal with you in your capacity as a shipowner. To meet you as a Governor is an unexpected pleasure."

"Bad pennies," said Grimes, "turn up in the most unexpected places."

"Ha ha. But I refuse to believe that the Terran World Assembly would appoint a bad penny to a highly responsible position."

"You'd be surprised," said Grimes. "And, in any case, governments are rarely as moral as those whom they govern." (*There are times*, he thought, *when I feel that I should have a Boswell, recorder in hand, tagging after me . . .*) "I hope that your government is an exception to the rule."

Venito chuckled. "Some say that we shouldn't have a government at all, not on this world. But after the first few years our founding fathers—and mothers, of course, Madam President—were obliged to admit that pure Anarchism doesn't work. A state of anarchy is not Anarchism. But we *are* free, unregimented, doing the things that we want to do as long as we do not infringe upon the rights of our fellow citizens. From each according to his ability, to each according to his needs. My own ability is trade, buying in the cheapest markets, selling in the dearest. All for the greatest good, naturally, of Liberia . . ."

He had been drinking, of course, not too much, perhaps, but enough to loosen his tongue. Grimes ignored the President's attempt to push him along to another group. There was one point that he wanted to clear up, a matter that had not been fully dealt with in the data that he had been given to study on the voyage out from Earth.

He said, "You must have made some interesting deals in your time. . . . Agricultural machinery, for example. . . ."

Venito laughed. "Yes. That *was* a good deal! The new colony on Halvan—and the ship carrying all their robot harvesters and the like months overdue! She's listed as missing, presumed lost, at Lloyd's. I think that the presumption still holds—but that's not important. . . ."

Only to the crew, thought Grimes, *and their relatives.*

"And we had still more refugees coming in and so I said to Lopez, 'Put these people to work in the fields—and I'll flog all our agricultural machinery at better-than-new prices!' And I did just that."

"Clever," said Grimes. "Ill winds, and all that. But it wouldn't have been so good for Liberia if you didn't have the indentured labor system, if your field workers were being paid decent wages."

"What is a decent wage, Your Excellency? Enough to buy the necessities of life—food, shelter, clothing—with a little left over for the occasional luxury. That's a decent wage. On this world nobody goes cold or hungry. What more do you want?"

"The freedom to change your job when you feel like it, for a start."

"But all our citizens enjoy that freedom."

"Yes. All your *citizens*, Minister."

"Citizenship has to be earned, Your Excellency."

The President not only had her hand firmly on his elbow; she pinched him quite painfully. He took the hint and allowed her to conduct him to a meeting with the Minister for Culture and the lady with him, the Chief Librarian of Liberia.

They knew his background, of course, and, talking down from their intellectual eminence, made it plain that they held spacemen in low esteem.

Chapter 12

The reception was over.

The President and Colonel Bardon, very much like husband and wife getting rid of the guests after a party and looking forward to holding a post mortem on the night's doings as soon as they were in bed, escorted Grimes out to the waiting car, which was at the head of the queue of vehicles. Most of these were trishaws.

The ADC was there, with the two soldiers. All three of them made a creditable attempt at standing to attention. Grimes wondered briefly how the two enlisted men had spent their evening; obviously they had found congenial company somewhere. He knew how the ADC had passed the time; that officer had been mainly in the company of two not unattractive girls who seemed to have monopolized the services of one of the wine waiters. Surely ADCs, Grimes had thought disapprovingly, should always be at the beck and call of their lords and masters. But this was Liberia where all animals—unless they had the misfortune to be refugees—were equal. (But surely a Governor was more equal than the others.)

"Good night, Your Excellency."

"Good night, Madam President." Grimes clasped her extended hand. "Thank you for the party."

"It was a pleasure having you."

"Good night, Your Excellency."

"Good night, Colonel."

Grimes removed his tall hat before climbing into the passenger compartment of the car. The driver turned his head to regard him sardonically.

"Feeling no pain, Gov.?" he asked. (He, too, must have spent a convivial evening.)

When in Rome . . . thought Grimes resignedly. He said, "I'll survive."

"More than your predecessor did . . ." muttered the chauffeur.

The ADC and the soldiers embarked. The doors slid shut. The car drove away.

Grimes drowsed most of the way back to the Residence.

Wong Lee was waiting there to receive him and so, in his suite, was Su Lin. As though by magic the girl produced a pot of fragrant tea, brought it to him on a lacquer tray as he went into his office and sat down at the desk. He sipped from the cup that she poured for him; the steaming liquid cleared his head. The old man and the girl watched impassively as he opened the first of the folders that Jaconelli had laid out for him.

This contained the information on the Terran staff of the Residence.

Jaconelli, Grimes read, had been born in Chicago. His solitary qualification was Bachelor of Commerce, the minimal requirement for any secretarial post. Surely a Governor, thought Grimes, should be entitled to at least a Master to handle his correspondence and affairs.

Harrison Smith, the ADC, was another Bachelor—of Military Arts. He was a graduate of West Point. His birthplace was Denver. His Terran Army career had been undistinguished; he had not played a part, however minor, in even a police action or a brush-fire war.

The Sergeant of the Governor's Guard, Martello, was another American. Although seven years older than his officer he, too, had been lucky enough to avoid action during his Army service.

The privates were a mixed bunch—one New Zealander, three Poms, a Swede and an Israeli. That all of them had reached early middle age without attaining noncommissioned rank did not say much for them.

The New Cantonese file was a thicker one—but only because there were more names in it. Wong Lee had the biggest entry.

The majordomo was old, even older than his appearance and manner had led Grimes to believe. He had actually been born on New Canton, where his parents had been the owners of the Heavenly Peace Hotel and the Jade Dragon Restaurant. As had been the custom of his people he had commenced his training in hotel and restaurant management at a very early age. In spite of his refugee status he had easily obtained such employment on Liberia although he was never allowed to become the owner of his own establishment. He had applied for the post of majordomo to the Governor when the first of such appointments was made by Earth. He had got the job and for many years had kept it.

All the others had been born on Liberia, some of mixed parentage. Among these was Su Lin, with a New Cantonese father and an Irandan mother. And young enough, thought Grimes, to be his own daughter. He looked up at her from the typed pages. She looked back at him and smiled. He frowned back at her.

Finally he got to the transcript of the telephone conversation that Jaconelli had had with the Bureau of Meteorology. The Secretary, pulling rank as the Governor's personal representative, had received an assurance from one of the Deputy Directors (*the* Director had been among those at the reception) that Captain Raoul Sanchez would be released at once from his normal duties and instructed to report at the Residence at 0900 hours tomorrow morning. *Tomorrow* morning? Grimes looked up at the wall clock. *This* morning.

He said, "Thank you, Mr. Wong. Thank you, Su Lin. I shall not be needing you any more tonight. Please see that I am called promptly at 0700 hours."

The old man bowed deeply and then glided out of the office. The girl remained.

Grimes said again, "Thank you, Su Lin. Please call me at 0700 hours."

She said, "But you have yet to retire, Your Excellency. And my duties are to attend you at all times."

"I am capable of putting myself to bed," Grimes told her.

"But, Your Excellency, I have been trained . . ."

"And so have I, from earliest childhood—to undress myself and even to fold and hang my clothes properly."

She laughed at this and it made her even more attractive. If Grimes had not been so well looked after on the voyage out from Earth he might well have yielded to temptation.

"Good night," he said firmly.

"Good night, Your Excellency," she said softly.

A little later, wrestling with the fastenings of his archaic finery, he regretted not having retained her services if only to help him to undress.

Chapter 13

She called him at seven, placing the tea tray down on the bedside table with a musical clatter and then whispering softly into his ear, "It is morning, Your Excellency. It is morning."

Grimes ungummed his eyes and looked up at her. There must be, he admitted, far worse sights with which to start the day. She smiled at him and poured tea from the pot with its willow pattern decoration into a handleless cup on which was the same design. As soon as he had struggled into a sitting posture, propped by the plump pillows that she had arranged for him, she handed him the cup. He handed it back to her. When he first awoke it was not a drink that he needed but the reverse. With some embarrassment—normally he slept naked—he got out of the bed on the side away from her and padded through to the bathroom. The pressure on his bladder relieved, he returned to his bed and slid the lower portion of his body under the covers. This time he accepted the cup and sipped from it gratefully. He saw that she had brought his pipe from where he had left it in the office and had filled it. She put one end of the stem into her mouth, applied flame to the bowl from a small, golden lighter that she brought from the side pocket of her tunic. When it was drawing properly she handed it to him.

Even an Admiral, thought Grimes smugly, *wouldn't be getting service like this . . .* He wondered if he, as a Planetary Governor, outranked an Admiral. *De jure*, possibly, if not *de facto*.

He sipped and smoked, smoked and sipped.

She asked, "What does Your Excellency desire for breakfast?"

"What's on the menu?" Grimes asked.

"Whatever Your Excellency wishes," she said.

A roll in bed with honey, he thought. Then, *Down, boy, down!*

He said, after consideration, "Grapefruit, please. Then two eggs, sunny side up, with bacon and country fried potatoes. Hot rolls. Butter. Lemon marmalade. Coffee. . . ."

"At once, Your Excellency?"

"No, thank you. I always like to shower and depilate and all the rest of it first. And dress. . . ."

"What will Your Excellency wear this morning?"

And just what was a Governor's undress uniform?

"I leave it to you. Something informal, or relatively so. . . ."

He put the almost empty cup down on to the tray with a decisive clatter, declined the offer of a refill. When she removed the tea things, carrying the tray through to the sitting room, he got out of bed. There was an old-fashioned bolt on the door to the toilet facilities; he shot it. He completed his morning ablutions, depilation and all the rest of it without interruption. On returning to the bedroom he found that the bed had been made and that clothing had been laid out on it—underwear, a ruffled shirt of orange silk, dark gray, sharply creased slacks. Highly polished, gold-buckled shoes stood by the couch.

He dressed and went through to where a low table had been set with crockery and cutlery, a covered dish of hot rolls, a butter dish and another with the marmalade. There was a pot of coffee, a bowl of sugar crystals and a jug of cream. A prepared half grapefruit awaited his attention, as did that morning's issue of *The Liberty Star*. He sat down, propped the newspaper against the coffee pot and made a start on the grapefruit. He read the account of Madam President's reception for the new Governor the previous evening. He was amused to see himself referred to as "an officer who achieved great distinction whilst in the Federation Survey Service" and as "a successful shipowner who has put his great administrative and business talents at the disposal of both his home planet and of Liberia." The piece on Grimes concluded with the pious hope that he, as an experienced captain both of spaceships and of industry, would not feel the urge, as had his predecessor, to meddle officiously in the smooth running of the world that he had been called upon to govern.

The attentive Su Lin—he had not noticed her return—removed the plate with the now empty grapefruit shell, replaced it with that occupied by his eggs and bacon. She asked him how he preferred his coffee. He told her that he liked it black. He held the paper in both hands as she poured.

The eggs, bacon and fried potatoes were just as he liked them. The rolls were crisp. The marmalade, when finally he got to it, was deliciously tangy. By this time he had turned to the INTERSTELLAR SHIPPING—ARRIVALS AND DEPARTURES columns. *Sobraon's* arrival and departure were listed as *Orbital Only*. *Willy Willy*, with the obnoxious Dreeble commanding, had lifted off, with passengers for Isa—a world rich in metals, Grimes knew, with mining and smelting as the major industries—while the Governor had been enjoying himself at the reception. One did not need to be clairvoyant, he thought, to know what sex those passengers belonged to or for what employment they had been recruited. *Bulkalgol* and *Bulkvega* were due out very shortly, with grain, one for Waverley and the other for Caribbea. After that it looked like being a slack time, for some weeks, at Port Libertad. One name among the *Future Arrivals* caught Grimes's attention—*Agatha's Ark*. He remembered that old flash of prevision he had experienced while *Sobraon's* temporal precession field had been building up.

He filled his pipe, brought the stem to his mouth. Before he could strike a match Su Lin was holding the flame from a golden lighter over the charred bowl. Grimes hated having his pipe lit for him but submitted to the attention. He did not mind, however, having another cup of the excellent coffee poured for him.

The Liberty Star, he discovered ran to a daily crossword puzzle. He got up from the breakfast table and sat down in one of the easy chairs. Without being asked the girl brought him a slim, golden stylus from the office. But the puzzle was not to his taste; it was not of the cryptic variety. Furthermore it required of the would-be solver an encyclopedic knowledge of Terran political history—names, dates and all. And that, thought Grimes, was not a subject in which he would ever be awarded full Marx. He savored the pun, knocked out his pipe in a convenient ashtray (it had been burning unevenly), refilled it and, Su Lin being temporarily absent, clearing away the breakfast things, lit it properly himself.

He got up and, trailing an acrid rather than an aromatic cloud of blue smoke, wandered out into the corridor and, to his pleased surprise, found his way to the main doorway of the Residence without too much trouble. Servants bowed to him as he passed, the guard on duty at the entrance to the building saluted smartly.

It was pleasant outside, the morning sun warm but not too much so, the light breeze carrying the scent of the gaudy flowers from the big, ornamental beds. The closely cropped grass of the lawn was springy under the soles of his shoes. Su Lin joined him, walking respectfully to his left and half a pace to the rear. He was conscious of her presence and found himself wishing that their relationship was not one of master and servant.

She broke the silence.

"Your Excellency," she said, "someone approaches from the air."

"Thank you," said Grimes. He had already heard a distant clatter, looked up and seen a dark speck in the sky. He stopped walking and stared at it. Su Lin produced from a pocket a thin, round case, about twenty millimeters in diameter. She did something to it and it opened out into a tapered tube. She removed the covers from each end, handed it to Grimes. He realized that it was a telescope, a sophisticated instrument with a universal focus. He raised it to his right eye, managed to bring the approaching aircraft into the field of it. It was a minicopter, little more than a bubble-enclosed chair with two long skids under it as landing gear and over it the almost invisible rotating vanes.

Grimes recognized the pilot. It was Raoul Sanchez. He raised his free hand to wave. The young pilot returned the salutation, altered course slightly so as to come into a landing close to where Grimes and the girl were standing. Almost immediately the little aircraft was surrounded by a small crowd of indignant gardeners, gesticulating and shouting in high-pitched voices, pointing at the barely visible scars that the landing gear of the minicopter had made on the surface of the lawn. Sanchez grinned and shrugged apologetically. A door slid open in the surface of the transparent bubble.

"Better keep off the grass, Captain," said Grimes. "You'd better shift to the drive before we have a riot on our hands."

"Willco, Your Excellency."

The gardeners scrambled back as the vanes started to spin again. The machine lifted, drifted slowly over to the broad drive, settled down again, the skids crunching audibly on the gravel. By the time that Grimes had walked to it Sanchez had unstrapped himself from the chair and disembarked. He was wearing a suit of faded, deliberately frayed denim and a red neckerchief. He bowed formally to Grimes.

He said, "Your aerial chauffeur, Your Excellency, reporting for duty."

Lieutenant Smith who, accompanied by two soldiers, had come on to the scene achieved an expression that was both sneer and scowl.

Chapter 14

Sanchez led the way around the sprawling Residence to what was almost a minor airport. He had been there before, of course, while his brother had been atmosphere pilot to the late Governor Wibberley. There were hangars—two of them occupied and the third, the very big one, empty. Outside this, at a suitable distance, was a tripedal mooring mast.

Smith said, with a gesture toward this construction, "Your airship will be delivered this afternoon, Your Excellency. One of the Army's Lutz-Parsivals. Colonel Bardon has appointed Lieutenant Duggin to be your pilot."

Before Sanchez could protest Grimes said, "I have made my own appointment, Lieutenant. Captain Sanchez will be flying me."

"But the Colonel . . ."

"Is not the Governor. *I* am."

"But Captain Sanchez is a spaceman . . ."

"And a qualified airshipman. Is that not so, Captain?"

"It is, Your Excellency," replied Sanchez as Smith said nastily, "So was his brother."

"That will do, Lieutenant Smith!" snapped Grimes while making a *Pipe down!* gesture aimed at the other man. "That will do. Captain Sanchez is my pilot. And now, Captain, shall we look at what toys we shall have to play with?"

He walked to one of the occupied hangars, into it. The craft housed therein was a small pinnace of a type carried by the larger warships of the Survey Service, a spaceship in miniature. That, thought Grimes, he could fly himself—although legally he couldn't, his Master Astronaut's Certificate having been suspended. (Of course there was his Reserve Commission but that was supposed to be kept a secret.) Sanchez opened a door in the pinnace's side, into the litle airlock. Grimes clambered on board, followed by Sanchez and Smith. He went forward first, to the control cab. With two exceptions the instrumentation on the console seemed to be in order. Certain switches, dials and screens had been removed and replaced by blank cover plates.

"No Mini-Mannschenn?" asked Grimes. "No Carlotti deep space radio?"

"They were removed, Your Excellency," said Smith, "when Colonel Bardon had this pinnace modified for the Governor's use."

"Modified *how*?" demanded Grimes.

"The space occupied by that equipment was required for the bar and for . . . for . . ."

"Mphm," grunted Grimes. He asked suddenly, "Does the Residence run to its own Carlotti transceiver?" (That was one of the many things, he thought, that he should have found out long before he arrived on Liberia.)

"No, Your Excellency," said Smith. "Surely you must have noticed that there are no Carlotti antennae on the roof."

"They could be in the cellar," said Grimes, "and work just as well."

Smith made a show of ignoring this and continued, "The only Carlotti equipment is at the spaceport. It is manned and maintained, of course, by Terran personnel."

And so the Governor, thought Grimes, *can communicate directly with Earth only by courtesy of the Garrison Commander*.

He completed his inspection of the pinnace. He was not overly impressed. He could not refrain from using his memories of *Little Sister* as a yardstick. When he made his way out through the airlock Su Lin was there to help him down to the ground. He waved her aside irritably and then, when he saw her hurt expression, rather hated himself.

He said, "It's all right, Su. I'm a spaceman. I'm used to getting into and out of these things."

With the others he made his way into the other hangar in use. The aircraft there was a helicopter, a rather beat-up Drachenflieger, no doubt one of Bardon's cast-offs. Sanchez looked at the machine disparagingly.

"Governor Wibberley," he said, "never used this. My brother reckoned that it wasn't safe."

"And he, of course," said Smith, "was an expert on aeronautical safety."

"*You* . . ." the pilot growled, his fist raised threateningly.

"Lieutenant Smith," snapped Grimes, putting a control room crackle into his voice, "you will refrain from making provocative remarks." Then, his voice a little milder, "Captain Sanchez, I will not tolerate brawling among the members of my . . . family. And now, will you take luncheon with me?"

"Thank you, Your Excellency."

"And will you, Lieutenant Smith, please inform us when the airship is approaching?"

"Very good, Your Excellency."

The party walked back to the main entrance to the building, Sanchez beside Grimes, Su Lin the usual half pace to the rear and Smith, sulking hard, well astern.

It was a leisurely and pleasant meal, with drinks before, served by the attentive Su Lin. The honeyed sand crawlers were especially good, reminding Grimes of the honeyed prawns that he had enjoyed in Chinese restaurants on Earth. With the meal there was rice wine, served warm in tiny cups. When it was over Grimes lit his pipe—waiting until the girl was out of the room—and Sanchez a slim, black cigar.

The pilot said, "I must apologize for having lost my temper with your ADC, Excellency."

"He asked for it," said Grimes. "I've been considering asking Colonel Bardon for a replacement, but . . ."

"Better the devil you know, sir."

"Precisely. You must have seen him, now and again, when you visited your brother here."

"Yes. I never did like him. He didn't like me. And my brother hated him. It was mutual."

"He's Bardon's man, of course."

"Of course," agreed Sanchez.

Su Lin returned with coffee.

"Is it switched on, Su?" asked the pilot.

"Yes, Raoul," she replied.

Grimes stared at them.

"Is *what* switched on?" he demanded.

"A device that I carry," she replied. "A—how shall I call it? A conversation modifier. It takes our voices and—scrambles? shuffles? To any listener you are telling Raoul about some of your deep space adventures and he is asking questions about them."

"And what are you saying?"

"I am urging Your Excellency to take at least one of these *chinrin* cakes with your coffee. *Chinrin* cakes, of course, were a great delicacy on New Canton. The refugees brought *chinrin* seeds with them when they came here and now we have our own little plantations of the shrubs."

"This modifier," asked Grimes curiously. "Does it have to be programmed?"

"Only in the most general of terms. It could almost be said to be intelligent. Perhaps it functions psionically. It could be a form of pseudolife but that I cannot say. I am not a scientist."

"Could I see it?" asked Grimes curiously.

To his surprise she blushed embarrassedly.

"When Su Lin said that she carried the modifier," explained Sanchez, "she didn't mean that she carried it *on* her . . ."

"An implant?" asked Grimes.

"Yes, sir. But not a *surgical* implant. If you know what I mean."

"Oh. So am I to understand that as long as she's around, and along as she has *it* switched on, the bugs with which the Residence must be crawling will be sending absolutely fictitious reports to Bardon's monitors. I suppose that the bugs *are* Bardon's?"

"Of course, sir," said Sanchez.

"Mphm." He turned to Su Lin. "So you're rather more than my faithful handmaiden, it seems—just as Wong Lee is rather more than my faithful majordomo. But this . . . this *thing* of yours . . . where did you get it?"

It was Sanchez who answered.

"Shortly after the late Governor Wibberley's so-called accident there was a salesman here from Electra—not that he called himself a salesman. Trade Representative was his title. He was wined and dined by Estrelita but didn't make any sales. He was allowed to wander around without supervision—after all, what harm could a woolly-witted scientist-engineer do? He enjoyed a liaison with one of our girls, an OAP member." He grinned. "She put the hard sell onto him and made a convert. Probably only a temporary one but still a convert. She told him about our problems and of the way in which the Governor, who had been taking too much interest in the state of affairs here, had been eliminated. . . ."

"Tanya Mendoza is a friend of mine," said Su Lin. "She came to visit me here. It was quite natural that she should bring her Electran friend with her and quite natural that I should show him around the Residence. He had a detector with him—although as far as Smith and Jaconelli were concerned he had nothing on him but the usual camera and recorder carried by tourists. He confirmed our suspicions that—as you have said—the Residence is crawling with bugs. He promised Tanya that he would do something about it, something that would not be obvious to the . . . the . . . buggers. Is there such a word?"

"There is," said Grimes, "although its real meaning is not the one that you have given it."

Looking at her face he saw that she was making some sort of physical effort. He was about to ask what was wrong when Sanchez said, "Very interesting, Your Excellency. Very interesting. . . ."

Then, from behind him, Smith said, "Your Excellency, the airship is approaching now."

So the device had been switched off, Grimes realized. So all conversation from now on was being faithfully and truthfully recorded.

He turned to face his ADC.

"We'll be right out," he said.

Chapter 15

The Lutz-Parsival came in slowly and cautiously.

She was a graceful ship despite her chubbiness, her metal skin gleaming brightly in the sunlight. On her tail fins was painted the insignia of Bardon's regiment, a rampant golden lion. He would have to get that changed, thought Grimes. To a kangaroo? Why not?

"He's handling her like a cow handling a musket," muttered Sanchez disgustedly.

Grimes was inclined to agree. The approach was overly careful and then, in the final stages, clumsy. The ship dropped too fast as the helium in the gas cells was compressed and then lifted steeply as water ballast was dumped to compensate, drenching the gubernatorial party.

"If this," said Grimes furiously to Smith, "is a fair sample of the Army's airmanship it's just as well that I've appointed my own pilot!"

"Your Excellency," replied the ADC, "Lieutenant Duggin is a little rusty. . . ."

"If we were made of metal," said Grimes, "we'd be getting rusty!"

With his hand he wiped the water from his face. He would have liked to take his shirt off to wring it out.

"Your Excellency," said Su Lin, "you must go back inside to change into dry clothing."

"It doesn't matter, Su. I'll soon dry out. I want to see what other comic turns that clown up there is going to put on for us."

The airship circled slowly, once again losing altitude. This time her descent could be measured in millimeter/seconds. It was a long and painful process. By the time that the dangling lines had been picked up by the ground party—soldiers of the Governor's Guard supplemented by New Cantonese gardeners—Grimes's clothing was merely damp. And then the pilot did not use his engines for the final approach to the mast but was towed into position by the mooring crew. At last the nose cone was secure in the socket. A ladder was lowered from the control gondola and down it scrambled the plump figure of the pilot, handling himself as clumsily as he had handled the ship. He shambled rather than marched to where Grimes was standing and threw a casual salute in his direction.

"Lieutenant Duggin, Your Excellency. Reporting for duty."

"Lieutenant Duggin, you are relieved from duty," Grimes told him. "Lieutenant Smith will make arrangements for your transport back to barracks."

"But I'm your pilot, sir."

"You are not. But if ever I require a bath attendant I'll send for you."

"But, sir. . . ."

"That is all, Lieutenant. Captain Sanchez, do you wish Lieutenant Duggin to make a formal hand over?"

"It would be advisable, Your Excellency."

"Very well, Captain. See to it, will you?"

He stood with Su Lin and Smith watching as the two pilots walked to the dangling ladder and mounted it. As it took their weight the airship sagged down from the mast and then resumed her horizontal attitude. No further ballast was dumped; no doubt there was an automatic release of pressure from the atmospheric trimming cell or cells.

"Wait here, Mr. Smith, to look after Mr. Duggin after he's handed over," Grimes told the ADC.

He walked with Su Lin back to his quarters in the Residence.

She brought him tea. He sent her away to get another cup so that she could join him in the taking of refreshment.

He asked, "Are you switched on?"

She said, "Yes, Your Excellency."

"And what are we talking about?"

"I am telling you about the New Cantonese festivals that we still observe on this world."

"Fireworks, processions of lanterns and dragons and all that?"

"Yes, Your Excellency."

"I hope to see at least one of your festivals."

"You will be an honored guest."

"Thank you, Su." He sipped from his cup. "Now you can tell me about the underground. What do you do, what do you hope to accomplish?"

"As far as we, and the other refugees, are concerned we want full citizenship. As far as Captain Sanchez and the OAP are concerned they want a return to the egalitarian principles of the original colonists of the planet. All of us are against the regime of Estrelita O'Higgins and Colonel Bardon and the vicious trades that they foster."

"Such as?"

"The shipping of girls—yes, and boys—to the brothels of various worlds where there is a demand for them, such as Isa and Venusberg. The pleasure houses—so-called—on this planet. The drug trade. And the profiteering in all the stores at which the refugees must purchase the essentials of life to ensure that nobody can possibly save enough money to become financially independent."

"So you want a revolution."

"Yes. Not necessarily an armed revolt, although it might have to come that." (And was this, wondered Grimes, his solicitous handmaiden with her limited but courtly English? She was reminding him more and more of a girl he had once known who had been President of the University of Kandral's Young Socialist Club and who had finished up as Vice President of the planet.) "We realize that once we take up arms against O'Higgins we shall also be taking up arms against Earth, against the Federation, as represented here by Bardon. If it is at all possible the change must be made by constitutional methods. The Governor is more than a mere figurehead. He has . . . How shall I put it? He has the power to hire and fire."

"Mphm?" Grimes knocked out and refilled his pipe. Su Lin reverted to her serving maid persona and lit it for him. He thought, *I shall have to try to break her of* that *habit.* "Mphm?"

"Governor Wibberley was conducting his own investigation of the state of affairs here. He had amassed considerable evidence of malpractices. He was almost ready to act. And then. . . ."

"So you want me, as Governor, to sack Colonel Bardon *and* President O'Higgins *and* all her ministers. . . ."

She said, "There have been precedents. There was one, in *your* country, on Earth, many years ago."

He said, "There's more than one Australian precedent. The Governor General, Sir John Kerr, sacked Prime Minister Gough Whitlam. Some years previously the Governor of New South Wales, Sir Philip Game, sacked Premier Jack Lang. . . ."

"You see."

He went on. "And many years before that the garrison in New South Wales deposed the Governor, Captain—as he was then—William Bligh."

"And wasn't Bligh," she asked, "the man who was always having mutinies? You've had a few yourself, haven't you?"

"Which doesn't mean that I like having them, Su."

She laughed. "I suppose not. But there must be ways of doing things constitutionally. And to do them without calling Earth first for approval—always supposing that Bardon let you get a message through."

"Messages did get through, after Wibberley's death," said Grimes. "That's why I'm here."

"As trouble shooter?" she asked. "Or as shit stirrer? In any case, Bardon's made sure that no more messages get through without his knowledge."

"Just who—or what—are you, Su Lin?" he asked.

"You have seen my dossier, Your Excellency."

"For what it's worth."

"There *is* a Su Lin," she told him. "But she is not on Liberia any longer. She was carefully selected out of all the New Cantonese as being almost my double. I required only minor body sculpture to make me her replica."

"Then what is your real name?"

"It doesn't matter. I rather like Su Lin, anyhow."

"Where are you from? You aren't from FIA, are you? Or are you? If you are I should have been told."

"I am not."

"The Sinkiang People's Republic?"

"No. The New Cantonese here are no worse off than they would be on New Sinkiang."

"Then where?"

There was a knock on the door. Grimes saw Su Lin's face go briefly tense as her vaginal muscles switched off the device that she carried.

Sanchez entered.

"I have taken delivery of the Lutz-Parsival, Your Excellency," he reported formally. "She seems to be airworthy in all respects, although I shall have to make a more detailed inspection later." (*To look for hidden bombs*, thought Grimes.) "I have left her at the mast, in the sunlight, to recharge the power cells."

"I think that I'd like to have a sniff round aboard her myself," said Grimes, "if you will be so good as to accompany me."

"Of course, Your Excellency," said Sanchez.

Chapter 16

"We shall have to give her a name," said Grimes to Sanchez as he and the pilot made their way along the catwalk running from stem to stern inside the airship. "LP17 is too . . . impersonal. Ships are more than just . . . *things*."

"What do you have in mind, Your Excellency?"

Grimes thought hard. There had been quite a few ships for which he had felt a real affection, most recently *Little Sister* and *Sister Sue*. He grinned.

"*Fat Susie*," he said. "She is rather plump, isn't she? I'll tell Mr. Jaconelli to organize painters for you to put the new name on the envelope. And at the same time they can change the insignia on the tail fins. I want a kangaroo instead of that tomcat of Bardon's."

"People might think," said Sanchez, "that you're naming the ship after Su Lin."

"She's not fat," Grimes told him. "But there was a fat Susie, not so very long ago."

(He wondered where she was now, how she was faring.)

He inspected the comfortable lounge with its wide out-and-down looking windows on either side, the not-too-Spartan sleeping accommodation, the little galley with a standard autochef. This, if he was going to make much use of *Fat Susie*, would have to be modified to his requirements. He spent some time in the control cab, familiarizing himself with the instrumentation. It would not take him long, he thought, to learn how to fly this thing.

"She'll do," he said at last.

He was first down the ladder with Sanchez not far behind him. As he dropped to the ground he heard the air pump start up to pressurize the helium in one of the cells to compensate for the loss of weight.

Sanchez, who would now be living in the Residence, dined with him that evening, the two men taking their meal in Grimes's sitting room. (He had decided to use the dining room only for state occasions.) They were waited upon by Su Lin. The meal was a good one, traditional New Cantonese cookery. The pilot wielded his ivory chopsticks with as much assurance as did Grimes.

There was no need for Su Lin to activate what Grimes thought of as the anti-bug; conversation consisted mainly of generalities and of astronautical shop talk. Finally Sanchez said good night and left. Su Lin brought more tea, for herself and Grimes.

She said, "I am switched on."

"Indeed? And what are we talking about, Su Lin? I have to call you that as I don't know your real name."

She laughed. "As far as the bugs are concerned you're living up to your reputation. Casanova Grimes, the terror of the spaceways."

"Do people really think of me like that?"

"Some of them do. Pirate, libertine. . . . Oh, you've a reputation all right."

"Mphm."

"If Bardon thinks that you're spending all your time womanizing he'll not be expecting you to start putting your foot down with a firm hand."

"Mphm."

He looked at her. It was obvious that she was enjoying being herself and not playing the part of a faithful handmaiden.

He said, "You were just going to tell me who you're really working for when Raoul came in."

"Yes, I was. Do you really want to know, Your Excellency?"

"As long as we're in private you can call me John."

"I am honored, John. I'm with Pat."

With Pat? Did she mean that she had an Irish boyfriend, Grimes wondered, and therefore out of bounds as far as he was concerned? But PAT was an acronym, he remembered. PAT. People Against Tyranny. He recalled the first time that he had heard of this organization; it was during a spell ashore between ships at Lindisfarne Base. A dictatorial planetary president had been assassinated and PAT had claimed the credit for this act of justice. There had been some discussion of the affair in the junior officers' mess.

"Aren't you running rather a risk telling me, Su?"

"I don't think so, Captain Grimes, Survey Service Reserve."

"My Reserve Commission is supposed to be a secret."

"It is—and PAT CC, Pat Central Committee, are among those keeping that secret."

"Do you mean to tell me that Admiral Damien is one of your members? If ever there was a tyrant, he's one!"

"So you say. But we have members everywhere. On Electra, for example. Silverman, the scientist/salesman, really came here just to check the bugs in the Residence and to supply me with the counter measure. But getting back to Damien—didn't it ever occur to you that, when he was O.C. Couriers and you a courier captain, he was always sending you on missions in the hope, usually realized, that you'd throw a monkey wrench into somebody's machinery at the right time?"

"You could look at it that way."

"And when it was necessary to put a stop to the privateering operations of Drongo Kane and the Eldorado Corporation—just who did Admiral Damien pressgang back into the Survey Service?''

"Me. All right, then. Since PAT seems to have been using me for the Odd Gods of the Galaxy alone know how many years, why have I never been asked to become a member?''

"Because you're an awkward bastard. You'd be as liable to throw a monkey wrench into our machinery as into anybody else's.''

"Then why are you spilling all these beans?''

"Because I was told to do so. It was decided that you should know that there is a galaxy-wide organization behind you—as long as you're doing the right things. And that if you do the wrong things—there's a nasty, mercenary streak in your nature—you'd better try to make a get-away to the Magellanic Clouds.''

Grimes got up from his chair and began to pace back and forth. He managed to light his pipe—on the run, as it were—before Su Lin could do it for him.

He said, "I don't like being manipulated.''

"You haven't been manipulated all the time,'' she told him.

"And this nasty, mercenary streak you accuse me of having. . . .''

"What shipowner doesn't have one?''

"Some more than others. More than me.''

"So you say.'' Her smile robbed the words of offense.

It did more than that, making her look very attractive. And, he knew now, there was no longer that master-servant relationship to deter him from entering into a relationship with her. But would she now renew the offer that she had made when, so far as he then knew, she was no more than a serving girl?

She was still smiling at him, on her feet and facing him. She did not break away when he took her in his arms—but she did not put her own arms about him. She did not turn her lips away from his—but she did not open them.

When the kiss—such as it was—was over she said, "As well as being mercenary, you're snobbish. You had the offer, your first day here, and you turned it down. And now that you know that there's no great social gulf yawning between us you think that we'll fall happily into bed together."

Now Grimes was really wanting her. He kissed her again, brutally, and, holding her to him, walked her backwards into the bedroom. He threw her on to the couch. She sprawled there, looking up at him. And was that contempt in her expression—or pity?

She said, "When I first met you, you were making the rules. Now I'm making them. You can have me when I'm ready—and not before. Once you've proven yourself to be as good a man as Governor Wibberley was. . . ."

"You mean that he and you. . . ."

"Try to get your mind off sex, John. He was a *good* man, a religious man. A Bible-basher you'd call him—but, unlike so many Christians, he really tried to live according to his faith, to comfort and succor the helpless. Even agnostics such as myself could appreciate him, to say nothing of the mess of Anarchists, Confucianists, Buddhists and the Odd Gods alone know what on this planet. We—the various undergrounds and PAT—hope that you will carry on his work, the restoration of hope and dignity to the refugee peoples, the suppression of Bardon's rackets. . . ."

"Get off your soap box, Su," said Grimes tiredly. "I'm here to do a job and I'll do it to the best of my ability. I'll expect some pay for my work—after all, I have that nasty, mercenary streak in me—but, if all goes well, I'll arrange it myself. It won't cost PAT anything. It won't cost *you* anything. And now, if you'll excuse me, I'd like to go to bed. By myself."

"I certainly do not intend otherwise."

She got up from the bed and walked slowly out of the room.

"Call me at the usual time," Grimes called after her.

Chapter 17

The next day Grimes had been looking forward to taking a test flight in *Fat Susie* but, while he was having his breakfast, Jaconelli brought him a list of the day's appointments. He was to be host at a luncheon, he learned, for Madam President and her ministers. After this he was to accompany her to the official opening of the new Handicrafts Center just outside Libertad. After that he was free—for what little remained of the day.

He spent the forenoon familiarizing himself with the Residence, guided by Wong Lee and with Su Lin and Lieutenant Smith in attendance. It was one of those buildings that seemed to have just happened, additional rooms and facilities being tacked on to an originally quite small house as required. The servants' quarters were underground, as was the kitchen. Grimes lingered here, using a pair of long chopsticks handed to him by the chef to sample tidbits from various cooking utensils. He did some more nibbling during his tour of the storerooms.

There were the vaults in which the records were stored—or had been stored. Filing cabinets were empty and the only information available from the read-out screens was purely domestic—food, light, heating and wages bills for the past decade and the like. Grimes found details of the last official luncheon given by his predecessor. Wibberley had been English and had fed his guests on pea soup, Dover sole (were there sole in Liberia's seas?), steak and kidney pie, trifle and a cheese board featuring Stilton, Wensleydale and cheddar. He wondered how the New Cantonese kitchen staff had coped with this feast. To judge by the two breakfasts that he had already enjoyed they had probably made a very good job of it—just as they would almost certainly do with the menu that he had ordered.

He returned to his quarters to change from shirt and slacks into an informally formal lightweight suit. Su Lin, the dutiful handmaiden, assisted him unnecessarily to dress. She walked with him out to the portico where, with Jaconelli and the ADC, he waited to receive the guests.

Bardon, wearing a dark blue civilian suit that was almost a uniform, rode in with Estrelita O'Higgins in the presidential limousine. The President was in superbly cut blue denim with scarlet touches. The ministers and their companions were similarly clad. Before luncheon there were drinks in one of the big reception rooms.

The Colonel cornered Grimes while the Governor was graciously circulating among the guests.

He said abruptly, "I hear that my Lieutenant Duggin isn't good enough for you, Your Excellency."

"Frankly, Colonel, he isn't," said Grimes. "In any case I'd already made my own appointment of an atmosphere pilot."

"I was hoping, Your Excellency," said Bardon, "that you, with a military rather than an academic background, would be more cooperative with the Garrison than the late Governor Wibberley was."

"A military background, Colonel? Piracy, you mean?"

"I was referring to your Survey Service career, Your Excellency."

"In the Survey Service, Colonel, we expected a reasonably high standard of ship-handling competence."

"Ship-handling, sir? An airship is not a spaceship."

"One did not need to be an airshipman to know that Duggin was not very competent."

"You are entitled to your opinion, Your Excellency."

Grimes wandered on, chatting with the other guests. Most of them, inevitably, asked him what he thought of Liberia and then, before he could make reply, told him what he should think.

And then the sonorous booming of a gong announced that luncheon was about to be served.

Grimes enjoyed the meal in spite of the company; he did not like fat cats and most of the guests could be categorized as such. The Residence chef and his assistants had done very well. Local crustacea, served simply with a melted butter dressing, could almost have been the yabbies that Grimes remembered from his younger days in Australia. The Colonial Goose—leg of hogget, well spiced—could not have been better. The tropical fruit salad, its components marinated in wine, was a suitable conclusion to the meal. There should have been kangaroo tail soup for the first course but the necessary ingredients had not been available on this planet.

It was Estrelita O'Higgins, sitting at Grimes's right, who brought the luncheon party to a close.

"Your Excellency, they will be waiting for us at the Handicrafts Center. Oh, there is no *real* hurry." She smiled. "Everybody of any importance is here. Nonetheless, we have our obligations. Our duties."

She asked for more coffee.

Finally the party made its collective way to the waiting cars. Grimes rode in his own official vehicle, accompanied by his ADC and with two soldiers sitting forward, with the chauffeur. Estrelita O'Higgins led the motorcade.

The new Handicrafts Center was a big, single-storied hall, one of those buildings that manage to show signs of dilapidation even before their completion. It looked like an unprosperous factory. Outside its main entrance, which was bedecked with wilted flowers, was a small crowd. There was a band which, at the approach of the official cars, struck up with a selection of Australian folk songs which, at first, Grimes found it hard to recognize; every one of them sounded like a military march. There were the schoolchildren with their little flags. Most of them, Grimes noted, were New Cantonese. There were older people—teachers?—and they, too, were mainly representative of the refugee population.

The cars stopped.

Estrelita O'Higgins, squired by Colonel Bardon, got out of hers. There was some not very enthusiastic flag waving and a ragged cheer. Grimes, accompanied by his ADC, disembarked. Was it his imagination or was the cheering a little louder?

The President, accompanied by Grimes, Bardon and the Minister of Industry, mounted a temporary, bunting-covered dais. She spoke into a microphone and her amplified voice came from the speakers mounted on the streetlamp standards. She told her listeners how Liberia—that generous host!—had supplied facilities for the fitting education of the children of those to whom refuge had been given.

God bless the Squire and his relations, thought Grimes, *and keep us in our proper stations.*

Manual Silvero, the Minister of Industry, said *his* piece. He extolled the virtues of labor. A fat, short, greasy man he looked, thought Grimes, as though he had never done an honest day's work in his life.

He concluded, "And now it is my honor to request His Excellency, Commodore John Grimes, to open this well-appointed, palatial, even, training establishment."

The President led the way down from the dais. Bardon indicated that Grimes should follow her. The others came after them. They walked to the entrance, which had a scarlet, silken ribbon strung across it. A young man—a native Liberian—approached them, bearing a plump, purple cushion. On it was a pair of golden scissors. Bowing, he presented the implement to the Governor.

Grimes took the scissors, worked them experimentally. They seemed to be in order. He walked the few steps to where the ribbon barred his way to the drab looking interior of the Handicrafts Center.

And was it accidental or did somebody possess both a sense of humor and an acquaintance with Australian folk music?

Click go the shears . . .

Click went the shears and the ribbon parted.

The children cheered (because they had to) and there was a patter of polite handclapping.

Chapter 18

Grimes returned to the Residence.

Sanchez was waiting for him in the portico.

He said, as soon as Grimes was out of the car, "I've taken her out, Your Excellency . . ."

Grimes wondered who *she* was.

"She handles quite well . . ."

"Oh. *Fat Susie*."

"Of course. What did you think I meant, sir?"

"Come with me to my office and tell me about it." Then, to the ADC, "I'll not be requiring you any more today, Lieutenant Smith."

"Very good, Your Excellency."

As soon as Grimes and the pilot were seated Su Lin materialized with a tea tray.

"Are you switched on?" Grimes asked the girl. He realized, too late, that this would be rather a foolish question, one that would cause the snoopers to wonder, to add two and two to make at least five, if she were not.

But she was.

Grimes said, "I want to wander around the city incognito. To see for myself without having to peer through a thick screen of officials, politicians and hangers on."

"Like that Caliph of Baghdad," said Raoul. "Haroun al Raschid or whatever his name was."

"Yes."

"Governor Wibberley used to do it," said Su Lin. "I would help him with his disguise. A denim suit, false whiskers. A voice modulator. . . ."

"But how did he—how do *I*—get out of this place unobserved?"

"Wong Lee has a car," she said. "It's a van, rather, with

the back enclosed. He runs into the city now and again, in the evening. He goes to the Golden Lotus Club. This is one of his recreational nights."

"And mine," said Grimes, suddenly making up his mind. "Su, could you disguise me? Is there a denim suit that would fit? Can you still lay your hands on the other things?"

"Of course."

"And would you come with me, Raoul?"

"It will be my pleasure, sir."

"Then what are we waiting for?"

He went through to his bedroom and got out of his informal suit. When he was down to his underwear Su Lin came back with a bundle of clothing and other things. She unnecessarily helped him on with the floppy-collared white shirt and the scarlet neckerchief, the blue denim suit, the black, calf-length boots. There was a full-length mirror in the wardrobe door and Grimes admired himself in it. He rather liked this rig—but he was still him.

The girl told him to sit in a chair, went behind him to carry on the work of disguise. He felt the sticky coldness as some adhesive was dabbed on to his skull behind his ears and then her hands as she firmly pressed the prominent appendages to the fast-setting gum. She came around to stand in front of him and looked down at him.

She said, "That's better. Now, open your mouth, please . . ."

He obeyed.

Her deft fingers inserted a pad, a tiny cushion covered in slick plastic, into each side of his mouth, under each cheek. He was, of course, aware of their presence although they were not uncomfortable.

"Now look at yourself," she told him.

He got up from the chair and did so. He stared at the chubby-faced stranger who stared back at him from the mirror.

He asked, "Don't I get a moustache?"

His voice was as strange as his appearance, high, squeaky almost. He could see his expression of surprise.

She told him, "The voice modulator is incorporated in one of the cheek pads. The way you look and the way you sound nobody will recognize you."

"Perhaps. But just about everybody on this world has face fungus of some kind."

"All right." She went back to the things that she had laid out on the bed and selected something that looked, at first glance, like a large, hairy insect. "This is self-adhesive," she told him. "You'll need a special spray, of course, to get it off."

Grimes looked at himself again.

That heavy moustache suited him, he thought. It was a great pity that his modulated voice did not go with his macho appearance. He supposed, ruefully, that he couldn't have everything.

He took the broad-brimmed black hat, with its scarlet ribbon, that the girl handed him, went through to the sitting room. Sanchez got up from the chair in which he had been sitting when Grimes entered. At first Grimes did not recognize him; the tuft of false beard on his chin was an effective disguise.

Sanchez asked, "Ready, Joachim?"

"Joachim?"

"You have to have a name."

"Joachim, then," agreed Grimes. "I rather like it." He patted his empty pockets. "What do I use for money?"

Su Lin handed him a well-worn notecase and a small handful of silver and copper coins.

She said, "At first you'd better let Raoul do the paying, until you get the feel of the local currency."

"That shouldn't be long," Grimes told her. "As a spaceman I'm used to paying for things, on all sorts of worlds, in all sorts of odd coins and pieces of paper or whatever. And now, as soon as I've found my pipe and tobacco, I'll be ready to go."

"You will *not* smoke a pipe, Joachim," said Su Lin severely.

"I've seen people smoking pipes in Libertad."

"And everybody knows that *you* smoke one. There were cartoons in the newspapers when your appointment was first announced; in every one of them you had a pipe stuck in your face. Pipe and ears—those are your trademarks."

"Mphm."

"Here's a packet of cigars, and a lighter. And now, if both of you will follow me, I'll take you to the truck."

Grimes thought that he had already acquired a fair knowledge of the geography of the Residence; he soon discovered that he had not. There was a door that he had thought was just part of the paneling in the corridor; beyond this was a corridor of the kind that, aboard a ship, would be called a working alleyway. There was a tradesman's entrance. Beyond this was the rather shabby van, in the driver's seat of which the old majordomo was sitting. Wong Lee was not wearing his livery but was looking very dignified in a high-collared suit of black silk, a round black hat of the same material on his head. He ignored Grimes and Sanchez as they clambered into the rear of the vehicle. The door shut automatically as soon as they were aboard. There was a roll of cloth of some kind on which they made themselves comfortable. The only light came from ventilation slits and that—it was all of half an hour after sunset—was fading fast.

The van started, so smoothly that the passengers were hardly aware of the motion. Raoul offered Grimes a long, thin cigar from his pack, took one himself. The two men smoked in companionable silence, broken eventually by the pilot.

He said, "Wong Lee's letting us off on the corner of May Day Street and Tolstoy Avenue. On the outskirts of the city. From there it'll be easy to get a trishaw. He'll pick us up on the same corner at 0100 tomorrow."

"And how do we fill in the time until then?" asked Grimes.

"Easily, Joachim. I'll try to give you an idea of the way in which the refugees are exploited here. We'll do a tour of the pleasure district."

"Combining business with pleasure, as it were," said Grimes.

"You can put it that way," said Raoul coldly, very coldly.

Grimes remembered, then, what he had been told when the pilot's shuttle craft brought him down from the orbiting *Sobraon* to Port Libertad, about the New Dallas girl called Mary Lou who had been one of the entertainers in the Pink Pussy Cat.

He said, inadequately, "I'm sorry, Raoul."

"There's no need to be, Joachim. I know that you're not the sort of man who'll get much pleasure from what we're going to see. You're no Holy Joe—as Wibberley was—but you have your principles."

"You hope," said Grimes, adding softly, "and *I* hope."

The van stopped.

The rear door opened on to a warm darkness that was enhanced rather than dispelled by the sparsely spaced, yellow streetlamps.

Grimes and Sanchez got out.

Without a word to them Wong Lee drove away.

Chapter 19

It did not seem to Grimes to be a place at which to wait for a cab—or its local equivalent—but, after a wait of no longer than five minutes, an empty trishaw, its operator pedaling lazily, drifted along, halting alongside them when hailed. Yet another New Cantonese, Grimes decided, a little man, scrawny in his sleeveless singlet and baggy shorts yet with muscles evident in his thighs and calves.

Grimes clambered into the basketlike passenger compartment, which was forward of the driver, followed by Sanchez who, before mounting, ordered, "Garden of Delights."

The trishaw operator grunted acknowledgment and, as soon as his passengers were seated, began pumping his pedals. The journey was mainly through quiet side streets and, Grimes decided, more or less toward the locality of Port Libertad, the glare of lights from which was now and again to the right and now and again to the left but always forward of the beam.

They came to a street that, by local standards, was fantastically bright and bustling. There were street stalls, selling foodstuffs, from which eddied all manner of savory aromas. There were brightly lit façades, establishments whose names were picked out in multi-colored lights. *The Pink Pussy Cat . . . The Dallas Whorehouse . . . The Old Shanghai . . . The Ginza . . . The Garden of Delights . . .*

The trishaw stopped.

Grimes got out and began to fumble for money. Sanchez forestalled him, tossing coins to the operator, who deftly caught them. The two men walked into the vestibule of the Garden of Delights where, sitting in a booth that was like a miniature pagoda, an elderly Oriental gentleman who could have been Wong Lee's slightly younger brother was sitting in receipt of custom.

Again Sanchez paid and led Grimes through a doorway, through an entanglement of beaded curtains, into a large, dimly lit room, the air of which was redolent with the fumes of the incense burners standing on tripods along the walls and between the tables. The decor, thought Grimes, was either phonily Terran Oriental or fair dinkum New Cantonese—but he had never been to New Canton and never would go there. (Neither would anybody else; the planet was now no more than a globe of incandescent slag.) There were rich silken hangings. There were bronze animals that could have been either lions or Pekingese dogs. There were overhead lanterns, glowing parchment globes encircled by painted dragons. There was music—the tinkling of harplike instruments, the high squealing of pipes, the muted thud of little drums.

There was a stage at one end of the hall. On it was a girl, gyrating languidly and gracefully to the beat of the music. She was attired in filmy veils and was discarding them one by one. (*And what the hell*, wondered Grimes, *did Salome have to do with China, or New Canton?*) Nonetheless he watched appreciatively. The girl was tall, high-breasted, slender-limbed. Her dance *was* a dance, did not convey the impression that she was disrobing hastily prior to jumping into the shower or into bed.

Grimes's attention was distracted momentarily by a waitress who came to their table. She was wearing a high-necked tunic that did not quite come down as far as possible, golden sandals and nothing else. She had brought two bowls of some savory mess, one of rice, what looked like a tall, silver teapot, two small silver goblets, two pairs of chopsticks. She poured from the pot into the cups, bowed and retreated.

"Your very good health, Joachim," said Sanchez, raising his cup.

"And yours, Raoul."

Grimes sipped. He had been expecting tea, was surprised—not unpleasantly—to discover that the liquid was wine, a hot, rather sweet liquor. He put the cup down, picked up his chopsticks and with them transferred a portion of rice to the sweet-and-sour whatever it was in his bowl. He sampled a mouthful of the mixture. It wasn't bad.

On the stage the dancer was down to her last veil. She swirled it around her—partially revealing, concealing, affording more glimpses, concealing again, finally dropping the length of filmy fabric. She stood there briefly, flaunting her splendid nudity. She bowed, then turned and glided sinuously from the stage. The orchestra (if one could call it that) fell silent. There was a pattering of applause.

Grimes looked around. There were not, he saw, many customers. There were men, dressed as he and Sanchez were. At two of the tables there were obvious spacers. At one of these the waitress was being mauled. Obviously the girl was not enjoying having those prying hands all over her body but she was not resisting.

"You'll not get shows like this out in the country, Joachim," said Sanchez.

(And that, thought Grimes, was the pilot's way of telling him that there could be bugs here. It was very hard, these days, to find a place that was not bug-infested.)

He said, "That was a lovely dollop of trollop. On the stage, I mean."

"She'll not be that way long, Joachim. The signs were there. Her eyes—didn't you notice?"

Grimes admitted that he hadn't paid much attention to her face.

"That faraway look. Dreamsticks. Soon she'll start to wither. The waitresses, too. But there are plenty more where they came from. Don't tell me that you haven't had the recruiters around your plantation yet."

"I thought that they were selling encyclopedias," said Grimes.

"Ha, ha!"

The music had started again, a livelier tune. The dancer

who came on the stage might have been beautiful once, still possessed the remains of beauty. But her movements were clumsy; her strip act was just that and nothing more. When she was completely naked she stood there, swaying, beckoning to various members of the audience. Grimes felt acutely ashamed when he, briefly, was the target of her allure. He was ashamed for his cloth when, finally, one of the spacers got to his feet and shambled to the stage.

"They aren't going to do it *here*?" he whispered to Sanchez.

"There are rooms at the back, Joachim. She'll want to go through his pockets in privacy. Her habit's expensive. But let's get out of here. It's not very often that you have a night on the town and there are more places to sample."

"Wait till I've finished my sweet-and-sour," said Grimes.

The Dallas Whorehouse was their next port of call. The girls there were all tall and blonde, the music a piano on which a tall, thin and very black man hammered out old-time melodies. He was far better than the instrument upon which he was performing. Grimes recognized "The Yellow Rose Of Texas" and, in spite of himself, was amused by the very well-endowed young lady who borrowed two twenty-cent pieces from a spacer sitting just under the stage and placed one over each nipple, after which she counter-rotated her breasts without dislodging the coins. When she was finished she deftly flipped them into the cupped hands of the spaceman.

"In a few weeks' time," said Sanchez sourly, "she'll have to use paper money—and stick it on with spit."

"A pity," said Grimes sincerely.

The pilot looked at his wrist companion. "Finish your beer, Joachim. I have to show you that the big city's not all boozing and wenching, otherwise you'll be going back home with a false impression."

"Give me time to finish the tacos and this chili dip," grumbled Grimes.

Chapter 20

The next place that they went to was a very dowdy house, one of a terrace, in a poorly lit side street. As they approached it Grimes wondered what sort of entertainment would be offered in such a venue; something unspeakably sordid, he thought.

There was a doorkeeper, a burly man wearing the inevitable frayed denims and the almost as inevitable heavy beard.

"Your contributions, comrades," he growled, gesturing toward a battered metal bowl on the table before him. There was a clink and rattle of coinage as Sanchez paid for himself and Grimes.

The two men passed through a curtained door into a hall, took seats toward the back. Grimes looked around curiously. The room, he saw, was less than half full. There were both women and men there, some of them obviously Liberians, some New Cantonese, some Negroid, some blondly Nordic. As yet there was nobody on the platform, behind which were draperies of black and scarlet bunting, at the end of the room.

Grimes was about to ask what was going on when a tall, heavily bearded man mounted the platform. He was followed by a fat woman, by two other men of average height and, finally, by a girl who was more skinny than slim, whose protuberant front teeth gleamed whitely in her dusky face. She took her seat at a battered upright piano; the others sat behind a long table on which were water bottles, glasses and what looked like (and were) old fashioned microphones.

The thin girl assailed the keyboard of her instrument. The people behind the table stood up. With a shuffling of feet and a subdued scraping of shifted chairs those in the body of the hall stood up. Everybody—excepting Grimes—started to sing.

The faith of our fathers lives on in our hearts,
The flame of their courage burns on,

Their banners still fly, let us lift them on high,
In the light of Liberia's sun . . .

There was more, much more. Grimes hummed along with the rather trite music while he listened to the words. This was a political meeting to which Sanchez had brought him, he decided, a gathering of the Original Anarchists. At last the song was over. Everybody sat down but the big, bearded man on the platform.

"Comrades," said this person. "Comrades, and honorary comrades . . ." (The New Cantonese? wondered Grimes. The refugees from New Dallas and other devastated worlds? So even the OAP was capable of discrimination . . .)

"Comrades. Honorary comrades. Again there is hope. Again Earth has sent us a Governor, one who may take our part, as Governor Wibberley did, against the tyranny of O'Higgins and Bardon. But I must warn you, all of you, not to place too much faith in him. After all, the man is no more than a common pirate. . . ." (Piracy, thought Grimes, wasn't exactly a common trade.) "We will support him if and when he confronts O'Higgins and Bardon. We will stand against him when he attempts to re-impose the rule of Imperial Earth.

"But what manner of man is this new Governor, this pirate Commodore Grimes? With whom shall we have to deal when the time comes? What say you, Chiang Sung?"

One of the New Cantonese got to his feet.

"I am only an under-chef at the Residence, Comrade. I have little contact with him. I have seen him, of course. He has inspected the kitchens. He was very affable. He appreciates good food. It will be a pleasure to work for such a gentleman. But Su Lin, his maidservant, can tell you more than I."

"And where *is* Su Lin?" demanded the fat woman. "Where is the Pekingese Princess? The airs and graces that she puts on when she's no more than a governor's trollop . . . Come to that—where is the Lord High Mandarin Wong Lee? With all due respect to Comrade Chiang Sung, we should exercise far greater discrimination."

"And where," demanded one of the smaller men on the platform, "is *Captain* Raoul Sanchez?" He went on, sneering heavily, "Oh, he came crying to us after that wench of his died and after his brother was murdered—or so he says.

But I suppose that now he's found himself a new girl and, as we know, he's inherited his brother's soft job he'll scrub us."

Grimes heard Sanchez growl softly and gave him a sharp nudge with his elbow.

He sat through a long and boring speech by the Comrade Chairman. The more he heard the less he was puzzled by the fact that the Liberian authorities tolerated the OAP. Probably many of the men and women at this meeting were government agents. Possibly these same agents, as dues-paying members, made quite heavy contributions to the OAP working expenses. He listened to horror stories from various refugees, men and women in domestic service whose masters and mistresses, according to them, were unduly harsh. Most of such tales left him unmoved. Those servants would not have lasted long in like capacities aboard any spaceship, naval or mercantile. Those who make a practice of insolence, dumb or otherwise, should not be surprised when their employers take counter measures.

The meeting came to a close just as Sanchez was beginning to fidget and snatch ever more frequent glances at his wrist companion. The pianist again battered the long-suffering keyboard. Everybody stood up.

Arise, ye prisoners of starvation,
Arise, ye wretched of the world,
For Justice thunders condemnation
And the flag of Hope's unfurled!
Then comrades come rally
And the last fight let us face,
Fraternity and Liberty
Unite the human race!

"Time we got going, Joachim," said Sanchez.

They made their way toward the door, accepting handfuls of leaflets as they did so. They were almost out and clear when they were accosted by a large, heavily moustached man.

"New here, comrades?"

"Yes, comrade," said Sanchez. "We're up from our plantation. Somebody told us that there was an OAP meeting so we thought we'd look in."

"Interested, comrades?"

"Yes. We have drifted away from the old ideals."

"I'd like to send you some more literature, comrades. Put you on our mailing list."

"We'd be pleased with that," Sanchez said. He pulled out his notecase, took out a card and gave it to the man. "And now, if you'll excuse us. We have a date. With two of the girls from the Whorehouse."

"But you're contributing to their degradation, comrades."

"Come off it, comrade. They like their work. Or they will with us—eh, Joachim? Come on, man. We mustn't keep the ladies waiting."

As they waited for a trishaw Grimes said, "Raoul, surely you could see that the man was some sort of under cover agent."

"Of course I did."

"But you gave him a card . . ."

"I didn't say that it was mine, did I?" He hailed an approaching trishaw. "Come on, Joachim. We mustn't keep Wong Lee waiting."

Chapter 21

Sitting in the back of Wong Lee's truck they talked.

"What did you think of the OAP meeting, sir?" asked Sanchez.

"Not much," said Grimes frankly. "Just an occasion to blow off harmless steam under the watchful eye of the authorities."

"You're right, sir. And the other places?"

"I've seen worse on other worlds."

"Including the encouragement to drug addiction?"

"Even that."

"But not in the same way, sir. On other planets there are pushers—but surely they are not employed by the government. The policy here, on Liberia, is that the refugees shall become so dependent on dreamsticks and other drugs that they lack the drive to achieve full citizenship."

"Are there any emancipists?" asked Grimes.

"Emancipists?"

"It's a term from Australian history, Raoul. During the days when New South Wales was a penal colony the emancipists were convicts who had been granted their freedom. More than a few of them became wealthy and influential men."

"We do have the equivalent here, sir, but there aren't many of them. There's Calvin McReady, who's one of our minor grain kings and all set to become a major one. There's Sin Fat, who owns the New Shanghai. But they regard themselves as Liberians, not as refugees, or ex-refugees. They are as money- and power-hungry as any of the native-born Establishment."

"So it was, all too often, in New South Wales," said Grimes. "But tell me, Raoul, why are you in the OAP? Is it only for personal reasons?"

Sanchez fell silent for a while, quietly smoking one of his long cigars.

Then, "There are more than personal reasons, sir. When I was a child I was taught the history of Liberia. After I left school—before, even—I could not help but see the disparity between the ideals of our founding fathers and what we have—despite all the lip service—now. . . ."

"Mphm. You went into an odd trade, didn't you, for one of your political beliefs. A spaceman has to accept discipline, take orders. Once he becomes captain he has to give orders."

"But I wanted to become a spaceman," Sanchez said. "I want to become a *real* spaceman, not a ferry master. Oh, I could never stand Survey Service discipline and spit and polish, such as you were once used to—but merchant ships are run on fairly democratic lines."

"Mphm," grunted Grimes dubiously.

"Of course, sir, what would be ideal would be a *little* ship, with no crew, of which I was owner-master. Something on the lines of that *Little Sister* of yours. . . ."

"Either accumulate at least a million credits or hire yourself out as yachtmaster to a billionairess who'll give you such a ship as a parting gift." Grimes laughed. "I did it the second way. I certainly couldn't have done it the first."

"But you must *know* people, sir."

"I do, Raoul, I do. Hinting, are you? Well, if all goes well I just might—only might, mind you—be able to get you a berth as a very junior officer in a deep space ship. After that it'd be up to you—getting in your deep space time, passing examinations and all the rest of it. There are no instant captains in deep space. But forget that we're spacemen. I'm a planetary governor who's been traveling incognito among his people. You're my guide. Tell me about the dives we were in tonight."

"First, sir, the Garden of Delights. It's owned by Colonel Bardon and Estrelita O'Higgins. The manager is one Chiang Sooey. Chiang is not yet a citizen but hopes to become one. The turnover rate of entertainers is high—Chiang likes them to take their pay in dreamsticks and the like rather than in money. . . ."

"And the dreamsticks. . . . Where do they come from?"

"One of the main sources of supply used to be the ships owned by Able Enterprises but recently a dreamweed plantation was started by Eduardo Lopez. . . ."

"The Minister for Immigration?"

"The same. There was an influx of refugees from Bangla—there was some sort of Holy War there. Dreamweed comes from Bangla. The people there use it but they're immune to its worst effects. They were recruited to work on the Lopez plantation. The occasional leaves they smoke or chew will not reduce their capacity for hard work."

"And the other people, the customers, who get hooked have to work like bastards to feed their habit."

"Yes. And burn themselves out. And now, the Texas Whorehouse. Owned by a syndicate of Bardon's officers. Managed by Lyman Cartwell, of New Dallas origin. Like Chiang Sooey, not yet a citizen but hopeful of becoming one. It's not at all likely; he's become a dreamstick addict himself."

"I take it that the clipjoints—how much do I owe you, by the way?—that we didn't patronize are all very much the same insofar as ownership is concerned."

"With the exception of the New Shanghai, of course.

And I'll let you have a detailed accounting as soon as possible, sir."

"Do that, Raoul."

"To date, sir, you've just seen the glamorous—*glamorous*, ha, ha!—side of the exploitation of the refugees. You've yet to see the conditions on the farms and plantations—the living quarters, the company stores . . ."

"It's time," said Grimes, "that you and I took *Fat Susie* out for an airing. A leisurely tour of my domain. . . ."

"I'd like that, sir."

Obviously the van was slowing.

It stopped and the rear door slid open.

Grimes and Sanchez jumped down to the ground, found themselves standing by the tradesmen's entrance of the Residence. Su Lin was waiting for them there. After a brief word of greeting she led them inside the building and through a maze of passageways to the Governor's quarters. She produced the inevitable tea. After this had been sipped she brought out a bottle of solvent and, applying it with gentle hands, removed Grimes's false facial hair. Sanchez attended himself to the stripping of his own disguise.

The pilot said good night and departed for his accommodation. The girl stayed with Grimes and insisted on preparing him for bed.

She did not offer to share his couch with him.

Chapter 22

After a not too early breakfast Grimes sent for Sanchez.

Su Lin was present while the two men studied charts spread on the desk in the Governor's office. Whatever the bugs picked up and reported would not be what was actually being said.

"I suggest, sir," said the pilot, "that we start by flying to the McReady estate. There are mooring facilities there."

"A surprise visit, Raoul?"

"More or less. We'll give him a call about an hour before we're due. That'll give him time to muster a few hands and to get his own blimp away from the mast and into the hangar."

"It sounds rather high-handed."

"You're the Governor, sir."

"But not an absolute monarch. Mphm."

"If we cast off at noon," said Sanchez, "we should arrive at about 0900 hours, McReady's time, tomorrow morning. The actual flying time will be seventeen hours, weather permitting. At this time of the year there shouldn't be much wind, either with us or against us. Would you mind standing a watch or two, sir? There's an automatic pilot, of course, but I'm old fashioned. I feel that the control room should be manned at all times."

"So do I," said Grimes.

"I can stand a watch too," put in Su Lin. "I may not hold any licenses or certificates but I can handle lighter than air craft."

"Did you fly with Governor Wibberley?" Grimes asked.

"No. I learned . . . elsewhere."

"But what gave you the idea that you were coming with us?"

"The Lord High Governor must have his personal maidservant in attendance, mustn't he? Who's going to make your tea and cook your meals?"

"I can handle an autochef," Grimes told her huffily. "When I was by myself in *Little Sister* I fed quite well. I don't need a huge kitchen, such as here, with hordes of chefs and scullions."

"Three watches will be better than watch and watch, sir," said Sanchez.

"I suppose so. But you're the expert, Raoul. Shall we need any crew apart from the three of us?"

"What for?"

"As long as you're happy," said Grimes, "I am. I don't want any of Smith's nongs in my hair. Come to that—I don't want Smith himself, even though he is alleged to be my ADC."

"He hates flying," said Su Lin. "Whenever possible he found some excuse to avoid accompanying Governor Wibberley on his flights."

"He knew what was going to happen," said Sanchez bitterly.

"Could it happen to me?" asked Grimes interestedly. "To us?"

"*Fat Susie* is clean," the pilot told him. "So far. And I've set up an intrusion recorder that will let me know if anybody has been sniffing around her during my absence."

"One of *your* electronic toys, Su Lin?" asked Grimes.

"Yes."

"Then all right, Raoul. Get *Fat Susie* ready for flight. I'll see Smith and Jaconelli and tell them that I shall be away from the Residence for a while."

"Perhaps you'd better tell Madam President and Colonel Bardon as well," suggested Su Lin.

Sanchez left.

Grimes picked up the telephone on his desk, was able to get in touch with the ADC and the secretary without any trouble. After a very short while they came into the office.

"Good morning, gentlemen," said Grimes.

"Good morning, Your Excellency," they chorused.

"Captain Sanchez and I are going to take *Fat Susie* out for a trial flight. I can't be sure when I shall be back."

"Will you require me, Your Excellency?" asked Smith.

"No, thank you. Somebody has to mind the shop during my absence, to maintain my liaison with the military. . . ." Smith looked relieved. "And you, of course, Mr. Jaconelli, will maintain liaison with the civil government. I'd like you both to pass out the necessary information regarding my temporary absence from the Residence."

"Will you be filing a flight plan, Your Excellency?" asked Smith.

"No. Captain Sanchez and I will just be swanning around, admiring the scenery, letting the wind blow us where it lists. . . ."

"It is a calm day, Your Excellency," said Smith.

"Just a figure of speech, Lieutenant."

"And should we wish to get in touch with you, Your Excellency?"

"*Fat Susie's* radio telephone system will be operative throughout."

Smith, Grimes noticed, was sneaking glances at the charts laid out on the desk. He wouldn't learn much. The one with the courses plotted on it was under all the others, the one on display was of the Lake Country, west of Libertad.

"I think that's all, gentlemen," said Grimes.

"Thank you, Your Excellency."

"And will you pack an overnight bag for me, Su Lin?"

"Very good, Your Excellency."

After having made sure that his tobacco pouch was full Grimes strolled out of the Residence and made his way to the mini-airport.

Fat Susie was swinging lazily at the low mast. The end of the ladder hanging from her control cab was just clear of the ground. Grimes caught hold of the side rails, got his feet onto the bottom step. He heard, above him, the air pump whine briefly as pressure in the atmospheric trimming cells was reduced to compensate. He climbed up to the cab, through the open door, went forward.

"Permission to board, Captain?" he asked Sanchez, who was feeding information into the auto-pilot.

"Glad to have you aboard, Commodore," replied the young man.

"What courses do you propose to steer?"

"With your permission, sir, north at first to make a circuit of Mount Bakunin. When it's erupting it's very spectacular—but it's been quiet for some years now. Of course, if it were erupting we shouldn't be going near it. After that we follow a great circle to the McReady place. That takes us over Rumpel's Canyon and, a bit farther on, the townships of Vanzetti and Princeps. . . ."

"Should be a scenic trip."

"Yes, sir."

Through an open window came the sound of a female voice.

"Ahoy, *Fat Susie! Fat Susie*, ahoy!"

Grimes looked out and down. Su Lin was standing there, two large suitcases on the ground beside her.

"Your Excellency," she called, "could you send a line down for the baggage?"

"I'll fix it, sir," said Sanchez.

Grimes watched with interest as the pilot opened a hatch in the deck of the cab, lowering through it a wire from a winch secured to the overhead. Su Lin hooked on both bags. By the time that they were inboard she was half-way up the ladder. She did not stay long in the control cab but went up into the body of the ship. Sanchez and Grimes were again discussing the navigational details of the flight when she came back.

"I've checked the autochef," she said. "It's very short on spices. No mace, no cummin, no tumeric. No . . ."

"You've time to get some from the kitchen, Su," said Sanchez. "But make it snappy." He turned to Grimes. "*Women* . . ." he said.

"Don't spoil the ship for a ha'porth of tar," Grimes told him. "Don't spoil the stew for a pinch of salt. Don't spoil the roast for a sliver of garlic. Don't . . ."

"Wasn't your Survey Service nickname Gutsy Grimes, sir?" asked Sanchez respectfully.

"It was. For some obscure reason people still find occasion to remind me of it. What time did you order the ground crew for?"

"They should be along now," said Sanchez.

And there they were, following in the wake of Su Lin, who was carrying a quite large bag. Again the winch was put to use and then, as soon as the girl was aboard, the ladder was retracted. Two soldiers clambered up the other ladder, that inside the metal tripod, to the head of the mast. Sanchez stuck his head out through a forward window of the cab, a portable loud speaker to his mouth.

"Let go!" he shouted.

There was a faint clang as the quick release shackle at the end of the airship's mooring wire was given a sharp blow.

"Lift!" called Sanchez.

Grimes, who had been given instructions on the drill by the pilot, used the airpump to reduce pressure in the midships trimming cell. *Fat Susie* drifted lazily astern, drifted and lifted, going up like an unpowered balloon. She cleared the Residence roof with ease. Grimes, looking out and down, saw that an almost horizontal part of it was being used as a sunbathing area by female members of his domestic staff. Apparently unembarrassed, one of the naked girls got to her feet to wave to the slowly ascending dirigible.

"Back inside, sir," ordered Sanchez. "I'm going to close the windows."

The transparent panels slid silently into place. Almost as silently the motors started. Sanchez put the wheel over, watching the gyro-compass repeater. When he was satisfied he switched to automatic.

Fat Susie, maintaining course and above-ground altitude, would find her own way to Mount Bakunin.

Su Lin came back into the control cab carrying an insulated container.

"I thought," she said, "that you would both like lunch here."

"The Governor," said Sanchez, "would like lunch anywhere."

"I resent that," said Grimes, but jocularly. From the steam that issued from the box when its lid was removed he thought that the girl had conjured up a meal of chili beef. He sat down on the settee, gratefully took the bowl and chopsticks that she handed to him.

Chapter 23

Grimes enjoyed the flight.

He had always loved dirigibles, maintaining that they were the only atmospheric flying machines that were real ships. And now he had one of his very own to play with—although it was a great pity that he was not master as well as being *de facto* owner. When he had time and opportunity, he thought, he would qualify as a pilot of lighter-than-air craft. Meanwhile Sanchez was instructing him in the elements of airship handling, allowing him to take the controls during the circuit of Mount Bakunin.

The snow-covered upper slopes of the great, truncated cone were dazzlingly white on the sunlit side, a chill, pale blue in the shadow. The frozen-over crater lake was like cold, green stone. The lower slopes were thickly forested and even the old scars of lava flows were partially overgrown with scrub. As was to be expected in the vicinity of a high mountain there were eddies and updraughts and downdraughts. Sanchez watched alertly while Grimes steered and Su Lin, acting as altitude coxswain, turned her own wheel this way and that. He said little, just an occasional "Easily, sir, *easily*. . . ." or "Not so fast, Su, or you'll put us in orbit. . . ." *Fat Susie* made her own creaking protests at the over-application of elevators or rudder but these diminished as Grimes and the girl got the hang of their controls.

And then course was set and its maintenance left to the automatic pilot. *Fat Susie* flew quietly and steadily into the darkening east, the flaming sunset astern. Dusk deepened into night and the stars, the unfamiliar (to Grimes) constellations appeared in the sky. Those directly overhead were, of course, obscured by the airship's upper structure but Su Lin was able to point out and identify those not far above the horizon.

"That's the Torch of Liberty," she said. "The bright red star at the tip of it is the Pole Star . . ."

"Mphm." (That constellation, thought Grimes, looked as much like a torch as that other grouping of stars, with Earth's Pole Star at the tip of its tail, looks like a Little Bear.)

"The Hammer and Sickle. . . ."

"I was under the impression," said Grimes, "that the founders of this colony were Anarchists, not Communists."

"They had to call their constellations something," put in Sanchez. "And that one does look like what it's called."

Su Lin went up and aft to the galley, returned after not too long with dinner for them all, a simple but excellent meal of lamb chops and some spicy green vegetable with a fruit salad to follow. Shortly after this Grimes retired to his cabin; he was taking the middle watch at the suggestion of Sanchez. "You'll want to see Rumpel's Canyon," the pilot had told him. "In the *dark*?" queried Grimes. "You'll see it all right, sir," Sanchez assured him.

Stretched out on the comfortable couch he had little trouble in getting to sleep, lulled by the slight swaying motion of the ship and by her rhythmic whispering. He awoke instantly, feeling greatly refreshed, as Su Lin, calling him for his watch, switched on the cabin light. She had brought him a pot of tea.

"Rise and shine!" she cried brightly. "Rise and shine, Your Excellency!"

She put the tray down on the bunkside table and returned to the control cab.

Grimes poured and sipped tea, then got up and went into the tiny toilet facility. He finished his tea while he was dressing. He filled and lit his pipe, then went out into the narrow alleyway toward the control cab. Looking up at the gas cells, their not overly taut fabric rippling from forward to aft, he wondered how it had been in the early days of airships when the only buoyant gas available was hydrogen. It must have been hell on smokers, he thought.

He clambered down the short companionway into the cab. Su Lin turned away from the forward windows, through which she had been peering, binoculars to her eyes.

"The canyon's coming up now," she said.

She handed him the glasses. He adjusted the focus and looked. There was the hard, serrated line of the land horizon, black against the faintly luminous darkness of the sky.

"More to your left," she told him.

A spark of light . . . A town or village? But there was an odd quality about it. It was pulsing as though it were alive. The ship flew on and now there was more than just a spark to be seen. A stream of iridiscence came slowly into view, a winding, rainbow river and then, most spectacular of all, a great cataract of liquid jewels.

At last the show was over, fading astern.

"Luminous organisms," said Su Lin matter of factly. "Found only in the Rumpel River. And now, sir, will you take the watch?"

"I relieve you, madam," said Grimes formally.

"She's on course and making good time. If any of the automatic controls play up the alarm will sound. Call Captain Sanchez—although that shouldn't be necessary. There's a bell in his cabin. Call him, in any case, at 0345. The clock's adjusted to McReady's time."

"So I see." Grimes lifted his hand and spoke into his wrist companion. "Advance to 0045 exactly on the word *Now*." He watched the changing seconds on the clock. "Now."

"I'm an old-fashioned girl," said Su Lin. "I prefer old-fashioned watches—not contraptions that can do just about anything but fry eggs. Good night, sir. Or good morning, rather."

"Good morning, Su," said Grimes.

His watch passed pleasantly enough. He looked out at the dark landscape streaming past below with the very occasional clusters of light that told of human habitation. He studied the instruments—gyro compass, radar altimeter, ground, air speed and drift indicators and all the rest of them. He looked into the radar screen and saw a distant target, airborne, and finally was able to pick it up visually, a great airliner ablaze with lights along the length of her, sweeping by on course, he decided, for Libertad.

Then, satisfied that all was in order and would remain so, he went briefly aft to the galley to make for himself a mid-watch snack—a pot of tea and a huge pile of thick ham sandwiches. He went to the galley again to make more tea, this time for Sanchez when he called him.

"You shouldn't have done that, sir," protested the pilot. "You . . . You're the Governor."

"Where are your Anarchist principles, Raoul? In any case—you're the captain and I'm only a watchkeeper."

Shortly afterward Sanchez relieved him in the control cab.

He said, "At least you and Su managed to keep your paws off the controls. I was half expecting that you'd go down for a closer look at the canyon."

"I'd have liked to, Raoul, but I was brought up to believe that the captain's word is law."

"And so, surely, is the Governor's."

"That," said Grimes, "I have yet to convince myself of."

All of *Fat Susie's* people were well-breakfasted, showered (and in the cases of Grimes and Sanchez depilated) when the airship made the approach to the McReady Estate. The morning was fine, almost windless, and below the dirigible the grainfields were like a golden sea. Reaping had been commenced and, like hordes of disciplined ants, the laborers, scythes flashing in the sunlight, were cutting a broad swathe through the wheat, the cut stalks being loaded onto hand-drawn carts. This sort of harvesting, thought Grimes, would be relatively inexpensive only if there were an abundant supply of slave labor—flesh and blood robots. And flesh and blood robots are superior to the metal and plastic ones in at least one respect; they are self-reproducing.

Ahead was what was practically a small town—the threshing sheds, the barracks, mess halls and the like. On a low hill was a sprawling building that seemed to be larger than the Governor's Residence, tall by Liberian standards, all of four stories. In the center of its flat roof was a mooring mast from which a dirigible, smaller than *Fat Susie*, a clumsy looking non-rigid, was just casting off.

"McReady to *Fat Susie*," came a nasal voice from the speaker of the transceiver. "The mast will be ready for you. The mooring crew is waiting."

"Thank you, Mr. McReady," said Grimes into the microphone.

He had little to do but watch as Sanchez brought the airship in. He thought that the pilot was maintaining full speed for too long—and restrained himself from back-seat driving. But a dirigible, he realized, would lose way very quickly once power was cut. Such was the case. It was Su Lin who started, by remote control, the small winches that let down the weighted lines for the mooring crew to grab hold of and the other winch that paid out the stouter mooring, flexible wire rope, from *Fat Susie's* blunt nose.

The men on the roof worked efficiently.

A dozen of them held *Fat Susie* in position while two more of them clipped the end of her bow wire to the other wire from the tower. Winches whined, then there was a muffled clang as the airship's stem came into contact with the swivel cone.

"We're here," said Sanchez.

The door on the port side of the cab slid open, the ladder extended downward until it was just clear of the roof surface. Grimes looked out and down to the people awaiting him, to the tall, blue-denim-clad man with the broad-brimmed hat decorated with a silver band, to the almost as tall blonde woman in her denim shirt and full skirt. Both of them, he saw, were wearing riding boots, with silver spurs.

He thought ironically, *Deep in the heart of Texas.*

Chapter 24

Grimes clambered down the ladder to the pebbled roof.

McReady removed his hat in a sweeping salute. The woman curtseyed. Grimes, bareheaded, acknowledged with a stiff bow.

"This is an unexpected honor, Your Excellency," drawled the man.

"I was passing," said Grimes, "and thought that I'd drop in."

The man chuckled and extended his hand. Grimes took it. The grip was firm but unexpectedly cold. And there was coldness, too, behind the pale blue eyes set in the darkly tanned, bluffly handsome features. And McReady's wife, thought Grimes as he shook hands with her, was cast from the same mold as her husband—handsome enough but a cast-iron bitch.

Su Lin came down, followed by Sanchez.

Grimes made introductions.

"This is Su Lin, my personal attendant . . ." The McReady couple nodded coldly to the girl. "And Captain Sanchez, my pilot . . ." There was more hand-shaking.

"And now, sir, how can we entertain you?" asked McReady.

"With your permission, sir, I'd like to look around your estate," said Grimes. "I want to get the feel of this world—just as a captain likes to get the feel of a ship to which he has been newly appointed."

"But why pick on *me*, Governor?"

"I want to see how outsiders, comparative newcomers, make good on Liberia. After all, this entire planet is a social experiment—and how things are turning out is of great interest to my lords and masters on Earth."

"You've a fancy way with words, sir. And you've caught me at a busy time; unless I get dug into my paperwork I'm goin' to be suffocated under a pile o' bumfodder. But I can spare you Laura. Laura, honey, will you give the Governor the five credit tour?"

"Surely, honey." Then, to Grimes, "Do you wish to start right now, or would you like refreshment first?"

"Now, if you wouldn't mind," said Grimes.

The "five credit tour" did not include a look over and through the McReady mansion. Grimes and his party were carried by an elevator down to the ground floor and then out to where two trishaws were already waiting. Laura McReady gestured and the driver of the first one dismounted, went through the motions of helping Grimes into the passenger carriage (he did not require such assistance but did not wish to hurt the man's feelings) and then assisted the woman to take her seat beside him. Su Lin and Sanchez boarded the other vehicle unaided.

"Do you wish to see the village, sir?" asked Laura McReady.

"The village?"

"It's what we call where the laborers live."

"That will do for a start, Ms. McReady," said Grimes.

She turned her head and barked an order. The driver began pedaling. The trishaws made their way along a rather narrow but well-surfaced road along the sides of which tall bushes, blue-foliaged and with huge scarlet flowers, were in luxuriant growth. Gaudy insects, gold and crimson and metallic green, hovered in clouds around each blossom. From somewhere came the monotonous song of something that might have been a bird but that probably was not.

The road wound through outcroppings of bare rock, rounded, weatherworn, that gleamed whitely in the sunlight, then through an orchard grown from seeds of Terran origin. The citrus scent was heavy in the warm, still air.

They came to the village—a long street with buildings on either side, with cross streets that were little more than lanes. Bright banners—red, yellow and blue, decorated with ideographs—depended from poles protruding horizontally from the ornate eaves of the single-storied structures.

"Shops," said Laura McReady. "Eating houses. And so forth."

Grimes sniffed the savory aromas that eddied from some of the establishments. "Eating houses? Do you think that we could look inside one?"

"If you wish, sir." Her voice was cold, disapproving. "I'm afraid that I can't recommend any of these places. Mr. McReady and I have always preferred to eat the kind of food to which we are accustomed."

The trishaws stopped. The driver of the leading one dismounted, opened the door of the passenger compartment on Grimes's side. Grimes jumped out before the man could extend a helping hand. Mrs. McReady, however, made a major production of dismounting from the vehicle like a great lady born to the purple. Even the Baroness Michelle d'Estang would not have put on such airs and graces. By the time that she had set her well-shod, silver-ornamented feet on the ground Grimes had been joined by Sanchez and Su Lin.

He led the way into the eating shop. There were a few customers there, seated around small tables. These, seeing who had come in, got hastily to their feet and bowed deeply. (To him, Grimes wondered, or to their mistress?) A middle-aged woman came out from the kitchen at the rear of the premises. She, too, bowed and murmured, "You have honored my humble establishment, Missy Laura. . . ."

"*Your* establishment? Surely it is owned by the McReady Estate, is it not?"

"I am the humble cook and manager, Missy Laura."

"And this gentleman here is the new Governor, Commodore Grimes. He wishes to sample your cooking."

"Please to take a seat, Missy Laura. This way, please . . ."

She led the party to a table, pulled out four chairs. Su Lin pushed back the one intended for her. Here she was no more than a servant. She accompanied the manageress into the kitchen. Before he took his seat Grimes looked around. The customers were still standing respectfully.

"Sit down, please," said Grimes to them.

They ignored him.

"Tell them to sit down, Ms. McReady," said Grimes to her.

"Yes, Your Excellency," she said sweetly—but her expression was not sweet.

She made a gesture and the customers resumed their seats.

She said to Grimes, "You must remember, Your Excellency, that these are only laborers."

"But human beings, nonetheless."

"You are entitled to your opinion, sir."

Su Lin and the plump manageress returned, bearing dishes of tiny spring rolls, bowls of rice and others of interesting looking pickles, chopsticks, a teapot and cups. Laura McReady condescended to take tea and, without speaking, implied that it was not to her taste. Grimes sampled a spring roll; it was delicious. He tried the pickles and liked them. Sanchez, too, was eating with a good appetite. Between them the two men cleared all the edibles on the table.

More tea was brought and with it a dish of small cookies. Grimes took the one nearest to him. It was still warm, hot almost. It must have been freshly baked. He broke the crust and was surprised to see a small square of folded paper inside. So, he thought, they had fortune cookies even on Liberia.

He unfolded the paper. The writing on it was in minuscule characters but very clear.

Pay heed to the manner in which people nourish others, and watch what they seek out for their own nourishment.

Wasn't that from the *I Ching*? He should have Magda with him here, he thought, to throw the coins and consult the Oracle of Change.

He tore the paper into tiny shreds, dropped them into the ashtray.

"What did it say, sir?" asked Raoul. "Mine says that there will be advantage in crossing the great water. I suppose that 'great water' is another way of saying 'deep space'."

Laura McReady sneered silently.

Their meal finished, the party walked out into the street, escorted to the door by the deeply bowing manageress. The question of payment wasn't mentioned; presumably the McReady Estate would be footing the bill. (They could well afford it.) Raoul Sanchez and Su Lin lagged behind, talking in low voices. Then the pilot overtook Grimes and Laura McReady, who were walking slowly along the footpath.

"Your Excellency. . . ."

"Yes, Captain Sanchez?"

"Perhaps we should inspect one of the other eating houses."

"His Excellency has already enjoyed a good lunch," said the McReady woman.

"We can inspect without eating," said Grimes. He suspected that there was some good reason for Raoul's suggestion.

"But when you have seen one you've seen them all," insisted Ms. McReady.

"Not necessarily," said Grimes.

She glared at him. Did he, he wondered, wield, as Governor, the punitive powers that he had possessed as a Survey Service commanding officer? Could he put this woman in the brig on a charge of Dumb Insolence?

Su Lin turned into one of the narrow cross streets. Sanchez followed her. Grimes and the McReady woman brought up the rear. She was almost literally seething with hostility. The girl paused outside the door of a place that was little more than a shack, waited until the others caught up with her. She lifted the bead curtain to allow Grimes, Sanchez and Laura McReady to enter before her.

The lighting inside was dim, the air musty. There were long tables and benches, most of them occupied. One of the diners saw who had come in, got to his feet, still holding his bowl in one hand, his chopsticks in the other, and bowed. There was a scraping and shuffling as other men and women followed suit. And it was not toward himself, Grimes noticed, that this obeisance was directed.

"Tell them to sit down, please," he said to Laura McReady.

She did so.

Su Lin went through to the kitchen. She returned carrying a steaming bowl and a pair of cheap, plastic chopsticks. These, with a bow, she handed to Grimes. He looked suspiciously at the mess in the bowl—like gray, slimy noodles it was, specked with green and yellow—and sniffed the sour vapor. It reminded him of the sort of mess on which he had been obliged to live, for far too long a time, during a voyage in a ship's boat, nutriment that was actually reprocessed sewage.

He lifted one strand with his chopsticks, brought it to his mouth and sucked it in. It was even worse than he had been expecting. He swallowed it, then handed the bowl and the eating implements back to the girl.

He said, "So this is how the poor live."

"Your Excellency," said Laura McReady, "the food served in this establishment satisfies the highest nutritional standards. If this were not so there would never be a good day's work done in the fields."

"Mphm." Grimes filled and lit his pipe, hoping that the fumes of burning tobacco would clear the taste of that . . . sludge from his mouth. "Once I had to eat stuff like this myself. I functioned quite well on it. But I didn't have to like it."

"These people, Your Excellency, are not like you and me. They don't know anything better."

"What about the ones in the first place?"

"Foremen and forewomen. Clerks and the like."

"More highly paid than the laborers in here?"

"Of course. You're more highly paid than . . . than a common spacehand, aren't you? But may I suggest, Your Excellency, that we continue this conversation outside?"

"Not in front of the children, eh?"

"You could put it that way," she said coldly.

They walked through the village, looking into shops in which both luxuries—sweetmeats, spices and pickles to lend savor to the staple diet, cheap jewelry to brighten drab clothing—and necessities were sold. They saw purchases being made and paid for by thumbprints on a screen-pad, recorded by some master computer. They visited a school, in which children, ranging in age from about four to fourteen, were being taught how to be good little field hands. They made the rounds of the barracks, the dormitories for males and females, the married quarters, the hospital. Somehow Su Lin had taken charge—and if Laura McReady's looks could have killed the girl would not have lived beyond that laborers' eating house.

Everything was well-maintained, spotlessly clean.

And everything was drab, drab.

For most of the people on the McReady Estate life was just a matter of going to work to earn the credited pay to buy the food to give them the strength to go to work to earn the pay etc.

Grimes found no evidence to indicate that drugs such as dreamsticks were available to the workers—but there were shops selling a limited variety of alcoholic beverages, most of which seemed to be industrial alcohol with the addition of crude flavorings.

He sampled the so-called rum and even he didn't like it.

Chapter 25

At Grimes's insistence the party then went to the fields to watch the progress of the harvest. Laura McReady did her best to dissuade him but at last, sullenly, gave the necessary orders to the trishaw drivers. On the ride out they passed, bound in the opposite direction, a steady stream of large, steam-driven trucks bound for the threshing floors in the village.

Having observed the nature of the cargoes of these vehicles Grimes asked, "Why don't you thresh on the spot and just bring the grain in?"

"Why should we, Your Excellency?" asked Mrs. McReady. Then she condescended to explain. "The straw and the husks are . . . processed. They, too, have nutritional value. You, yourself, have just sampled some of the food made from such materials."

"Oh," said Grimes. "So that was origin of the sludge we tasted. I thought that it came from something worse."

"Why should we waste good organic manure?" countered the woman.

Grimes pursued the subject.

"So your slaves get the husks and you get the grain. For export."

"Not slaves, Your Excellency. Indentured labor."

"Mphm."

They came to one of the fields, to where a line of steam trucks was awaiting cargo. They dismounted and watched for a short while the huge-wheeled handcarts being pushed in from the slowly receding line of reapers, each piled high with golden, heavy-headed stalks. Men and women, sweating in the afternoon sun, naked save for brief loincloths, tipped the loads out onto the road and then, gathering up huge armfuls of grain-bearing straw, staggered up ramps to the truck beds to restow the harvest. Human beings, thought Grimes, reduced to the status of worker ants. . . . But worker ants do not toil under the watchful eyes of overseers. And these overseers, men and women bigger and tougher-looking than the common laborers, were armed with whips, short-handled but with at least two meters of lash. Usually they just cracked these threateningly while shouting in high-pitched voices—and then Grimes shouted in protest when one of the overseers drew a line of blood on the sweating back of a frail girl.

"The lazy little bitch," said Laura McReady, "deserved it. Look at the load she's carrying!"

"Even so . . ." protested Grimes.

"Your Excellency, you are the Governor. Before you became Governor you were a spaceman. With all due respect to you, what do you know of the management of a large agricultural enterprise?"

"Very little," admitted Grimes. "But I'm learning. And I don't like what I'm learning, Mrs. McReady."

"We all have to learn unpleasant lessons, Your Excellency."

And I shall be teaching some, I hope, thought Grimes.

He led the way onto the field itself, walking between the furrows, his feet sinking into the soft soil. The incoming handcarts swerved to avoid him—or to avoid Laura McReady, who was walking close behind him. Her they knew but they would not know the new Governor. He came up to the line of reapers, stooped and sweating as they wielded their flashing sickles. He heard the cracking of the overseers' whips and their shouted orders. He saw a woman, not young, one of the gatherers, straighten up briefly from her labors and stand there, her face turned up to the uncaring sky. For some reason (and who could blame her? thought Grimes) she was weeping quietly.

She stood in tears amid the alien corn . . . Where did that come from? Not that it mattered. What did matter was that a woman was standing there, in tears, the helpless victim of a harsh economic system and of political hypocrisy.

"Su Lin," he said, "will you ask her what is wrong?"

"What does it matter, Your Excellency?" asked Laura McReady.

"It does to her, madam," said Grimes.

Su Lin went up to the woman and, in a soft voice, spoke to her in her own language. The answer came in a rather unpleasant whining voice, punctuated by sobs.

"She says, Your Excellency," Su Lin told him, "that her husband was promoted to threshing floor foreman. Now he has no time for her. He has taken up with one of the girls working under him."

"You can't blame *me* for that," said Laura McReady smugly.

Grimes ignored this.

"Tell her," he said to Su Lin, "that I am sorry. Very sorry."

And what the hell good will that do? he asked himself.

And what the hell good will that do? Mrs. McReady, to judge from the expression on her face, was obviously thinking.

She asked, "And now have you seen enough, Your Excellency?"

"For the time being," said Grimes.

"Then may I suggest that we return to the manor house?" She added, without enthusiasm, "You and Captain Sanchez will be dining with us, of course."

"Thank you," said Grimes. "And Su Lin?"

"Your servant, Your Excellency, will be able to take a meal with our own domestic staff."

And make sure that you keep your pretty ears flapping, Su, thought Grimes.

Following the line of furrows they made their way back to the waiting trishaws.

Chapter 26

After their return to the manor house Grimes, Sanchez and Su Lin went back briefly into the airship. There the two men showered and changed—not that they had much to change into, just fresh suits of blue denim enlivened by scarlet neckerchiefs. They held a brief conference in the control cab before making their way down to the roof.

"The setup here," said Grimes, "reminds me of what I have read of the plantations in the American deep South before the War Between The States. Instead of Negro slaves there are New Cantonese indentured labor—but the only essential difference is that of skin pigmentation. . . ."

"And nobody is strumming a banjo and singing Negro spirituals," commented Sanchez drily.

"But Commodore Grimes is right," said Su Lin. "The situation is analogous."

"Not exactly," Sanchez insisted. "Far from exactly. Where are the Yankee generals at the head of the Union armies, marching south to free the slaves?"

"It wasn't quite like that, Raoul," said Grimes. "In fact, according to some historians, the question of slavery was only a side issue. The major one was that of secession. And I don't think that Liberia has any desire to secede from the Federation." He got up from the settee, looked out and down from one of the control cab windows. "There's some sort of functionary down there. He seems to be waiting for us. We'd better go and join our gracious hosts at the tucker table."

The McReady butler, a tall, thin, pigtailed man in black-and-white brass-buttoned livery, bowed deeply to Grimes as he stepped from the foot of the ladder to the roof surface.

He said, "The Lord and the Lady are awaiting you, Your Excellency. Please to follow."

He led Grimes and the others into the elevator cage, scowled at Su Lin when she was standing too close to her master, scowled at her again when she moved to stand by him. The downward journey did not commence until the grouping of the passengers was to the butler's satisfaction—he standing in solitary state by the control panel, Grimes and Sanchez in one corner, Su Lin in another.

The downward journey was swift and smooth. The door opened. The butler was first out, bowing deeply to Grimes as he disembarked, saying, "Please to follow, Your Excellency." Then, to Su Lin, "Wait here, woman. You will be sent for."

She smiled submissively and bowed to the upper servant. She winked at Grimes.

The butler, with a slow and stately walk, led the way along a corridor the walls of which were paneled with some dark, gleaming wood, floored with the same material. There were no pictures or other decorations. They came at last to a hinged door which the butler opened with a flourish. Beyond this was a large room, paneled as was the corridor but with wall ornaments. There were the mounted heads of horned beasts and others ferociously fanged. There were highly polished firearms—antique projectile weapons, modern lasers and stunguns. There were, even, crossed cavalry sabers.

McReady and his wife got up from the deep, black-leather-upholstered armchairs in which they had been sitting. They were dressed for the occasion—the man in a silver-braided and -buttoned black jacket over a ruffled white shirt, a kilt in a tartan that Grimes could not identify (he was no expert in such matters), long socks in the same tartan, highly polished black, silver-buckled shoes. Laura McReady was in high-necked, long-skirted, long-sleeved black with a sash in the same tartan as that worn by her husband.

Both of them looked at the formally informal attire of their guests and allowed themselves the merest suggestion of a sneer.

"Your Excellency," said the woman, "we must apologize. We assumed that you, as the Governor, would be dressing for dinner."

"The rank is but the guinea stamp," quoted Grimes. "A man's a man for a' that."

"Indubitably," said McReady. He repeated the word, making it sound anything but indubitable. "But be seated, please. A drink or two before dinner, Your Excellency?"

"That will be a pleasure," said Grimes.

He and Sanchez lowered themselves into deep armchairs, facing the others across the black, gleaming surface of the low round table. There was a decanter already there, a bowl of ice cubes and, standing on ceramic coasters, four glasses, two of which had already seen used.

"Whisky, Your Excellency? Captain Sanchez? On the rocks?"

"That will be fine," said Grimes.

"Thank you," said Sanchez.

The whisky, rather to Grimes's surprise, was not Scotch. It was bourbon. He didn't mind. It would have been improved by light conversation during its intake. Words were exchanged, of course, but it was obvious that the McReady couple were trying, without enthusiasm, to be on their best behavior and were annoyed that their guests, sartorially, had themselves made no great effort. After the second drinks—insofar as Grimes and Sanchez were concerned—had been disposed of a gong sounded somewhere outside.

The butler appeared and bowed.

"Lord McReady, dinner is served."

"Your Excellency," said McReady, "shall we proceed to the dining room?"

The dining room was a huge barn of a place, gloomy, the only lighting being from the candles set in ornate silver holders on the long, polished table. The McReady family, thought Grimes, must have a thing about black wood. McReady stood by his high-backed chair at the head of the not very festive board; Laura McReady indicated that Grimes should take one halfway down the table on McReady's right. She moved to her own chair at the foot of the table, leaving Sanchez to find his way to a position facing Grimes.

Everybody sat down.

Grimes, his eyes now accustomed to the near darkness, looked around curiously. There were paintings on the walls, ancient-looking oils, uniformly gloomy, horned beasts standing around drearily in a drizzle, another horned beast—a

Terran stag?—understandably perturbed by the harassment of hounds. He had been expecting that the McReady estate would be Little Texas; it was turning out to be, inside the manor house at least, Little Scotland. And what would be for dinner? Haggis? He hoped not.

But there was no kilted piper to play in "the chief of all the pudding tribe." There was only the liveried butler supervising the activities of the New Cantonese maids, pretty little girls in short-skirted uniforms. Somebody, somewhere, had switched on music—and that had no Scottish flavor. Grimes recognized one of the tunes—"The Yellow Rose Of Texas." He wished that the local representatives of the Clan McReady would be consistent.

The first course was a soup that Grimes categorized as lukewarm varnish. The second course was some sort of flavorless fish, steamed, with a bland, uninteresting sauce. This was followed by boiled mutton accompanied by vegetables with all the goodness stewed out of them. Finally there was an overly sweet fruit tart smothered with custard. The wines, Grimes had to admit, were not too bad. Without them the meal would have been quite impossible.

Throughout there was desultory conversation.

"And what do you think of Liberia, Your Excellency?"

"I have hardly been here long enough, Mrs. McReady, to form an opinion."

"Have some more of this mutton, Your Excellency. It's from our own flocks."

"I don't think that I have room, Mr. McReady."

"Oh, but you must. Haven't I heard somewhere, Your Excellency, that your nickname in the Survey Service used to be Gutsy Grimes?"

"Just a slice, then."

"Governor Wibberley used to enjoy his visits here. It was on his way back to the Residence from our estate that he was so tragically killed."

"Oh."

Grimes looked across the table at Sanchez. Sanchez looked at him.

"That is an unusual name that you have given your airship, Your Excellency."

"How so, Mrs. McReady?"

"*Fat Susie* . . ."

"She's named after a girl I once knew," said Grimes.

"And did you *call* her Fat Susie? To her face?"

"No."

"And was she fat?"

"Well, she was . . . plumpish."

"And where is she now?"

Damn the woman, thought Grimes. *She sits there like a statue all through the meal and now, once the subject of my murky past crops up, she's putting me through the third degree . . . And what was the* official *story of Susie's disappearance?*

"I don't know," he said truthfully.

At last the meal was over.

The party retired to what McReady called the gun room for coffee and brandy and cigars. (Grimes refused the latter and stuck to his pipe.) Mrs. McReady made deliberately half-hearted attempts to stifle her yawns. Grimes said that it was time that he was getting on his way. He thanked his hosts for a very enjoyable day and evening. There was a brief session of not very warm handshaking. The butler escorted the Governor and his atmosphere pilot up to the roof where, black against the darkly luminous sky, *Fat Susie* swung at the mooring mast like an oversized windsock.

Su Lin was waiting for them aboard the airship.

She said, "Look what I found!"

She showed Grimes and Sanchez a small sphere of black metal.

"Where was it, Su?"

"Tucked in between the main gas cells."

"What is it?"

"Just a ball, an empty ball, not hidden very cleverly and bound to show up on the metal detector I used. Just a warning."

"I wish it were a bomb," said Grimes viciously, "so that I could drop it on those bastards!"

"Not selective enough," she told him. "There are quite a few nice people in the servants' quarters."

"And I suppose that you had a nice meal," said Grimes.

"Very nice, as a matter of fact. Satay, and . . ."

"Don't tell me. But if this . . . *thing* is just a warning

how did they know that *you* were going to go through the ship with a fine tooth comb and find it?"

"Not me," she said, "but *you*. You are the ex-Survey Service Commander, the pirate Commodore. They're hoping that you will make a better job of cleaning up the mess here than your predecessor did." She laughed. "You know, I think that the dummy bomb was planted not by the baddies but by the goodies."

"A warning nonetheless," said Grimes.

"Too right," she said.

Chapter 27

As a matter of courtesy Grimes kept in radio contact with both President O'Higgins and Colonel Bardon. There seemed to be no great need for him in the capital—no schools or bridges to be opened, no official dinners or luncheons to attend. During his conversations he was deliberately vague about *Fat Susie's* flight plan. "Just swanning around," he would say. "Just letting the wind blow me wherever it listeth. . . ."

And that, for much of the time, he was actually doing. During his younger days on Earth he had acquired some expertise as a hot air balloonist and he found his old skills returning. Now he was the instructor and Raoul his pupil. With main engines shut down and only the air pumps in operation he would decrease or increase altitude in the search, usually successful, for a fair wind. The dirigible drifted over the countryside, going a long way in a long time and quite often in the right direction.

Her descents to ground were unscheduled, dropping down with very little prior warning onto the manor houses of the vast estates, her people receiving grudging hospitality ("What the hell is *he* doing here?" Grimes overheard on one occasion) from those whom Grimes, remembering his Australian history, categorized as squatters. In long ago Australia, however, there had been three classes of colonist—the wealthy squatters, the small farmers and the laborers who, in the very earliest days, had been convicts. More than one governor had sided with the little men against the big landowners. Some of them had been socially ostracized by the self-made aristocracy. One of them, the immensely capable but occasionally tactless Bligh, had been deposed by his own garrison, the New South Wales Corps, the officers of which were already squatters or in the process of becoming such.

On Liberia things were only a little different, although there were no small farmers. The status of the refugees was almost that of those hapless men and women who had been shipped out to Botany Bay in the First Fleet and its successors. Bardon's Bullies were not at all unlike the personnel of the New South Wales Corps. They were up to the eyebrows in every unsavory and lucrative racket.

There was the Lopez dreamweed plantation in the foothills of the Rousseau Ranges, an expanse of low, rounded hills covered with a purple growth that, from the air, looked more like the fur of some great animal than vegetation. The swarming, brown-skinned laborers, gathering the ripened leaves, could have been lice. There was the sprawling, red-roofed manor house with, at its highest point, a latticework mooring mast. There was a ship at this mooring, a large dirigible with military markings, crossed swords below the Terran opalescent sphere on its dark blue ground. It seemed to be taking on cargo of some kind, bales piled on the small area of flat roof space being hoisted, one by one, into its interior.

"And now, sir," said Sanchez, grinning widely, "we shall embarrass them by making our presence known. Give them a call, Su."

"*Fat Susie* to Lopez Control," said the girl into the transceiver microphone, "*Fat Susie* to Lopez Control. Do you read me?"

"Lopez Control here," came the answer at last in a very bored voice. "What do you want?"

"Request mooring facilities."

"You'll just have to wait, *Fat* . . ." There was a long pause, then, "What did you say your name was?"

"*Fat Susie*. And, in case you're wondering, the Governor, Commodore Grimes, is on board."

Loading operations had ceased, Grimes saw, looking out and down through his binoculars. Loading operations had ceased but work had not. The remaining bales on the rooftop were being rolled into a large penthouse—from which, no doubt, they would hastily be taken down and stowed somewhere out of sight.

A fresh voice issued from the speaker of the transceiver.

"*R273*, Major Flattery commanding, to *Fat Susie*. My compliments to His Excellency. I am casting off now so that you may approach the mast. May I ask how long you will be staying here?"

"Tell him," said Grimes, "that I don't know."

Su Lin passed on the message.

"*Fat Susie*," said Flattery, "please inform His Excellency that I am on urgent military business and have a schedule to keep. I would like to know how long I shall be delayed."

"Tell him," said Grimes, "that I am on governmental business."

"*Fat Susie*," said the major (he must have overheard Grimes's instructions to Su Lin), "please inform His Excellency that I shall be obliged to inform Colonel Bardon that my schedule has been disrupted. Over and out."

R273 cast off, drifted lazily astern from the mast. Flattery was in no hurry to start his engines. Sanchez, coming in against the wind, passed closely to the larger ship. Grimes could look into the control cab, saw a ferociously moustached face scowling at him through one of the windows. Major Flattery, he assumed. He waved cheerfully. Flattery did not acknowledge the salutation.

The mooring party—dark-skinned men in startlingly white loincloths and turbans—was waiting for *Fat Susie*. She was brought to the mast smartly enough, hooked on. A tall, thin man, in white tunic with a scarlet sash, white-trousered but barefoot, stood at the foot of the ladder, extended a hand to assist Grimes as he stepped down from the platform. Then he put his hands to his turbaned forehead and bowed deeply.

"Sahib. The Burra Sahib and the Burra Memsahib await you."

Amn't I a Burra Sahib? wondered Grimes.

He followed the man into the penthouse with Su Lin a couple of steps behind him. Sanchez was staying with the ship; it had been decided not to ignore the warning, dummy bomb that had been planted at the McReady estate. The rooftop shelter was a big one, being intended for the handling of freight as well as passengers. Grimes sniffed suspiciously. The air still carried a sickly sweet aroma. Dreamweed. It would not be wise, he thought, to inhale too deeply.

There was a large car for cargo, a much smaller one for passengers. Inside this cage the air was free of taint. The downward journey was smooth and swift. The vestibule into which they emerged had a tiled floor, black and white in a geometrical pattern which was repeated on the tiled walls. From somewhere came the tinkling music of a fountain accompanied by bird song. This could have been a recording but Grimes didn't think that it was.

The butler led Grimes and Su Lin through a succession of arches, bringing them at last to a large, airy room, the floor of which was covered with beautiful carpets. There were others, even more beautiful, on the walls, tapestries almost, with strutting peacocks, prowling tigers and brightly clad horsemen doing unkind things to fierce looking boars with their long lances.

At a low table Eduardo Lopez and Marita Lopez were sitting on piles of cushions, sharing a narghil. The fat little man, in white silk shirt and trousers, with crimson cummerbund and slippers, could have been an old-time Oriental potentate. His wife, in gauzy white trousers and bodice, could have been an overblown harem beauty.

"Lopez Sahib," announced the butler, "the Governor Sahib and . . ." He paused to look doubtfully at Su Lin. "The Governor Sahib and his servant."

Lopez put down the mouthpiece of the pipe onto the inlaid surface of the table. He got slowly to his feet. His wife remained seated.

"A good day to you, Your Excellency. Had we been expecting you we would have arranged a proper reception."

"I like to keep things informal," said Grimes.

Meanwhile Su Lin had collected more brightly covered cushions, had put them down by the table.

"Please be seated, Your Excellency," she said to Grimes.

Grimes sat, cross-legged. Lopez resumed his own seat. He, his wife and Grimes were the points of an equilateral triangle about the round table. Grimes sniffed the fumes that were drifting from the bowl of the water pipe. Mainly tobacco, he decided, but with some addition.

"You will smoke, Your Excellency?" asked Lopez. He clapped his hands. "Ram Das! A pipe for the Governor Sahib!"

"I'll use my own, thanks," said Grimes hastily. "And my own tobacco."

Su Lin made a major production of filling and lighting the vile thing for him. Mrs. Lopez went into a paroxysm of coughing.

When she was quite finished Lopez inquired, "And how may we serve you, Commodore Grimes? And may I presume to ask why you are honoring us with your presence?"

"A sort of captain's inspection," said Grimes. "A tour of spaceship *Liberia*. Just finding out what lives where and what does what. After all, this world is my new command."

"It could be argued," said Lopez mildly, "that Madam Estrelita O'Higgins is the captain of spaceship *Liberia*."

"A sort of staff captain, perhaps," Grimes said. "And, carrying on with the astronautical analogy, Colonel Bardon is the master at arms. But I am the master. My name is on the register."

"I am not a spaceman," said Lopez, "but I think I see what you mean. I do necessarily agree with you."

For what seemed a long time the Lopez couple and Grimes smoked in silence, Su Lin and Ram Das watching them impassively. Then Grimes asked a question.

"What was that army dirigible doing here, Mr. Lopez?"

"Major Flattery is a personal friend, Your Excellency. He was paying a social call."

"Indeed? His ship seemed to be loading some sort of cargo."

"It is our custom," said Lopez, "to make small gifts to our departing guests."

"Indeed? And I suppose that these same guests make gifts to you in exchange. Like folding money."

"A plantation owner," said Lopez coldly, "expects to make some small profit."

"Talking of plantations," said Grimes, "I would like to inspect yours."

"I have nothing to hide, Your Excellency," stated Lopez. "Ram Das, ask Mendoza Sahib to attend me here. At the same time arrange for two trishaws to be waiting in the portico."

"To hear is to obey, Sahib."

The butler silently left the room.

Chapter 28

Grimes looked curiously at Mendoza when that gentleman eventually made his appearance. He could have been a survivor from the long defunct British Raj in India. He was tall and thin, deeply tanned, black-haired and with a pencil-thin moustache. His eyes were startlingly blue against the dark skin of his face. He was clad in spotless white—shoes, trousers with a knife-edge crease, a high-necked, gold-buttoned tunic. Under his left arm was a white sun helmet.

He stiffened to attention as he faced his employer.

"Sir?"

He could have been a subaltern of some crack Indian regiment of the old days called before his colonel to be given his orders.

"Ah, Mr. Mendoza. This gentleman is the new Governor, Commodore Grimes . . ."

Mendoza bowed stiffly in Grimes's direction. Grimes disentangled his legs and, with Su Lin's assistance, got to his feet. He extended his hand. After what seemed to be a long hesitation Mendoza took it. It was like, thought Grimes, getting a fistful of cold, wet, dead fish.

"The Commodore," said Lopez, "would like a tour of the plantation. I assume that his . . . er . . . servant will accompany him."

"Yes," said Grimes, "Su Lin will be coming with me."

"You spacemen!" chuckled Lopez. It was a dirty chuckle. He flinched under Grimes's hostile glare then went on hastily, "I beg your pardon, Your Excellency, but members of your profession do have a reputation, you know."

"If a world such as New Venusberg," said Grimes coldly, "were obliged to depend upon spacemen for its prosperity it would very soon go bankrupt."

"Yes, yes. Of course. I was merely jesting. And now, if you will accompany Mr. Mendoza, he will show you everything that you wish to see. Dinner will be awaiting you on your return. Do you appreciate Oriental cuisine, such as Indian curries?"

Grimes said that he did. Then he and Su Lin followed Mendoza from the room, leaving Lopez and his consort to the enjoyment of their shared pipe.

The trishaws were waiting in the portico, each powered and piloted by a scrawny man, each of whom had an almost black, dusty skin. Two pairs of yellow eyes regarded Grimes and the girl incuriously, looked to Mendoza with a mixture of respect and fear. Fear was predominant.

"Will you ride with me, Your Excellency?" asked the plantation manager. "Your servant can bring up the rear."

Grimes would far sooner have ridden with Su Lin but the arrangement proposed by Mendoza made sense. He would be able, when sitting alongside the visitor, to point things out and to explain. (He would be able, too, to distract Grimes's attention from things that he should not be seeing.)

He climbed into the passenger basket of the leading trishaw while the driver sat impassively, his gnarled feet on the pedals. Mendoza joined him. The man was redolent of some male perfumery. Grimes sniffed disgustedly. He would much sooner have been smelling Su Lin's clean scent.

Mendoza gave orders in a language strange to Grimes. Then, "Jao!" he snapped. "Juldi jao!"

"Atcha, Sahib!"

The trishaw took off like a rocket, its spinning wheels spattering the loose gravel of the driveway to port and to starboard. Grimes turned his head to look astern. The vehicle with Su Lin was following.

"We shall pass, first, through the laborers' compound,"

said Mendoza. "As you will see, Your Excellency, our workers are well and adequately housed."

Well and adequately housed they may have been, although Grimes had his doubts. The trishaws sped between rows of barrack-like buildings, drab gray, of poured concrete construction. The windows were tiny, unglazed, some screened by dirty rags fluttering lethargically in the light breeze. There seemed to be children everywhere—black, skinny, naked brats of both sexes. But they were not running and shouting and screaming as children should. They were squatting silently in the dust, staring at nothing. There were a few adults abroad—withered, ancient crones shuffling on their various errands, old men sitting in doorways conversing among themselves in low voices.

These adults, despite their apparent age, seemed to be showing far more life than did the children. They stood up as the two trishaws passed, salaaming deeply. And Grimes thought that he read hate in their yellow eyes.

"Mr. Mendoza," he said, "shouldn't these kids be at school?"

"School, Your Excellency? What for? Whatever skills they will need when they join our work force they will learn from their parents."

"Shouldn't they be . . . playing?"

"Playing, Your Excellency?"

"Yes. I've seen children on more worlds than you've had hot dinners and, more than once, I've cursed the noisy little bastards. But these. . . . Anybody would think that they were doped."

"They are, Your Excellency."

"What!"

"It is their way of life. Their parents start them on the dreamweed almost as soon as they are weaned. By adolescence they have built up at least a partial immunity and are able to function as members of the work force."

"What a life!" exclaimed Grimes.

"They have never known any better, Your Excellency. And who can say that they are not happy, sitting there and dreaming their dreams?"

"Would you want *your* children to grow up like that, Mr. Mendoza?"

"I have no children, Commodore Grimes. It is extremely unlikely that I shall ever be a father. To me the necessary preliminaries, undertaken with a woman, would be extremely distasteful."

His voice must have carried. From the following trishaw came Su Lin's scornful laugh.

The manager lapsed into sullen, haughty silence. The vehicles sped on, hardly slackening speed when, once they were clear of the compound, there were hills to negotiate. The road was now a winding one, threading its way between hillocks on each of which the fleshy stems and leaves of the dreamweed flourished. In this locality the crop was not yet ready for harvesting; the predominant colour of the vegetation was a greenish blue. As they progressed, however, Grimes saw an increasing number of purple leaves.

And then they came to an area in which the harvest was in full swing. On either side of the winding roadway rose the glowing purple mounds, over which crawled the small, dark-skinned people, their white loincloths in vivid contrast to the almost-black of their thin bodies. They were working in pairs—usually it was the man who wielded the knife, hacking the fleshy leaves from the thick, convoluted stems while a woman filled a basket with the yield. Filled baskets stood by the roadside, awaiting collection. Overseers moved among the workers. These wore white jackets and turbans as well as loincloths. Their skin was lighter than those of the laborers, their build heavier. They carried short whips.

The air was heavy with a sweet yet acrid aroma. Grimes wondered if it were safe to breathe. He asked Mendoza as much.

"Perfectly safe, Your Excellency," the manager told him scornfully. "The dreamweed has to be taken orally—chewed and swallowed. If you care to look you will see the field hands doing just that. Doesn't it say in the Bible, 'Thou shalt not muzzle the ox that treads the corn'?" He barked an order to the trishaw driver and the vehicle slowed to a crawl, as did the one carrying Su Lin. "On the other hand, it is not desirable that the ox make a pig of himself. As that man there is doing."

The person indicated was working far more slowly than the others. The leaves that he was hacking from the stems he was stuffing into his busily chewing mouth while his woman, holding her almost empty basket, watched.

An overseer was making his way around and over the tangle of stems, shouting angrily. The man paid no heed, although his woman put out a hand to try to catch his wrist as he was raising another bundle of leaves to his mouth. He shook her off, went on chewing. The overseer was now within striking range. He raised his whip and used it, slashing the addict across the face. The laborer screamed shrilly. He brought up his long, heavy knife to ward off the whip that was descending for a second blow. And then there was a flurry of fast action, after which the whip-wielder was staring stupidly at his right wrist from which the bright red, arterial blood was spurting, then at his hand, still clutching the whip, on the ground at his feet. The woman was wailing loudly; it seemed odd to Grimes that so loud a noise could come from so small a body. But she was soon quieted. The knife silenced her, slashing down onto the juncture of scrawny neck with thin shoulder.

There was blood everywhere.

On the hillock both workers and overseers were scrambling desperately away from the scene of the maiming and the killing. Down in the road the trishaw drivers were attempting to turn their vehicles so that they could return to the safety of the compound. The madman, purple froth spattering from his working mouth, his yellow eyes glaring, was jumping down the hillside toward them, miraculously avoiding being tripped by the tangled roots and stems.

Su Lin's trishaw was around, making off downhill. Grimes's trishaw was turning. As it did so it heeled over. Mendoza fell heavily against Grimes—and Grimes fell out on to the roadway. He scrambled to his feet. He would have run but, in his fall, he had twisted his right leg. He was weaponless. He looked around frantically. A stone to throw at the fast advancing homicidal maniac . . .

But there weren't any stones, and it was a very long time since, as a very junior officer in the Survey Service, he had taken a course in unarmed combat.

He decided that if he were to die all his wounds would be in front. He would not turn his back on his murderer. And perhaps—perhaps!—he might be able to cow the man into submission with his best quarterdeck glare . . .

The killer was down on the road now, loping toward Grimes. Grimes stood there, facing him.

"Stop!" he barked.

And the man did stop and momentarily—but only momentarily—the light of sanity gleamed in his yellow eyes. Then he came on again, the bloody knife upraised.

"Stop! Drop that knife!"

The man came on.

Grimes heard running feet behind him. So Mendoza, he thought, had returned to sort things out. Presumably he was used to such emergencies and, probably, armed.

But it was not Mendoza. It was Su Lin. She ran past Grimes as he shouted at her, "Get back, you stupid bitch! Get back!"

She had something in her right hand, something small that gleamed golden in the sunlight. Grimes recognized it. It was the lighter that she had used to ignite the tobacco in his pipe.

He staggered after her. He had to save her from the madman, even though it cost his own life.

The maniac screamed, dreadfully. Before he threw up his hands, his knife dropped and forgotten, to cover his face Grimes saw the two-meter-long flame, a thin pencil of intense radiance, that slashed across the mad, staring eyes, searing and blackening them. There was a sickening stench of burned flesh in the air. Then the man, hunched and moaning, turned and shambled blindly away. Sightless, he could not keep to the road. He crashed into the dreamweed plants, tripped and fell heavily. His thin, high whining was a dreadful thing to hear.

Su Lin, the lethal lighter back in a pocket, stopped to pick up the knife.

"What . . . What are you going to do?" asked Grimes.

"Finish him off quickly," she said. "It will be the kindest way."

She was right, of course.

Grimes made no attempt to stop her but did not watch.

Chapter 29

The two trishaws returned.

Mendoza got out of the leading one, walked past Grimes and Su Lin to where the huddled form of the dead maniac was sprawled face down, the hilt of his knife protruding from his back. Two of the overseers were squatting by the corpse, talking in low voices. The manager went to them, was obviously questioning the men. He returned to the governor and the girl. His expression, decided Grimes, was an odd combination of condemnation and disappointment.

He said, "This is a serious matter."

"Too right it is," said Grimes. Then, "And where were *you* when the shit hit the fan?"

"A man is dead, Your Excellency."

"For all the help that you were, I could be dead too. As for your dead man—he is responsible for one death himself. Possibly two."

"But this is a serious matter, Your Excellency. This woman may be your servant but she is a native of this world—and not a citizen. Only citizens may carry weapons."

"Only citizens, Mr. Mendoza?" Grimes gestured toward the dead man. "Was *he* a citizen? What about his knife?"

"A working tool, Commodore."

"And a murder weapon."

Mendoza ignored this.

He said to Su Lin, "Give me your flame-thrower, girl. It will have to be produced as evidence when you are brought to trial."

Grimes thought hard and fast.

He said, "It is not hers to give to you, Mr. Mendoza."

"What do you mean?"

"It is *my* lighter. During my career as commodore of a privateer flotilla I found it convenient to carry on my person gadgets such as that lighter—seemingly innocent but capable of being used in self defense . . ." While he was speaking he was filling his pipe. "I had to use it once," he went on untruthfully, "to quell a mutiny . . ."

"Then what is *she* doing with it?"

By this time the bit of Grimes's pipe was between his teeth. Su Lin lit it for him, using a flame of normal dimensions and intensity.

"You see what she's doing with it," Grimes said through a cloud of acrid smoke. "She regards this as part of her duties."

"Like stabbing a blinded man in the back, Your Excellency."

"He would not have lived," said Su Lin. "Not only was he blinded but his brains were fried."

"This is a matter for Mr. Lopez," said Mendoza stiffly.

"Naturally," agreed Grimes. "After all, it was one of his employees—or slaves—who would have murdered me had it not been for Su Lin."

"It was one of his employees who was murdered by your servant, Your Excellency. At the very least there will be a heavy claim for compensation."

"Quite possibly," said Grimes. "I shall have to look into the legal aspects. I am not as young as I was and being attacked by homicidal maniacs puts a severe strain upon my nervous system. It is likely that I shall require the services of an expensive psychiatrist to undo the mental damage that I sustained." He drew deeply from his pipe and then exhaled the smoke. "But no doubt Mr. Lopez is rich enough to pay both the doctor's bill *and* the damages that I shall demand."

"Your Excellency," almost sneered Mendoza, "is quite a space lawyer."

"As far as this planet is concerned," growled Grimes, "I am the law—and the prophets. The members of my personal staff answer only to me, and don't go forgetting it. Come, Su Lin, we will share a trishaw back to Mr. Lopez's not so humble abode. Mr. Mendoza can do as he pleases."

The two of them clambered aboard one of the waiting vehicles.

"Home, James," ordered Grimes, "and don't spare the horses."

To his surprise the man understood. It was a pity as it

meant that he and the girl were not able to compare notes during the ride back to the Lopez establishment.

Understandably Mr. Lopez was not pleased when he heard Grimes's story. He would have been far happier, Grimes could not help thinking, if Mendoza had returned alone with the news of the murder of yet another troublesome planetary governor. And yet, Grimes knew, the messy affair had not been planned. How could it have been? But Mendoza had been quite prepared to let nature take its course and would have been commended rather than otherwise if Grimes had been hacked to pieces.

"A sorry business, Your Excellency," sighed Lopez.

"It could have been sorrier still as far as I'm concerned," said Grimes coldly. And then—he might as well put the boot in while he had the chance—"I was far from impressed by the conduct of your Mr. Mendoza. Any officer of the Survey Service behaving as he did would face a court martial on the charge of cowardice in the face of the enemy."

"My trishaw driver bolted," Mendoza said.

"So did Su Lin's. But she managed to jump out and run back to help me."

"Ah, yes," murmured Lopez, "there is the matter of the weapon that she was carrying, quite illegally."

"Not a weapon," Grimes told him. "A lighter. *My* lighter."

"A very special sort of lighter," insisted Lopez.

"*Anything* can be used as a weapon," said Grimes. "You should see what the average petty officer instructor in the Survey Service, a specialist in unarmed combat, can do with a rolled-up newspaper. And when I was privateering one of my officers could do quite dreadful damage with a pack of playing cards."

"You realize, Your Excellency," persisted Lopez, "that I shall be obliged to make a full report to President O'Higgins's chief of police and to Colonel Bardon."

"Report away, Mr. Lopez. I am Colonel Bardon's superior officer. And, legally speaking, I rank above the president. As far as I am concerned *my* servant took steps, effective steps, to save my life while yours, Mr. Mendoza, was rattling down the road as fast as his trishaw could carry him."

"The driver panicked!" almost shouted Mendoza.

"That's *your* story. Stick to it, if you feel like it. I could hardly care less."

There was what seemed to be a long silence, broken at last by Lopez.

"Well, Your Excellency, what has been done has been done. I suppose that now you will wish to return aboard your airship to freshen up before joining Madam Lopez and myself for dinner. . . ."

"I shall return aboard my airship," said Grimes, "and then I shall order my pilot to cast off."

"But I have instructed my chef to prepare a meal, a very special meal, for the occasion of your visit."

"You'll just have to eat it yourself. Come, Su Lin."

The butler escorted them from from the oriental opulence of Lopez's reception room up to the roof. Grimes regretted having missed what probably would have been a superb curry. But, he consoled himself, there might have been some subtle poison in the portions served to him, or, possibly, a stiff infusion of dreamweed essence.

He was relieved when he emerged into the late afternoon sunlight, looking up to the gleaming bulk of *Fat Susie* swinging at the mast. Sanchez looked out from an open control cab window and waved cheerfully. Grimes raised a hand to return the salutation.

Now there would be that blasted ladder to negotiate. The wrenched muscles of his right leg were still painful and he could move the limb only by making a conscious effort.

"Your Excellency," said Su Lin, "I will ask Captain Sanchez to send down a cradle for you."

"You will not."

Slowly, painfully, he went up the ladder, taking as much weight as possible on his arms, Su Lin close behind him. He clambered at last into the control cab.

"What's wrong, Commodore?" asked Sanchez anxiously.

"Just a twisted leg, Raoul. It could have been worse."

"Very much worse," said the girl.

"But what happened?"

"I'll tell you later. Meanwhile, get us the hell out of here."

"The mooring mast is not manned, sir."

"You can actuate your release gear from the cab, can't you? As long as nothing fouls it's quite safe."

Sanchez did as ordered and *Fat Susie* drifted slowly astern, away from the roof of the Sanchez mansion, a winch whining as the short length of wire cable was reeled in. Only Ram Das, the butler, was there to see them go.

"You must rest now, Your Excellency," said Su Lin.

"All right."

"Where do we go, Commodore?" asked Sanchez.

"I'll leave it to you, Raoul. Surprise me."

Walking slowly and painfully he made his way aft to his quarters.

Chapter 30

Stripped, prone on his bunk, Grimes submitted to the ministrations of Su Lin.

He murmured, "What did I ever do to deserve you? Devoted handmaiden . . . Highly efficient bodyguard . . . And now masseuse . . ."

Under her kneading fingers the soreness and stiffness were dissipating. But there was another stiffness, of which he was becoming embarrassedly conscious. *As long as she doesn't ask me to turn over . . .* he thought.

But she did not.

She slapped his naked buttocks and said cheerfully, "You'll survive, Commodore. But you usually do, don't you?"

"If I didn't," he told her, "I shouldn't be here." He flexed his legs experimentally. "Thanks to you, I shall be able to stand my watch."

"All part of the PAT service," she told him. "And, talking of watches, it's almost time that I was relieving Raoul. You'll be fit to take over at midnight, will you? Good. Then you had better get some sleep."

"I'll do just that," he said.

Sleep was a long time coming—and when it did he was plagued by nightmares—or, rather, by a recurring nightmare. In it he would be standing there, helpless, on the hot road, under a blazing sun, while the madman came at him with bloody machete upraised. Each time he woke up just as the sharp, gleaming blade was descending on his unprotected head.

And then Su Lin was there, switching on the light, putting the tea tray down on his bunkside table.

"Are you all right, Commodore?" she asked. "Do you feel fit enough to take over? If not, Raoul and I can manage between us."

"I'm feeling fine, Su Lin."

"You don't look it."

"I'm a little tired, that's all. The tea will perk me up. Get back to control like a good girl. I'll be with you shortly."

"As you say, Commodore," she said doubtfully.

The tea did refresh him.

He dressed, then made his way forward and then down into the cab. *Fat Susie* was ambling along at cruising speed, almost silently, only the occasional click and whine of servo-mechanisms telling that the auto-pilot was functioning, maintaining course and adjusting attitude and altitude as requisite.

He looked at the chart and at the dotted line of the extrapolated track ahead of the airship's actual position, a trace that, astern of her, was unbroken.

"We're flying over the Unclaimed Territory, as they call it, now," said Su Lin. "No doubt, eventually, it will be tamed—with wheatfields and vineyards and . . . dreamweed plantations. It all depends, I suppose, on what sort of influx of refugee labor—slave labor—there is over the next few years. . . ."

"Assuming, of course," Grimes said, "that things continue going on as they have been going on. But aren't we supposed to be throwing a spanner into that machinery?"

She grinned. "We are, Commodore."

"Just what is down there, anyhow?" asked Grimes.

"In places, a jumble of rocks. Deep canyons. Savage animals. Even more savage plants."

"Savage plants? You have to be kidding, Su Lin."

"I'm not. I thought that you had been given a thorough briefing on this planet before you were sent here, *Governor*."

"I was given a fine collection of spools to study on the way out. I studied them. But they were all concerned with history, politics, economics and sociology."

"I'll see to it that you get a briefing on Liberia's natural ecology when we get back to the Residence. Who knows? It might come in useful some day. It will be interesting, at least."

"As you say." Grimes was still looking at the chart. "I suppose that these names given to the various natural features should tell me something. Mount Horrible . . . Bloodsuckers Canyon . . . Shocking Valley . . . But that sounds more comic than sinister . . ."

He was interrupted by an insistent beeping from the radar. He went to the console, looked into the PPI. Yes, there was a target, an airborne target. just abaft the starboard beam, all of forty kilometers distant. He pushed the extrapolation button. The airship, as he assumed that it must be, was flying on an almost parallel course in the same direction.

Su Lin had gone to the radio telephone transceiver.

"*Fat Susie* to unidentified aircraft to my starboard. Do you read me?"

The reply came with no delay.

"*Citizen Marat* to *Fat Susie*. I read you loud and clear. Where bound, *Fat Susie?*"

"Cruising, *Citizen Marat*. Where are you bound? Over."

"Libertad to Rousseauville with mail and passengers. Over."

Grimes, now, was staring out through the starboard window of the cab, binoculars to his eyes. He realized that he could not see the line of the land horizon against the dark luminosity of the sky. And, at this range, he should be able to see the other airship's running lights—but there was nothing there. And something seemed to have blotted out those stars at lower altitudes. He looked ahead. There the stars were dimming, were being obscured.

So *Fat Susie* had driven into a belt of cloud. So what? Radar and radar altimeter were working perfectly. The only traffic was bound in the same direction at the same speed. The extrapolated course was well clear of any mountains.

He heard Su Lin say, "A very good night to you, *Citizen Marat*. And *bon voyage*."

"Bon voyage to you, *Fat Susie*." And then the male voice of the other watchkeeper chuckled. "Are *you Fat Susie*?"

"Just Su," she replied. "And not fat."

"I'd like to meet you some time."

"Good night," she said firmly. "Over and out."

"Wolves of the air," commented Grimes. "Off with you now, Su Lin. Get your head down. I have the watch."

Grimes, although he had done his share of atmosphere flying, was a spaceman, not an airman. He did not like this pushing ahead through thick fog. (Cloud, he told himself, cloud, not fog. The air would be clear enough at ground level, clear enough if he pushed *Fat Susie* up and through this vaporous ceiling.) He considered reducing altitude, then decided against it. Airships are not designed for hedge-hopping. Should he lift? But that would mean the dumping of ballast. And Sanchez had set the course, had set it in three dimensions, and might be annoyed, when called to take over the watch, to find that Grimes had been playing silly buggers all over the sky while he slept. All right, all right, Grimes was the pilot's employer. But he, Grimes, was not the master. Sanchez was.

Should he call Sanchez?

And then, Grimes told himself, *he'd have valid grounds for thinking of me as an old woman. Damn it all, I'm a shipmaster. I've commanded far bigger vessels than this little gasbag. As commodore, I've commanded a flotilla. (And,* he thought wryly, *made a jesusless balls of it.*)

Apart from the visually invisible *Citizen Marat* there was no other traffic. There would not be, Grimes knew, over this region of the planet. Grimes consulted the radar. The other airship was on a slightly converging course but she was drawing ahead. Furthermore, she was maintaining an altitude at least a thousand meters in excess of *Fat Susie's*. She would cross ahead of *Fat Susie* safely enough and without incident.

The watch wore on. The air in the control cab, from the fumes of Grimes's pipe, was almost as thick as the air outside. The airship maintained course and altitude without a human hand at the controls. In the PPI the glowing blip that was *Citizen Marat* was now ahead, was still edging over to port. Grimes stared into the screen, drowsy, hypnotized by the steady rotation of the sweep.

But there was something wrong!

The range was no longer opening; it was closing fast. A glance at the auxiliary screen showed that the other ship was losing altitude rapidly. What the hell was she playing at?

It was one of those occasions when Grimes wished that he had three pairs of hands. Somehow he managed to push the General Alarm button and, a split second later, to initiate the process of switching from automatic pilot to manual control. *Fat Susie*—the stupid bitch!—seemed reluctant to yield the dominance of her functions to a mere human. It seemed ages before the illuminated sign, AUTO, over the wheel and the gyro compass repeater flickered out to be replaced by MANUAL. And all the time there was the urgent stridency of the alarm bells to engender panic.

Sanchez and Su Lin were in the control cab. Neither had taken time to dress. Sanchez stared out through the windows at nothingness, then went to the radar.

"Holy Bakunin!" he muttered. "How the hell did you . . .?" Then, "Turn away, man! Hard-a-starboard!"

Grimes, at the wheel, spun it rapidly to the right. He felt *Fat Susie* heel over, heard her creaking protests. From above and abaft the control cab there was a peculiarly muffled crash—and, almost immediately afterwards, a noise that could only be that of the discharge of at least one medium caliber automatic cannon. *Fat Susie* lurched, shuddered. Grimes, clinging to the now useless wheel, managed to keep his feet. He stared out through the port window, saw that the colliding airships had, fortuitiously, found a pocket of clear air in the cloud blanket. By the crimson glare of his own vessel's port navigation light he could see a great hulk backing away, under reversed thrust, from its victim.

He could read the name . . .

No, not the name. The single letter and the three numerals.

Wherever the real *Citizen Marat* was, this was not her.

This was the army's *R273*, the rigid dirigible that had cast off from the Lopez mooring mast to make room for *Fat Susie*.

The clouds enveloped her once more and she vanished from sight.

Fat Susie, her main gas cells ruptured, fell almost like a stone.

Chapter 31

"Up into the ship!" shouted Sanchez.

"Why?" asked Grimes stupidly.

"Because the control car is going to hit first, you fool!"

Su Lin was already mounting the short ladder. Grimes followed her. Sanchez followed him. They reached the catwalk that ran fore and aft between the gas cells, these containers wrinkled now, collapsing upon themselves. There was no place else to run. The vertical ladder that gave access to the outside of the envelope was blocked by fold upon fold of limp fabric.

The lights were still burning, running from the emergency power cells. They gave some small comfort. The three members of *Fat Susie's* crew huddled together in their cave of wrinkled cloth, blocked now at either end, waiting for the crash.

"It can't be long now," said Sanchez at last.

His voice was oddly high, almost a soprano.

He's scared, thought Grimes. *I didn't think that he'd be the type to show such fear . . .*

He said philosophically, "What goes up has to come down, I suppose."

His own voice was high and squeaky, even in his own ears.

The helium, he thought. *There's a lot of it in the atmosphere we're breathing. It's making us sound like refugees from the papal choir . . .*

"She was a good little ship," said Sanchez regretfully. "I'd like to get the bastards who did this to her."

"I'd like to get the bastards," said Grimes, "who did this

to us. Did you see the markings on the other dirigible before she backed away?''

''I did,'' announced Su Lin, her voice faint, almost as inaudible as a bat's sonar squeak. ''I did. It was the Army ship that we saw at the Lopez plantation. It was no more *Citizen Marat* than I am.''

''You're the wrong sex in any case,'' quipped Sanchez,

There was no doubt about that, thought Grimes. He was acutely aware of the girl's nudity pressed against him.

He said, changing the subject, ''I wonder what premiums Lloyd's would charge to insure the life of a Liberian governor?'' He was about to add, ''Especially one who travels by airship . . .'' when *Fat Susie* struck.

It was an amazingly gentle contact. The catwalk lifted beneath their feet, throwing them together but not violently. From somewhere beneath them there came the sound of a muffled crash. And then there was silence, broken only by the sound of their breathing and the hiss of escaping helium.

The lights did not go out but their illumination was dimmed by the layers of fabric through which it had to shine.

They were huddled together, the three of them, in a sort of cave, the walls and ceiling of which were formed by the fabric of collapsed gas cells. Luckily air was getting in from somewhere. At the same time the helium was getting out. Their voices were reverting to normal timbre.

''Where's that fancy lighter of yours, Su Lin?'' asked Grimes. ''We can use it to burn our way out.''

''Unluckily,'' she told him tartly, ''I don't have any pockets in my birthday suit. The lighter's where I left it when I turned in. On my bunkside table.''

''And the door to your cabin,'' said Sanchez thoughtfully, ''should be right behind where you are standing now . . .''

Wriggling, squirming, they managed to turn around. Su Lin's body, Grimes realized, was slippery with perspiration. So was Sanchez's, on the other side of him. They were facing a featureless wall of limp fabric. They tried to lift it up and clear, but it was anchored somehow at its lower edge. They tried to pull it down, then to pull it sideways. Grimes was almost envying the nudity of his companions. His own clothing was becoming soaked. He could feel the sweat puddling in his shoes.

During their struggles with that impenetrable curtain Su Lin's hip was pressing heavily against his right side. There was something hard in his pocket of which he became painfully conscious. His pipe, of course. His pipe—and the old-fashioned matches that he preferred to other means of ignition.

"Raoul," he asked. "This fabric . . . Is it flammable?"

"Of course not."

"Will it melt, if heat's applied?"

"I don't know. I just fly airships. I don't build them."

"Then there's only one way to find out. Su Lin, can you shift a bit to your right? A bit more . . ."

"Normally I should appreciate this," grumbled Sanchez, against whom the girl was now pushing.

Grimes got the box of matches, after a struggle, out of his pocket. It felt damp to his touch. Had his perspiration made them useless? He got one of them out of the box, struck it. It fizzled sadly and went out. He dropped it, extracted a second one. He was careful not to touch either its head or the striking surface with his fingers. This one did burn, but unenthusiastically. The oxygen content of the air in their little cave must, thought Grimes, be getting low, depleted by their consumption of it during their exertions.

Carefully, carefully he brought the feeble flame into light contact with the fabric. It began to smoke and bubble. A vile, acrid stench assailed their nostrils. The match went out. Grimes let it fall, got a third one from the box. By the time that it had burned away there was a small hole with fused edge, just large enough for Su Lin to get her index finger into. She tried to tug downwards but achieved nothing.

Grimes used seven more matches to enlarge the hole in an upward direction. (There were now only three left; he should have put a full box in his pocket before going on watch.) He could, now, get his right hand into the vertical slit. He pulled, sideways, with all the strength that he was able to exert in this confined space. The fabric was stubborn—but there was room, now, for Sanchez to get his left hand into the hole to join the struggle.

Suddenly there was a ripping noise. Slowly, slowly the rent was enlarging while the two men panted from their combined effort. Luckily fresh air, in appreciable quantities, was getting in now.

They paused, to breathe deeply.

Between them the girl said, "Give me a hand, you two. I think I can squirm through . . ."

She did that. With her gone there was room for Grimes and Sanchez to move with much greater ease. They could hear her scuffling progress on the other side of the curtain. They heard her grunt with effort. Was something jamming the door to her cabin? They heard, faintly, what they hoped was a sigh of relief.

At last she was back.

"Stand clear!" she called. "Stand clear!"

The jet of flame—not as long as when the lighter had been used as a weapon but still as glaringly incandescent—swept downwards, and then up. It went out.

She said, "Come in. This is Liberty Hall. You can spit on the mat and call the cat a bastard."

The ship—what was left of her—was theirs again.

They gained access to their cabins.

Sanchez and Su Lin got dressed, then they and Grimes sat in the little wardroom with stiff drinks. They felt that they deserved them but were careful not to overindulge. Grimes wanted to take a torch to go outside to assess the damage but the others vetoed the suggestion.

"We're still alive," Su Lin told him. "If we go outside the ship, at night, we very soon shan't be. This is the Unclaimed Territory. Remember?"

"And as for viewing the wreck," said Sanchez, "that can wait until daylight. One thing *is* certain—*Fat Susie* will never fly again."

"Mphm," grunted Grimes, filling and lighting his pipe. Then, "What time is sunup, Raoul?"

The pilot looked at his watch, just a timekeeper without any fancy functions.

"About an hour," he said. Then, with a wry grin, "Where *has* the night gone to?"

"I'll make some tea," said Su Lin briskly.

She got up from the settee, went from the wardroom into the adjoining galley. After a brief absence she returned.

"Raoul," she said, "there's no fresh water . . ."

Sanchez got up and went back with her into the airship's kitchen. They returned, eventually, to the wardroom. Their faces were grave.

"Commodore," said the pilot, "there's good news and bad news. The good news is that this was a crash that we shall be able to walk away from. The bad news is that we owe our soft landing to the fact that we lost considerable mass during our descent. Our fresh water tanks must have been holed."

"If our luck holds," said Su Lin, "we might find that we're not too far from a stream . . ."

"And that the stream doesn't harbor any life forms big enough to be a serious menace to us," Sanchez said.

"Meanwhile," the girl went on, "we have beer, and table wines, and lolly water. Even if there's no water handy it'll be at least a week before we die of thirst."

"You're a pair of cheerful bastards," grumbled Grimes.

"Don't complain," the girl told him severely. "We're alive. There's no reason at all why we shouldn't stay that way."

"I'm surprised," said Grimes, "that Major Flattery didn't stick around to make sure that we were all very dead."

"I was myself—but, thinking it over, I can see why he just made us crash, *here*, and then flew off," said the girl. "I can see what the official story will be. Steering gear failure and a midair collision, contributed to by the bad airmanship of the vessel sustaining major damage. Flattery's own ship was damaged too, so much so that he could not make an immediate search for survivors—if any . . . In the fullness of time a proper search will be organized—but everybody will be quite sure either that we were all killed at once by the crash or, shortly afterwards, by the local flora and fauna. . . ."

"Why should Flattery make a report at all?" asked Grimes, "except to his boss, Colonel Bardon . . . As far as the rest of Liberia is concerned Governor Grimes will be enjoying himself flying hither and yon about his domain. Eventually there will be a public urinal or something to be ceremoniously opened and people will start to ask, 'Where *is* the Governor?' And Lopez Sahib will have been the last person to have seen me, and he will say that *Fat Susie* was last sighted proceeding east—whereas we were proceeding north. . . ."

"And years from now," said the girl, "when the Unclaimed Territory is opened up for exploitation, somebody will find what's left of *Fat Susie* and what's left of us. If anything."

"And I shall be blamed, posthumously," Sanchez said. "Pilot error. That's what they'll say."

"And what they'll say about me," contributed Grimes, "is that my famous luck finally ran out . . ."

They all laughed, enjoying, briefly, their indulgence in gallows humor.

Then Grimes asked, "Could we make our way back to civilization by foot?"

"Not if we're where I think we are—where I'm reasonably sure that we are—we couldn't. Not even if we had weapons. Did *you* bring any private pocket artillery with you, Commodore?"

"No."

"Su Lin?"

"Only my all-purpose lighter. And there are some quite useful knives in the galley—not that they'd be much use against the local predators. And you, Raoul?"

"There's a laser torch in the workshop. Normally it runs off the mains, although it has a power cell. But the power cell has a limited life."

"We could recharge—or could we?—from the power cells that are supplying juice for the emergency lights," said Grimes.

"And *they*, too, aren't exactly everlasting," Sanchez told him.

"Even so, once the sun is up they should be recharging themselves."

"Yes. Of course. Assuming that things weren't too badly damaged by the collision and the crash. As soon as it's light we'll go outside and see just how well off—or badly off—we are."

Chapter 32

Dawn came, the light of the rising sun striking through but diffused by the tattered fabric that obscured the outside of the wardroom windows. Su Lin led the way into the galley where each of them selected a knife. Grimes did not like knives; he made no secret of his preference for doing his killing from a distance, lobbing missiles and directing assorted lethal rays at some enemy whom he would never meet face to face while, of course, this same enemy would be reciprocating in kind.

These sharp blades, however, were better than nothing—not as good as Su Lin's versatile lighter but the charge in that would not last forever.

The three of them made their way aft, frequently having to hack their way through the tough fabric of the collapsed helium cells. They cut their way into the workshop. They found not only the laser gun—it looked like a weapon, a pistol, but its range would be pitifully short—but also two long-handled spanners, a big screwdriver that might be used as a stiletto, and a hammer.

Egress would not be possible through the control car; comparatively gentle as their fall had been at the finish, that compartment had taken the brunt of the impact. The thin metal skin forming the envelope must, Grimes knew, have been pierced by the sharp prow of Flattery's airship and by the fire of the major's automatic cannon—but none of them could do more than hazard a guess as to where the bigger rents would be. So, even though they were conscious that they were using power which might be badly needed for defense, Sanchez cut through the metallic integument, burning what was, in effect, a large inverted U, a panel that was easily bent out and down.

Fat Susie had found her last home on top of a low, rounded hillock. No, not a hillock. It was an island in the middle of a river. It would be an easy swim to either bank. Furthermore, that stream would be a valuable source of fresh water.

Grimes was the first out through the improvised doorway although the others tried to restrain him. He stood there in the warmth of the morning sun, savoring the fresh air, the light breeze that carried the not unpleasant tang of some vegetable growth. He straightened up from his knife-fighter's crouch, an attitude which he felt must look more than a little foolish. He wished that he had a sheath into which to stick the long, sharp blade.

Su Lin joined him, her golden lighter, ready for action, gleaming in her right hand. Sanchez—the captain, last to leave his ship—jumped down. Unlike the others he did not stand admiring the scenery. He stared up at *Fat Susie*, a great, gleaming beached whale that had been run down and almost cut in two by some passing vessel.

"The bastards!" he muttered with great feeling. "The *bastards!*"

"But not very efficient ones," commented Grimes. "They should have made sure of us."

"But they have, Commodore. They have. This is the Unclaimed Territory."

"All that I see," Grimes told him, "is a quite pleasant little island in the middle of a river, with the eastern and western banks within easy reach of even such a poor swimmer as myself. The banks are well wooded—and that looks like fruit on some of the trees. Is it edible, I wonder?"

Su Lin muttered something about Gutsy Grimes.

"We have to eat, don't we?" Grimes said. "*Fat Susie* wasn't stocked for a long voyage. We have to live off the land." He grinned. "Unless we resort to long pig," he finished.

"The Governor's talking sense, Su Lin," Sanchez admitted. "What do you know, really know, about the Unclaimed Territory? Apart from hearsay, that is. . . ."

"What do *you* know, Raoul?" she countered.

"Not much. Not one quarter as much as I should. It's a reserve of native life-forms, some of them nasty. . . ."

"Like that?" asked Grimes.

He indicated with his knife something that, moving silently, was almost upon them. It didn't look like much to worry about. It could have been an almost deflated air-mattress, garishly striped in blue, green and orange, flung carelessly down upon the mossy ground. But it was motile, flowing over the irregularities of the surface.

"Just a glorified amoeba . . ." he said.

Foolishly—as he was very soon to realize—he squatted, prodding the wetly glistening surface with the point of the blade. He wondered dazedly what had hit him as he was hurled violently backwards. He sprawled there, paralyzed. He was dimly aware that Su Lin had her lighter out, was directing its shaft of intense flame at the . . . *thing*. There was a strong smell of burning. Grimes was expecting it to be of seared meat but he was surprised. The smoke that irritated his nostrils, that made him sneeze, that made them all sneeze, was one that he would have associated with a grass fire.

He heard rather than saw the flurry of activity as the creature, flapping madly in its death throes, died.

Then Su Lin was beside him, kneeling by him, her strong, capable hands stroking him gently.

"Commodore! Are you all right?"

"What. . . . What hit me?"

"It was an electric shock. I should have remembered what these things look like. . . ."

"What . . . things?"

"Shockers, they call them . . ."

He managed to sit up.

"Then this must be the Shocking River that I saw on the chart. And the shockers themselves . . . Like electric eels and rays back on Earth, and similar animals elsewhere. . . ."

"Yes. But these aren't animals. They're plants. They use their chlorophyl to convert sunlight into electricity. . . ."

Grimes was recovering now, his interest diverting his attention from the pain that persisted in his cramped muscles.

"Plants, you say? Motile plants . . . But why motile?"

"So that they can move from shadow into sunlight to recharge their batteries, crawl back into the shade to avoid an overcharge." She laughed. "I gave this one an overcharge, all right! Too, very often, their victims are thrown away from them by the shock. Then they have to ooze toward them and over them to envelop and ingest them."

Grimes shuddered. He did not fancy being enveloped and ingested.

"By why," he persisted, "are their victims such mugs as to touch them in the first place?"

"Why were you such a mug, Commodore?"

"Mphm. And, come to that, why did I get a shock? The knife has a wooden handle. It should have been a fairly effective insulator . . ."

He was still holding the weapon. He dropped it to the ground, saw the metal studs that secured the hilt to the blade.

"Yes, Su Lin, I was a mug. But *why* are the local animals mugs too?"

"They are attracted by the gaudy coloration—which duplicates, almost exactly, the coloration of other plants, non-motile and without built-in solar power plants, which are very good eating. I hope that we find them so—as we might be here for a very long time."

"If you will excuse me from the natural history lesson," said Raoul, "I'll carry on with my survey of the ship."

"Do that," said Grimes. "Su Lin and I will explore the island, what there is of it, and see what it has to offer in the way of a balanced menu."

"We will keep together," said the girl firmly. "As far as I can recall, from what I have read, the shockers are the least dangerous of the life forms that we are liable to encounter. So, while one is poking around the wreckage, the other two will be keeping a lookout. I shall have my lighter and the Commodore will have the laser pistol."

"I wish it were a *real* pistol," said Grimes.

"We have to make do," she said, "with what we've got."

Chapter 33

There were flying things that sailed through the air with lazy, undulant grace—until they swooped. They were all great, flexible wing, long, sharp beak and huge, bulbous eyes. These creatures, the humans soon discovered, were attracted both by movement and by color. They saw one of them dive from the air onto a shocker, saw it stunned into immobility and, slowly, slowly enveloped by the crawling plant. They were attacked themselves, three times. On the first two occasions pairs of the creatures were easily driven off by the slashing jet of fire from Su Lin's lighter, set to maximum intensity. The third attack was by a solitary flyer, hungrier or more aggressive than the others. It came boring in, vicious beak extended, like some nightmare airborne lancer, until Su Lin, standing her ground, succeeded in blinding it. (*Her favorite technique*, thought Grimes with a shudder. *I'd sooner have her on my side than against me. . . .*) Whining shrilly the thing veered away, flapping clumsily, and fell into the river. Almost immediately its struggling body was attacked by the denizens of the stream—and very shortly thereafter a covey of aerial predators swooped down, not (of course) to rescue their mate but to prey upon the aquatic carnivores that were ripping his (?) body to shreds. Long, writhing, segmented, many-legged bodies were impaled on the sharp beaks, carried into the sky and then dropped from a great height to fall with armor-shattering impact onto a rocky outcrop on the far side of the water.

"That could have happened to us," muttered Sanchez, at last tearing his eyes away from the distant, grisly feast.

"But it didn't," said Grimes, "Thanks to Su Lin. But I suggest that, from now on, we move *very* slowly. It might help."

It did—but working in slow motion was tiring. And although the flying things now seemed to be ignoring them (perhaps they were intelligent and had come to the conclusion that the strange, two-legged beings on the island were better left alone), there were other . . . nuisances. There was a sort of huge worm that, unexpectedly, would extrude its blind head from the mossy ground and attempt to fasten its sucker mouth upon their booted feet and ankles. There was a small army of crab-like things, each with a carapace all of a meter across, each armed with a pair of vicious looking pincers, that marched out of the stream and up the hill in military formation, that milled about in confusion on finding the way blocked by the wreckage of *Fat Susie*, that finally made its way around the stranded airship and then down the hill and into the water.

There was a straggler.

This Grimes killed with the laser pistol. The smell of roast crab made his mouth water.

"That was very foolish, Commodore," chided the girl. "The rest of them might have come back to attack you."

"But they didn't, did they? And I'm very fond of crab."

"These things only look like crabs. Their flesh might be poisonous to us."

"There's only one way to find out. Standard Survey Service survival technique. You take only a very small taste of whatever it is you're testing. If, at the end of an hour, you're suffering no ill effects then it's safe and you can tuck in."

While he spoke he was using his knife to lever up the top of the carapace, like a lid. The smell was stronger, more tantalizing. He scooped out a pea-sized portion of the pale pink, still steaming, flesh with the point of the blade. He was raising it to his mouth when she put out a hand to stop him.

"No, Commodore. Not you. You're the Governor. I'm the guinea pig." Her long fingers plucked the morsel of meat from the knife, brought it to her mouth. "H'm. Not bad, not bad at all. Now, I'll put this thing in the shade. If I'm still healthy at the end of an hour it will be our lunch . . ."

Slowly, painstakingly they continued to make their way about the wreck. They found that a relatively large area of the solar energy collecting screens on top of the envelope was undamaged. Power would be no problem. Hopefully neither food nor water would be—as long as they could fill buckets from the river without being dragged into it and eaten. (None of them had any desire to see the things that had attacked the downed flier at close quarters.) They might even, constructing a raft or canoe from the dirigible's metal skin, be able to get away from the island by crossing the stream or by drifting down-river. But what then? Could they hope to make their way overland or by water to human settlement? So far they had seen only a small sample of the Unclaimed Territory's flora and fauna, and only those creatures that operated by day.

What came out at night?

Yet, thought Grimes, there just could be a way. It all depended on what was in the workshop, what materials there were for making emergency repairs. Too, they would have to gain access to the wrecked control car so that they could study the charts.

"I'm still alive," said Su Lin, breaking into his thoughts. "It's lunch time. I can whip up some mayonnaise, and . . ."

But when they went to pick up the crab-thing they found that the worms had gotten to it first, sucking the shell dry and empty.

Chapter 34

Back in the wardroom they took lunch, eating rather uninteresting sandwiches (Grimes bitterly regretted not having had the crab put in a safe place) and washing them down with mineral water. After the meal and a brief smoke Grimes suggested that they get in a supply of fresh water. There were buckets available; there were some large empty plastic bins that could be filled. Sanchez volunteered to do the actual bucket filling and insisted that it was his duty. While he stooped on the river bank, bending out and down and over, Su Lin and Grimes kept watch—she of the sky and he of the water. Her weapon had a far greater range than his, the laser tool.

The winged creatures did not bother them. The many-legged swimmers did, once they became aware of the humans' existence. Grimes drove off the first attack, by a single predator, without any difficulty. He discovered that if he kept the water boiling or almost so it was a good deterrent. The ugly, vicious things did not venture from the merely warm into the very hot. He was beginning to congratulate himself when, very fortunately, he took a glance upstream. The water centipedes—as he had decided to call them—were coming ashore, were advancing toward them, their two-meter-long bodies wriggling sinuously along the bank. Hastily he and the others retreated up the hill, temporarily abandoning the buckets. Luckily the aquatic predators could not stay long out of their native element. They returned to the river.

But they waited there, their writhing bodies gleaming just under the surface, stalked eyes upheld like periscopes.

Grimes had seen in the workshop some pairs of rubberized work gauntlets. Accompanied by Su Lin and Sanchez he went to get three pairs of these.

"A good idea, sir, now that it's too late," complained Sanchez. "I could have done with these when I was having to dip my hands into that near-as-dammit boiling water . . ."

"They're to insulate against more than heat," Grimes told him.

Su Lin laughed appreciatively; she was quicker on the uptake than the pilot.

They went in search, then, of shockers. It was quite easy to distinguish them from those other gaudy plants that they imitated. If a thing wriggled sluggishly when it was lifted, it was a shocker. If it didn't wriggle and was securely rooted to the ground it wasn't. They were able to build a barricade of the electric plants up-river from where the buckets had been left. Then Grimes, with the laser, heated the water to near-boiling point again, simmering a centipede that was evincing hostile attentions toward him. The other creatures, as before, came ashore upstream. They tried to cross the living, garish carpet to get at their prey. They twitched and died.

Grimes wondered if they were edible—but the motile plants

had already made that decision. Very soon the long, twisted bodies were enveloped and the process of ingestion had commenced. Grimes shrugged. Those centipedes hadn't looked very appetizing. Hopefully, perhaps tomorrow, at the same time as today, there would be another procession of crabs. . . .

Anyhow, something had been accomplished. The wreck of *Fat Susie* was now well stocked with water.

"What now, Commodore?" asked Sanchez wearily.

"We get down into the control car to fetch out the charts, Raoul."

"Come off it, sir. Can't it wait until tomorrow? We've put in a very busy day, and it will be advisable for us to keep watches all through the night. We've seen only the daytime beasties—Bakunin alone knows what the nocturnal ones are like!"

"Was Bakunin a xenobiologist?" asked Grimes interestedly.

"Just somebody to swear by, sir—the same as your Odd Gods of the Galaxy."

"We'll continue this theological discussion later," said Grimes. "Right now I want those charts. I want to see what chance we have of getting out of here."

"But we can't even get ashore from this blasted island!"

"Can't we?" asked Grimes gently. "Can't we?"

"Of course we can," said Su Lin, "as long as the Commodore's famous luck hasn't run out."

"I don't think that it has," said Grimes softly. "I don't think that it has. . . ."

They had to cut their way into the control car, using the laser tool. Fortuitously—a case of Grimes's luck!—the aperture that they burned in the deck was directly over the chart table. Fantastically none of the charts sustained fire damage. They took these to the wardroom, spread them out on the carpet, studied them.

"We're here," said Sanchez definitely, drawing a circle around the representation of an island in a wide river with a soft pencil.

"Are you sure, Raoul?"

"Yes, sir. It's not far from where Flattery attacked us. We made very little headway after that—for obvious reasons."

"Mphm. Now find me a small scale chart, one with the Shocking River and this island on it but showing the terrain beyond the Unclaimed Territory."

"This one should do, Commodore."

"Good. Now, how was the wind today?"

"I . . . I didn't notice. . . ."

"Did you, Su Lin?"

"No."

"Well, I did. It's been northerly all the time—no more than light airs during the forenoon but, by now, quite a stiff breeze. Presumably—and hopefully—this weather pattern will persist. From where we are now the shortest distance to what is laughingly referred to as civilization is due south."

"But we still have to get off the island, sir!" protested Sanchez. "And then, when we do, we have to cross at least a thousand kilometers of broken terrain *crawling* with all manner of *things*. . . ."

"I know that, Raoul. Now, am I correct in stating that I saw, in the workshop some tubes of a very special adhesive?"

"Yes, sir."

"Used when you're slapping patches on to ruptured helium cells."

"That's what it's for, sir."

"And did I see some cylinders of compressed helium?"

"You did." Sanchez laughed. "I see what you're driving at, Commodore. A balloon with the envelope made from pieces of our burst gas cells glued together. And suppose we get winds with an average velocity of, say, twenty kilometers an hour . . . A fifty-hour flight—and we're out of this mess!"

"And probably into a worse one," grumbled Su Lin, but smiling as she spoke.

But the supply of adhesive, they discovered, was sufficient only for making the odd repairs. There was not nearly enough to gum together pieces of fabric to make a balloon large enough to support three persons. The helium situation was better—but what would they have to put the lighter-than-air gas in?

Grimes said, "With luck we might be able to make a

reasonably airworthy one-man balloon. With luck that one man might make it, then come back to rescue the others . . ."

"A one-woman balloon," said Su Lin.

"After we've made the thing," said Grimes, "we'll decide who's to go."

Chapter 35

Sanchez stood the evening watch, Su Lin the middle and the morning watch was kept by Grimes. Before they broke up—two to go to their beds and the other to commence his tour of duty—they discussed procedure. Would it be better for the watchkeeper to stay inside the ship or should he go outside? They agreed that an open-air vigil could well be tantamount to suicide. Then there was another question. Should lights be rigged to illuminate *Fat Susie* from the outside, or not? None of them knew much about the flora and fauna of the Unclaimed Territory. Would night prowlers be scared away by lavish illumination or would they be attracted to it?

"We didn't have any unfriendly visitors last night," argued the pilot. "The only lights were those inside the ship—and most of the ports were well screened by wreckage."

"Any nocturnal animals," said Grimes, "could well have been scared away by the descent of a huge monster from the sky. It might not be long before they accept *Fat Susie* as part of the scenery. If we rig lights outside it will make her look unnatural and delay acceptance. Too, if we do have to go outside to fight something we shan't be fighting in the dark."

"That makes sense," said Su Lin. "But the watchkeeper should stay inside the ship, on the catwalk handy for the cabins, and, on no account, go outside by himself. And the watchkeeper will have with him what seems to be our most effective weapon—my lighter." She grinned at Grimes. "And I hope that you, Commodore, will use matches to light your pipe. I don't want the lighter's charge reduced unnecessarily."

They found suitable and powerful lights and ran them, on wandering leads, outside the ship. They stood there, while the darkness deepened, waiting to see if anything would be attracted. They soon came to the conclusion that the gearing lamps would be useful in an unexpected way. Up the hill, from all sides, oozed the shockers, coming to recharge their solar batteries. They soon formed a tight cordon about the wreck, seemingly content to remain there, quiescent, soaking up the radiation. They were far more effective a barricade against intruders than anything that might have been constructed from the available materials could be.

After a not very satisfactory supper Grimes and Su Lin retired to their cabins, leaving Sanchez in charge.

The girl called Grimes at 0345 hours, bringing him the usual tea tray. After a sketchy toilet he dressed, then joined her on the catwalk.

She said, "It's been a quiet night. Either the lights have been scaring things off—or they've been electrocuted. If you don't mind, Commodore, I'll get my head down. We shall have a busy day."

"Off you go," Grimes told her.

He made his way through the ship to the hole that had been cut in her metallic skin, looked out. The external lights were burning brightly, the garish carpet of shockers was still in place. Here and there were sluggish stirrings, lazy undulations. A few of the carnivorous, mobile plants were bulging. They had fed, obviously. On what? On something quite big, that much was obvious. Something that, quite possibly, might have gotten inside the wreck and fed on its human occupants.

Would it be possible, wondered Grimes, to . . . to harvest? Why not? They were plants after all, not animals . . . to harvest the shockers, keep them in captivity and export them at a nice profit? The Survey Service would be a potential customer. Grimes recalled occasions in his own career when he had been involved in the exploration of newly discovered plants. Efficient sentries such as these creatures would have been very, very useful.

Get-rich-quick Grimes, he thought. *That's me*.

At the moment there was only one snag. As Governor of this world he could not, legally, engage in any profit-making enterprise. As Governor? He laughed aloud. If things didn't go as he was hoping he would soon be the late Governor Grimes.

He went back inside, smoked his foul pipe. He went into the galley and constructed a multi-tiered sandwich, made tea. He thought, as he was munching his snack, *We shall have to institute a system of rationing until we find out just what around here is edible.*

The watch wore on.

At 0600 hours he called Sanchez.

Shortly thereafter the two of them went to the hole in the envelope. They could not watch the sun rise as that was on the other side of the ship. They saw the shockers slowly oozing away from the shadow cast by the twisted hull. Artificial light they liked when there was nothing else—but they preferred the real thing.

"So we can get out," said Grimes, "without having to wear rubber boots . . ."

Until it was time to call Su Lin the two men busied themselves in the workshop, carrying the tools and some of the materials that they would need out of the ship. They did not think that any of the local life-forms would be interested in gas cylinders, shears or tubes of adhesive. They kept a watch for fliers, some of which were already sailing through the sky like, Grimes thought, the manta rays that he had seen in the tropical seas of Earth. Only once did one swoop down upon them but it sheared off at once as soon as Grimes directed a jet of flame, from Su Lin's lighter, in its direction.

Then the girl was called and they had breakfast. She, officiating as cook, looked at Grimes suspiciously.

"I could have sworn," she said, "that there was more bread than this when we finished supper last night. And there were those hard-boiled eggs that I had plans for. And what's this in the gashbin? An empty sardine can . . ."

"I'll get you another crab this morning," promised Grimes.

"You'd better, Commodore. You'd just better . . ."

After the meal—fried eggs (there would be no more after this) and bacon (in short supply but not finished)—they got down to work. Working mainly inside the ship they cut large sections from the fabric of the collapsed helium cells, trying to keep these as big as possible. Sweating with the exertion they—Grimes and Sanchez—lugged these out of the ship, spreading them on the mossy slope while the girl, her weapon once again in her possession, kept watch. They were troubled only by the great worms. Su Lin managed to kill one of these before it could withdraw its ugly, sucker-equipped head back into its burrow. They dragged it out of the hole, carried the still-twitching body—it was like a huge, greatly elongated sausage—into the wreck. There was a chance that its flesh might be edible.

Grimes, using his versatile wrist companion, utilizing its computer functions, had made his calculations the previous evening, had drawn plans and diagrams on the backs of the charts salvaged from the control car. The workshop yielded rulers and tapes and sticks of crayon. Finally, making ample allowance for overlap, it was possible for Grimes and Sanchez to begin cutting out elliptical sections from the gas cell fabric. They worked slowly and clumsily. At last Su Lin could stand it no longer.

"Here, Commodore," she told him, "take this." She handed him the golden lighter. "*You* keep watch. Dressmaking, with the preliminary cutting, is one of my skills. Obviously it's not one of yours."

"I never said that it was," Grimes told her.

So, while the others, on their hands and knees, worked he acted as sentry, scanning the sky and the ground and the river. Right on time the procession of crabs emerged from the water, led by the crustacean whom Grimes was now referring to as The Grand Old Duke Of York.

"Why do you call it that?" asked Sanchez curiously. (He and the girl had stopped work to make way from the procession.)

Su Lin laughed. She recited, in a sing-song voice,

"The Grand Old Duke Of York
He had ten thousand men,
He marched them up to the top of the hill
And he marched them down again . . ."

Meanwhile Grimes had opened fire on the stragglers. This time he got two of them. Work on the balloon envelope was suspended while these were carried into the ship and stowed in the galley for future reference.

Eventually, leaving Sanchez to work by himself, Su Lin went to prepare the midday meal, calling the two men when it was ready. She had boiled one of the crabs, serving it with a sort of sweet-and-sour sauce. It was delicious. The only fly in the ointment was that with her method of cookery she had seriously depleted the fresh water supply. So more had to be brought up from the river, using the same technique as on the previous day.

Nonetheless the work progressed steadily. A wrinkled, empty sausage skin was taking shape. (Grimes found it hard to believe that it, when fully inflated, would be spherical—but each segment of the envelope had been cut according to the formulae presented by the computer function of his wrist companion.) The supply of adhesive was holding out better than he had expected. When sunset came upon them the job was almost finished. All that remained was to gum into place two more panels and to fit a valve cannibalized from one of *Fat Susie's* gas cells.

Sanchez wanted to go on working under artificial light. Grimes would not permit this. It would be far too easy, he said, for something to swoop down upon them from the gathering darkness overhead, unseen until it was too late to take defensive measures. Su Lin was in complete agreement with him. So the empty, almost-finished baloon was rolled up and placed just outside the doorway cut in the airship's metal skin. It was too bulky for them to lift it inside. It had been bad enough having to lug it from its original position.

The sun was well down when they were finished and dusk was fast deepening into night. The lights were switched on. From inside the wreck they watched the shockers, attracted by the harsh illumination, making their slow and undulant way up the slope. Did the things have a memory? Grimes wondered. Did they recall that they had fed well the previous night? But he just somehow could not accept the idea of a sentient plant.

Before long the castaways were partaking of their evening meal. Su Lin had found time during the day to test the flesh of the huge worm that Grimes had killed earlier. It was non-poisonous but, even with the exotic sauce that she had concocted, not very palatable. Presumably it was nutritious and a strictly rationed one glass of red wine apiece took the curse off it.

As before, they kept watches. But this time, by arrangement, Grimes called the others earlier. They wanted to make an early start on the balloon construction. After a very sketchy breakfast they went outside, emerging from the ship a few minutes before sunrise.

Sanchez was first out and yelled loudly in horror and anger.

"What's wrong?" demanded Grimes.

The pilot pointed.

On top of the rolled up envelope were two of the shockers. Obviously they had eaten only very recently; their bodies bulged in the center like that of a boa constrictor immediately after a very heavy meal. And what juices would have been oozing from them, what corrosive digestive fluids and excretory matter?

Su Lin hurried back inside for the work gloves. The three of them put these on and, with rather more haste than caution, removed the carnivorous plants from the top of the roll of balloon fabric, throwing them to the ground. They were all expecting to find a ragged hole eaten through the material—but it seemed to be undamaged. They felt the surface of the tough plastic with their fingers, prodded it and pinched it. The real test, Grimes knew, would not be until the balloon was inflated. And if all was well insofar as gas-tightness was concerned there was a way in which the aerostat could be furnished with protection from aerial attack during its flight.

But he would not, he decided, say anything to the others until the process of inflation was initiated. A lot would depend on how much of the fast-setting, stick-anything-to-anything adhesive was left.

There was an assault by the fliers while the last panel was being glued into place. Grimes beat this off—but when the last attacker had been disabled (those bulging eyes were very vulnerable) he noticed that the lance of flame from the lighter was neither as bright nor as long as it had been.

He said as much to Su Lin.

She replied, "I warned you that the charge wouldn't last forever. When it's exhausted all we shall have is that almost useless laser and the knives." She added, "This balloon of yours had better work, Commodore."

Then the envelope was finished and the equatorial band, made from strips of gas cell fabric, carefully positioned, held in place by sparing dabs, little more than specks, of the adhesive. Above it was a criss-crossing of webbing. Other strips of material would depend from the band when the balloon was ready for flight. These were attached to one of the light, wickerwork chairs from the wardroom. The aeronaut would travel in something approaching comfort.

The two ends of the filling pipe were connected to their respective valves.

"All systems Go!" said Sanchez, squatting by the gas cylinder.

"Not yet," said Grimes.

"But we have to fill this thing, sir," said the pilot.

"All in good time. But, first of all, *Little Susie* must be fitted with her defensive armament."

"*Little Susie?*" asked Sanchez.

"She has to have a name, hasn't she?"

"Defensive armament?" asked Su Lin.

"Yes. Shockers. We've found out that they can't harm the fabric. We've seen a flier killed by one of them."

"But with their bright coloring they'll attract the fliers, sir," the pilot said.

"The fliers, Captain Sanchez, are going to be attracted to anybody or anything invading their airspace. I don't fancy trying to fight them off with a galley knife. Come to that—even if I had a decent pistol I couldn't deal with anything up on top of the envelope. Not without shooting holes through my own means of support."

"Get your gloves on again, Raoul," said the girl. "We'll do as the man says and collect a few shockers." She asked Grimes, "Will the adhesive hold them in place?"

"I don't know," he said. "There's only one way to find out. If the glue won't work we'll just have to lash them on to the envelope somehow."

Chapter 36

The inflation of *Little Susie* was still further delayed.

Grimes didn't like the way that the fliers were hovering not overly far overhead, circling watchfully, gliding and soaring against the rising wind, maintaining their position relative to the island. It seemed to him that the airborne predators were far too interested in what was going on.

He said, "It will take three of us to handle this operation. It should be more—but three bodies is all we have. Somebody will have to stand by the valve on the helium cylinder, ready to shut off immediately. The other two of us will be kept busy handling the lines. Nobody will be able to keep a proper lookout."

"We'll just have to carry on and take a chance, Commodore," said Sanchez.

Grimes looked at the young man severely.

"As a spaceman, Raoul, you should know that chances aren't taken, except when the circumstances are such that there's absolutely no option."

"As now, sir."

"No. I admit that we have not had time to explore this island thoroughly—but you must have noticed, as I did, that at the northern end there is quite a miniature jungle of low bushes. In spite of their proximity to the water they are *dry* looking bushes. But not *too* dry. . . ."

Get on with it! said the young man's expression although he remained silent.

"All animals," went on Grimes pedantically, "fear fire. That holds good on every world that I have visited. I am sure that this one is no exception. My proposal is this—that we start a fire among those bushes, hopefully not too fast-burning but one with plenty of smoke. The wind will blow the smoke right over us. As we work we shall require goggles and handkerchiefs, well wetted, to tie over our noses and mouths. The fliers—unless they are related to the legendary phoenix—will not be at all inclined to dive into the heart of an apparent conflagration. . . ."

"Not so apparent, Commodore," said Sanchez. "But it's a good idea. As long as *we* don't get barbecued."

"We'll try just a small sample of shrubbery first," Grimes told him. "And, at the same time, we'll make sure that this mosslike growth is not flammable. We don't want to have to work with flames licking around our ankles."

"Especially," said Su Lin, "since our getaway craft will carry only one person . . ."

Grimes's plan worked.

The undergrowth at the northern end of the island was flammable but not explosively so; in fact, even with the laser in use, it was not all that easy to start the brush fire. Once Grimes got it going, however, it kept on going. A column of black, almost intoxicatingly aromatic smoke arose, drifting up the slope to cover the activities of the balloon crew, rising into the cloudless sky at an acute angle. Overhead, the fliers departed down wind. Were they really frightened? wondered Grimes, or were they hopeful that land animals fleeing the conflagration could be swooped upon as they ran in panic? The other local predators were doing well for themselves. The shockers, incapable themselves of swift motion, trapped the little, many-legged things that ran over them. In the river the water centipedes were feeding well.

Luckily there were very few sparks. Even though helium, unlike hydrogen, is an inert gas, any large burning fragment could have melted a hole in the envelope fabric. But the slowly swelling balloon was unscathed.

Grimes and Su Lin tended the guy lines, straightened out folds in the slowly distending fabric. They had to work, he said later, like one-armed paperhangers. *Little Susie* slowly took shape, lifting from the ground as she acquired buoyancy. And, although dwarfed by the bulk of the wrecked airship, she was not so little. She was not beautiful either. Despite the careful calculations and the painstaking implementation of these during the cutting and gluing of the segments she was a sadly lopsided bitch. But she was, thought (and hoped!) Grimes, airworthy. She strained at her mooring lines, anchored to the ground by grapnels from *Fat Susie's* stores. She was eager to be off.

"Shut off and disconnect," ordered Grimes, his voice muffled by the wet handkerchief covering his mouth. "After all this trouble we don't want to burst her. And now, Su Lin, if you'll be so good as to pack me a tucker box I'll be off. Expect me back when you see me. I'll be as quick as I can mustering help."

"But you're not going, Commodore," said Sanchez.

"I'm not going?" (All the time Grimes had assumed that he would be piloting the balloon.) "*I'm* not going? Damn it all, it's my job."

"It is not, Governor Grimes," Su Lin told him. "Raoul and I have talked this over. *You* are the Governor. You are the best hope we have, such as it is, of cleaning up the mess on this planet. You're too precious to risk."

"Me, *precious!*" Grimes exploded. "Come off it, girl!" He turned to Sanchez. "*You* know, Raoul, that I'm a quite fair balloonist. Didn't I teach you quite a bit about the art of free ballooning?"

"Yes, Commodore, and I learned from you. And I am, after all, a qualified airshipman."

"Even so . . ."

"There's another point," said the girl. "We don't know, we have no way of knowing, where the balloon is going to come down. With a little bit of luck it might be somewhere that's just lousy with OAP members and supporters. On the other hand, it might be somewhere crawling with police, police informers and staunch supporters of Bardon and O'Higgins. Even if the descent is made unobserved, by night, the balloon pilot will still have to feel his way around cautiously, to find people whom he can trust. What chance would you have of doing that, Commodore? For a start, you're an obvious outworlder with an Orstrylian accent that you could cut with a knife. Raoul's a native. He knows people. He knows his way around . . ."

It made sense, Grimes had to admit.

But he didn't like it.

He and Sanchez stood in the billowing, eddying smoke through which the afternoon sun gleamed fitfully. They looked up at the misshapen *Little Susie*, bobbing fretfully at her moorings.

"A poor thing, but mine own," murmured Grimes. "Look after her, Raoul."

"I hope she looks after me," said the pilot.

"You know," went on Grimes, "this is the first time in my life that I've actually designed a ship. I really should be risking my own neck on her maiden flight, not yours . . ."

"You and Su Lin," consoled Sanchez, "will be running plenty of risks staying here."

"Mphm. Why remind me?"

"Sorry, Commodore. What will you do if I'm not back with help within, say, ten days?"

"Then we make a raft or a canoe and try to make our escape down river. In fact, I think we'll make a start on the project tomorrow."

"And that will be a ship, designed and built by yourself, that you will have the pleasure of commanding. But I hope, sir, that it never comes to that." The pilot laughed. "You seem to have a *thing* about the name Susan. Your spaceship, the one in which you went privateering, is *Sister Sue*. The airship is *Fat Susie*. The balloon—*Little Susie*. What will you call the canoe or raft?"

"*Wet Sue*," said Grimes after a moment's thought.

"That sounds Chinese. It should please Su Lin . . ."

"Were you talking about me?" asked the girl, coming out of the ship with a plastic bag of foodstuffs and a flagon of water.

"Not exactly," said Grimes.

"Oh. Well, here're your provisions for the voyage, Raoul. As long as this wind holds they should last you as far as the nearest cantina."

If you get there, thought Grimes.

"*Bon voyage*, Raoul," said Su Lin. She put the food and drink into the chair suspended below the balloon (the added weight didn't seem to worry it) and then threw her arms about the pilot and kissed him soundly. Grimes felt a stab of jealousy. "*Bon voyage*, and look after yourself."

Grimes made a show of checking everything before lift off.

"Food . . . Water . . . Ballast . . . Now all we need is the crew. . . ."

"All present and correct, sir!" reported Sanchez briskly, saluting.

"Good. You know the drill, Raoul. That bag of assorted stones is your ballast. Don't throw it all away in one grand gesture. You'll probably have to jettison some weight after sunset when the helium cools and loses buoyancy. But don't be a spendthrift. Once weight has been dumped you'll not be able to get it back. Conversely, gas valved is lost forever . . ."

"Understood, Commodore."

"Then, good luck, Raoul." He extended his hand. Sanchez took it. "Good luck. You'll need it."

"We all need it, sir."

Sanchez hung the flagon of water from one arm of the chair, the bag of food—bread, cold meats and fruit—from the other. He took his seat, buckled on and adjusted the safety belt.

"Ready?" asked Grimes.

"Ready."

"Trip for'ard grapnel."

Sanchez yanked sharply on one of the three mooring lines. The grapnel flukes swiveled, came free of the soil.

"Trip port and starboard grapnels!"

This time it was Grimes and Su Lin who jerked upwards on the lines. The grapnels lost their grip. The balloon lifted. Su Lin did not jump back and clear smartly enough and a fluke fouled her clothing, catching in the loosely buttoned front of her tunic. She was lifted from the ground. Grimes caught her dangling legs, held her. Cloth ripped. *Little Susie* continued her ascent, taking with her Su Lin's upper garment.

Grimes actually ignored the half-naked girl whom he was holding tightly in his arms, stared up and after the rising balloon. She was rising steadily, carried along in the stream of smoke that was still coming from the brush fire. The fliers, well down wind, were staying clear of the reek of the burning. But would they continue to do so?

The diminishing balloon was drifting into clear air.

Su Lin disengaged herself from Grimes's arms—he was

hardly aware that she had done so—and was absent from his immediate presence very briefly. Then she was pressing something into his hands. It was a pair of binoculars that she had brought from the ship.

Grimes thanked her briefly, then put the powerful glasses to his eyes. The hemisphere of the balloon that he could see was holding its shape. There were (as yet, anyhow) no leaks, no ripped seams. Sanchez was sitting stolidly in his chair. But, Grimes saw as he adjusted the binoculars to obtain a wider field at the expense of magnification, the fliers, the circling, soaring and swooping carnivores, were closing in. The only weapon that Sanchez had with him was a long knife—and that was supposed to be used in lieu of a ripcord rather than to ward off attack. Too, his view obscured by the bulging gasbag, the pilot quite possibly was not even aware of his danger.

And what use would the shockers be as defensive weaponry? Grimes could see them plainly enough, gaudy patches on the silvery grey envelope. He had applauded his own cleverness in having them attached to *Little Susie's* skin but now was having his doubts. Contact with them might well be lethal but their bodies would never be tough enough to stop a direct, stabbing assault by one of those long, murderous beaks.

So far there was no direct assault.

The fliers were making rings around the balloon with contemptuous ease, flying in ever diminishing circles. (Surely Sanchez must have seen them by now—but what could he do about them? Did Anarchists pray to Bakunin?) Closer they were coming to the helpless aerostat, closer and closer. And then a leathery wing brushed *Little Susie's* taut skin—no, not her skin but the garishly colored plant attached to it.

Grimes watched the airborne predator falter in its flight and then fall, its great wings still outspread but unmoving. Dead or merely stunned, it was parachuting down. It did not reach the ground. The others were upon it, tearing it to shreds as it dropped. Grimes was reminded of maddened sharks feasting upon the injured but not yet dead body of a member of their own species.

Little Susie drifted on, steadily diminishing in the field of

Grimes's binoculars. Smoke was coming from her. *Smoke?* Yes. Grimes could just see that there was something dangling below the pilot's chair, a bundle from which the thick fumes were issuing. Clothing? Possibly. Perhaps Sanchez' jacket, probably Su Lin's shirt.

The pilot's ingenuity was to be commended, but . . . Weight was being sacrificed. As a result, gas might have to be valved. And then, with sunset (not far off), ballast would have to be dumped.

Was Sanchez sufficiently proficient a balloonist to juggle his buoyancy and ballast and still stay aloft for long enough to complete his voyage?

Grimes, he admonished himself, *don't be a back seat driver*.

Then *Little Susie* was no more than a speck in the sky, and then she was gone. She had not fallen, Grimes told himself. She was still aloft, still flying steadily south. She was just out of sight, that was all.

"This wind is chilly," said Su Lin.

He turned to look at her. She had her arms crossed over her naked breasts. She was shivering. Her creamy skin was speckled with smuts, some of them large, from the dying fire upwind. Her handkerchief mask and her goggles were still in place.

The effect was oddly but strongly erotic.

"There is nothing more that we can do today," she said. "I am going inside. Are you coming?"

Why not? Grimes asked himself. *Why not?*

He followed her into the ship.

Chapter 37

She did not make her way to her own cabin but into that occupied by Grimes. She sat down on the bunk, stripped off her goggles and the improvised mask, dropped them carelessly to the deck. This was out of character; she was usually fanatically tidy. She . . . slumped. But her breasts were proudly firm, the prominent nipples erect.

She said, "Well, Grimes, this is it. The girl from PAT and the Survey Service's prize trouble shooter alone at last. And for how long? Until Raoul returns at the head of the United States Cavalry to rescue us from this howling wilderness. *If* he does return, that is . . ."

"He'll be back," said Grimes with a conviction that was not altogether assumed.

"But when, Grimes, *when*? And how do we pass the time until we're rescued?"

"We have to keep ourselves supplied with food . . ."

"You would say that."

"We can't live on fresh air and sunshine. And then we have to make a start on building some sort of raft or canoe to get us out of here, down river, if Raoul doesn't come back."

"As far as I'm concerned," she told him, "mucking about in boats has never been one of my favorite pastimes. Especially in homemade boats on rivers *crawling* with large, vicious carnivores . . . Did it escape your notice that this stream runs through Bloodsuckers Canyon on its way to the sea?"

As she spoke she was easing her heavy boots off her feet—her slim, graceful feet with their crimson-lacquered toenails.

"We have to do something to pass the time," said Grimes.

"For a Governor, for a pirate Commodore, for a Captain in

the Survey Service Reserve you're remarkably dim. Or are you putting me on?"

"The thought of that had flickered across my tiny mind," said Grimes.

She laughed. "So the man is capable of double entendres. There's hope for him yet. . . ."

Slowly Grimes was removing his sweaty shirt. It was not quite at the stage when it could be stood in the corner but it was not far from it. And, on the bunk, the girl was sliding her trousers down her long, shapely legs. Above the waist her body was besmirched with smoke and smuts; below her navel her skin gleamed with a creamy translucence. The lush blackness of her pubic hair was in vivid contrast to the rest of her and was the focus of Grimes's mounting desire.

But, even though now naked himself, he hesitated before joining her on the not-too-narrow couch.

"Are you still . . . bugged?" he asked. "Or should I say anti-bugged?"

"I've room for only one thing at a time," she told him. "And, right now, that one thing is *you*."

It was good, very good, but Grimes could not shake off a feeling of guilt. Here was he—and here was Su Lin—reveling in the release of tensions, the all-over skin to skin contact, the intimate moist warmth, the murmured endearments and finally—from the girl—the screamed obscenities. (This rather surprised him; he had expected that one of her race would be a *quiet* lover.) He could not help thinking of Raoul Sanchez, dangling from that crudely cobbled gasbag in the perilous sky, with no one to comfort him through the coming night.

Tenderly and skillfully Su Lin aroused him again.

This time he thought only fleetingly of the young pilot. After all, he was *there* (wherever *there* was) and Grimes was here. Worrying about Sanchez would not make his voyage any safer.

And then, looking up, they saw through the port that darkness had fallen. They did not bother to dress at once. More important was to switch on the outside lights and then to make sure that there were enough shockers, attracted by the illumination, to form a protective cordon about the ship. (To judge from their numbers few, if any of the motile plants had been destroyed by the brush fire, which now seemed to be completely out.) Satisfied that they were about as safe as ever they would be they heated water, refraining from extravagance, and shared a sponge-down. Attired in clean clothing they had a not-too-bad dinner of what Grimes described as tarted-up bits and pieces, washed down with a quite decent local variety of claret. They drew up a watch-and-watch roster.

Grimes—who should have been drowsy but was not, who was feeling exceptionally fit and alert—took the first tour of duty while Su Lin slept in his bed.

Chapter 38

The night passed.

Grimes, who (thanks to his father's influence) was already something of a maritime historian, began to feel considerable sympathy for those long-ago Terran seamen to whom watch and watch had been routine. He recalled having read somewhere that Bligh—the much and unjustly maligned Bligh! —had been, by the standards of his time, an exceptionally humane captain. He had put his crews on three watches, four hours on and eight hours off. And now Grimes, following in Bligh's footsteps for the second time in his career, was having to revert to the bad old ways and, thereby, was missing out on his beauty sleep.

He didn't like it.

Neither did Su Lin.

"Midnight already?" she complained.

"No," he told her. "It's one bell. 2345. You've fifteen minutes before you're on watch."

"At least you've made tea. Thank you." She sipped from the steaming cup and grimaced. "What did you do? If I weren't a lady I'd refer to this as gnat's piss."

"One for each person and one for the pot," he said.

"What! I'll not believe that you used three spoonfuls of tea to make this feeble brew!"

"Who mentioned spoonfuls? One tea leaf for each person, one for the pot. There's precious little dry tea left in the cannister."

"I think I'll be able to find another packet or two. But you're right. We shall have to be economical. . . ."

Grimes would have liked to have stayed with her, to have watched her as she slid her elegant nudity from under the bed coverings. But he feared that if he did so there would be no middle watch kept. Regretfully he went back out into the alleyway. Before long, dressed in shirt, slacks and calf-length boots, she joined him there.

"All quiet," he told her. "All lights burning brightly. The shockers have been capturing occasional nocturnal beasties but I didn't see what they were. If you're happy, I'll get my head down."

"I have been happier," she told him. "On the other hand—I've been unhappier. . . ."

She kissed him briefly, then broke away before things could develop. He went into his cabin, stripped rapidly and slid between the sheets that were still warm from her body.

It seemed that only seconds had passed when she called him at 0345.

The pot of tea she brought was better—but only a little better—than the one that he had made. There was only one packet of tea remaining in the stores and they would have to make it last.

They shared breakfast—fried rice with the protein component being what was left of the worm. They knew that they must soon make a serious attempt at living entirely off the country but were inhibited from foraging by the activities of the fliers which, almost immediately after dawn, maintained a patrol over the island. And they were now almost weaponless. The charge of Su Lin's lighter was so depleted that it was now useful only for the ignition of the tobacco in Grimes's pipe. (And how long could he make his tobacco last?) The laser tool was effective only at very short range. Knives would not be of much use against something that could dive, without warning, from the sky with at least two meters of sharp, horny beak extended before it.

Water was not, yet, an immediate problem. There were still bottles of various mineral waters in the stores—but once these were gone they would have to go down to the river again. While there had been three of them, one could watch the sky, another keep an eye on the stream and the third one fill the buckets.

"Sometimes," said Su Lin, "I wish I were a mutant. One with eyes at the back of my head."

They spent the day mainly inside the wreck. Grimes, once again using the backs of the charts on which to make calculations and draw plans, tried to work out ways and means of using what wreckage was available to make some sort of boat or raft. A coracle would have been easy—had there been any of the adhesive left. But this had all been used in the manufacture of *Little Susie*. The sheet metal of the skin was very thin and could be bent into shape by hand. The laser pistol was actually a welding tool. Yet a canoe made this way would be almost as flimsy as a coracle and would offer hardly more protection against the aquatic predators.

At sunset Grimes had a sudden rush of brains to the head. Using the laser he killed—at least, he hoped that had killed it—one of the shockers when the creatures, attracted by the lights, took up their stations about the ship. Handling it with heavily gloved hands, careful not to let the still twitching mass touch any other portions of their bodies, they got the thing into the galley, put it onto one of the work surfaces. It overlapped considerably, the edges of it hung down almost to the deck.

Su Lin carved off a slice, then cut from this a very small portion. She chewed thoughtfully. When she spoke, Grimes saw that her teeth were stained green.

She said, "There's moisture here. And possibly—hopefully—some food value. Of course, there must be. The thing eats meat itself. . . ."

After an hour had elapsed she was suffering no ill effects. She and Grimes dined on shocker salad, washed down with shocker juice. (The thing's "battery" yielded a quite refreshing, only slightly acid fluid.) They were well-fed enough but they still felt hungry. Too, probably their diet, although rich in vitamins, would be deficient in many other essentials.

There was another night of watch and watch.

Just before sunrise, before the fliers resumed their diurnal patrol, Grimes was lucky enough to kill a shocker just after it had killed a thing that, he said later, looked like a cross between a spider and an Airedale terrier. He was able, at some risk, to get the animal's body into the wreck before any of the other carnivorous plants could reach it.

This provided them with meat for the day's meals.

The flesh was tough but Su Lin found that marinating it in juice squeezed from a dead shocker tenderized it. The meat was almost flavorless—but it was meat.

It would be possible for Grimes and Su Lin to hold on until Raoul Sanchez returned with help.

If he returned. . . .

If not they would either have to live out their lives as castaways or risk their lives on a hazardous voyage down-river in some cranky, homemade canoe.

Chapter 39

"Don't . . . stop . . ." she murmured.

But Grimes's body, clasped to hers by her strong arms and thighs, had become motionless. He tried to raise his head from where it had been beside hers on the pillow.

He demanded, "Do . . . you . . . hear . . . it?"

"Hear what? I can hear your heart thumping away like a runaway steam engine . . ."

"Not . . . my heart. Or yours . . . Listen!"

She heard it then. It was very faint, coming from far away. It was the irritable mutter of an inertial drive unit. A small one, thought Grimes, such as are fitted to ships' boats and pinnaces. And there had been a pinnace in one of the hangars at the Residence.

The mutter was now more of an interrupted snarl.

The thing was getting closer.

So Raoul had made it after all.

Grimes tried to disengage himself.

She asked, rather tartly, "Aren't you going to finish what you started?"

He said, "My name is Grimes, not Sir Francis Drake."

She said, "I wasn't aware that we were playing bowls."

They laughed together.

And then doubt assailed Grimes. What if this approaching pinnace or whatever were not piloted by Raoul Sanchez? What if this were Bardon or some of his minions coming to make sure that the troublesome Governor was well and truly dead?

Then this might be the last time.

She said, "I thought you were in a hurry to rush out to repel boarders."

He said, "A man can change his mind, can't he?"

He completed the act—but it was not as good as it should have been. All the time he was aware of that rapidly approaching pinnace. He rolled off her, hastily pulled on a pair of trousers, picked up the almost-useless laser pistol from the table on which he had left it, went out to the catwalk and then made his way to the hole that had been cut in the metal envelope. He was just in time to see the ship's boat coming in to land.

A ship's boat?

And what was the name on the bows?

No, not a name. Just letters and a number.

AA #1.

The boat touched ground, crushing at least half a dozen of the shockers. A scent like that of new-mown grass filled the air. The cacaphony of the inertial drive unit abruptly ceased. Slowly the outer airlock door opened. From it stepped a woman, not young but far from old, with short, iron-gray hair and matching eyes, dressed in a uniform that was, essentially, a short-skirted business suit, well-tailored from some gray fabric that looked (and probably was) very expensive, with touches of gold braid at the collar and on the sleeves.

She looked at Grimes and at the scantily clad girl standing behind him.

She asked pleasantly, "Have I interrupted something, Commodore?"

And then she, herself, was interrupted as four of the fliers, briefly scared off by the racket of the boat's inertial drive unit but now, with that engine shut down and silent, returning in search of prey, swooped. She would have been skewered had not Raoul Sanchez, jumping out of the airlock, knocked her to one side and then delivered a dazzling exhibition of laser play.

Before the remainder of the circling predators could launch a fresh attack he yanked the woman to her feet, hustled her through the opening cut in *Fat Susie's* skin and then literally fell in after her.

"Who is your friend, Raoul?" asked Su Lin.

The pilot scrambled to his feet, then said courteously, "Allow me to introduce Captain Agatha Prinn, of *Agatha's Ark*. Captain Prinn already knows Commodore Grimes, of course."

"Of course," she agreed. "We're old flotilla mates. And now the Commodore is a Governor and I'm still a star tramp skipper. But didn't somebody say once, 'Uneasy lies the head that wears a crown'?"

"You're more of an absolute monarch aboard your ship, Agatha," Grimes told her, "than I am on this planet. But tell me, do you still have that young El Doradan officer, the Count von Stolzberg, with you?"

"You mean Ferdinand, your son. . . ."

"How did you know . . .?"

"Everybody knew. But no, he's no longer with me. A pity. He was a good spaceman. But after the Inquiry into the privateering racket we were told that any El Doradan officers must be repatriated. . . ."

"Excuse me, sir and madam," put in Sanchez, "I really think that this old pirates' reunion can be deferred for a while. What's of pressing urgency is what's happening now on Liberia, not what happened when you were scouring the interstellar spacelanes under the Jolly Roger!"

Grimes glared at the young man, then laughed.

"All right, Raoul. Come into the wardroom and tell us

your story. And is there any beer left, Su Lin? Good. This calls for a celebration. Raoul back in one piece, and Agatha with him . . ."

"It's thanks only to Captain Prinn that I am back," said Sanchez.

The flight of *Little Susie*, said Sanchez, had not been too bad an experience. The worst of it had been the way in which he had almost been kippered, sitting in his chair with the smoldering rags—Su Lin's shirt and then his own clothing—directly beneath him. But the smoke had scared off the fliers.

During the first night he had been obliged to drop most of his ballast. The next day, to prevent the balloon from rising to a dangerous altitude, it had been necessary to valve helium. But the wind had been stronger than anticipated and he had made good time. By late afternoon he was out of the Unclaimed Territory. He didn't know quite where he was but, sighting a village on the horizon, decided to make his descent before he was over the settlement. He came down in a wheatfield, one some weeks away from its future harvesting. There was nobody to see his landing.

He extricated himself, with some difficulty, from the smothering folds of the deflating gasbag. He was, he realized, armed only with a galley knife and practically naked; he had stripped himself to his underpants to keep his deterrent fire going. As long as he was airborne he had not felt the cold as he had been traveling at the same speed as the wind. Now that breeze on his bare skin was very chilly.

He made his way toward the lights of the village, finding the going difficult in the fast-gathering darkness. At last he stumbled onto a road. Then he made better progress.

There was nobody abroad. He walked past the slave barracks—the *refugee* barracks, he corrected himself—and heard the sound of voices and of Oriental music and smelled the enticing aromas of exotic cookery. Now he was hungry as well as cold.

He kept on until he was in the village itself. There was the inn. He saw the sign—THE TORCH OF LIBERTY. It was then that he thought that some of Grimes's famous luck had rubbed off on himself. The parents of Miguel, one of his crew aboard the Met. Service tender, were innkeepers. The name of their cantina was The Torch of Liberty. Like their son, they were members of the OAP, the Original Anarchist Party. Raoul knew that there must be many Torches Of Liberty throughout Liberia—but somehow he was sure that this was the right one.

He went round to the back door.

He knocked cautiously.

He went on knocking.

At last the door opened and Miguel was standing there, demanding, "Who is it? What do you want?"

"I still can't get over the fantastic coincidence," said Raoul.

"No fiction writer," Grimes told him, "would dare to use the coincidences that are always happening in real life. But go on."

Miguel was on leave.

Miguel saw to it that Sanchez was fed and clothed and plied with restorative drinks. He listened to the pilot's story. He was of the opinion that the planetary authorities should be ignored and that Grimes should be rescued from the island as secretly as possible. The best way of achieving this, he said, would be to "borrow" one of the Met. Service tenders from Port Libertad and fly directly to the site of the wreck.

Meanwhile, Sanchez learned, already the news had been put about that Governor Grimes and his small entourage had perished in an airship crash. Searches had been mounted—but not one of them had covered the Unclaimed Territory. The Met. Satellites were making continual photographic surveys of Liberia—but the processing of the films was being carried out by Bardon's people. Almost certainly the fire on the island had been seen from orbit but it was being ignored.

Miguel and Raoul flew to Port Libertad in Miguel's 'copter. Both of them in Met. Service uniform, they attempted to take over one of the tenders. But the spaceport guards—Bardon's people—were suspicious. One of them had recognized Sanchez. There had been shooting, a chase. The two men had split up. Perhaps Miguel had escaped; Sanchez hoped that he had. Raoul, by this time little more than a mindless, hunted animal, had run up the ramp into the after airlock of one of the deep space ships in port. . . .

Agatha Prinn took up the tale.

"I was just strolling ashore," she said, "I'd just gotten as far as the airlock, in fact, when I heard shooting. I wondered what the hell was going on. And then this young man came bolting up the ramp, brushing past me. I was curious, naturally. And, having been to this world before, I was inclined to think that anybody in trouble with the authorities couldn't be all that bad. So I told my second mate—he was shipkeeping officer—to keep an airlock watch and to swear to any police or guards or whatever that no strangers had come aboard while, in my own quarters, I heard young Raoul's story.

"And what a story it was!

"As you know, Commodore, we tramp masters neither know nor care who heads the governments of the various worlds that we visit. We deal only with Customs, Immigration and Port Health officials. We never meet Prime Ministers or Presidents or Governors. At first I couldn't believe that *you* were the Governor Grimes of Liberia. But it all tied in. Jughandle ears, ex-Survey Service officer, ex-owner-master, ex-commodore of privateers.

"I've already told you that I've been to this world before, more than once. On any planet, this one included, I like to take one of my boats for a sightseeing cruise around. I log it as Boat Drill, of course. So the Port Authorities didn't feel it worth their while to make close inquiries when, this morning, I told them that I was about to go on my usual sightseeing tour." She laughed. "As a matter of fact one puppy, laughing himself sick over his alleged humor, did ask me to keep my eyes skinned for Governor Grimes and *Fat Susie*."

"And now you've found him," said Grimes.

"And now I take you and your people back to *Agatha's Ark*. I've plenty of spare accommodation. I'll keep you out of sight until we lift—and then you can use my Carlotti equipment to bleat to your bosses back on Earth about what's been happening."

"Why can't I bleat now?" asked Grimes.

"Because it's not legal for any ship to use deep space radio while in port. You should know that. You're Governor, aren't you?"

"Mphm. Well, if you don't mind, Agatha, I'd like you to take us back to the Residence. I'm still Governor—and I want to play hell with a big stick as long as I'm in office. There's Major Flattery for a start. I shall demand that he be arrested and put on trial.There's the dreamweed trade. There's . . . Oh, I could go on and on . . ."

"You can go on and on, Commodore, once you're up and clear from Liberia."

"But that wouldn't be the same, Agatha. Look at what happened in New South Wales. Governor Bligh was deposed—and then what could he do? He got no support from his Lieutenant Governor in Tasmania. He returned to England and was, to all intents and purposes, swept under the mat. Oh, Major Johnston was, eventually, brought to trial but received little more than a rap over the knuckles—and that after leading an armed mutiny!

"I have to stay here.

"I have to exert my authority. I have to show Estrelita and her boyfriend Bardon who's boss."

"As you please, Commodore," said Agatha Prinn. "I wish that I could be of some real help—but *Agatha's Ark* is no longer a privateer. The only arms aboard her are a few privately owned laser and projectile pistols."

"Just take me back to the Residence," said Grimes, "and I'll play it by ear from then on."

Chapter 40

They managed to scamper the short distance between the wreck and the ship's boat without being attacked by anything. Once inside the small craft they made a careful search and were relieved to find that no hostile life form had taken up residence while the boat had been left unattended. Then, with

Agatha Prinn at the controls, they lifted from the island and set course for the Residence.

Captain Prinn wanted to deliver Grimes at his own front door but he talked her out of it. It would be better, he said, if he and the others were dropped within easy walk of the gubernatorial palace; that way they could make entry without their being expected by Jaconelli and Smith. Too, Agatha would not be liable to reprisal by the authorities if there were nothing to associate her with the Governor.

"But they must know," she protested. "They must know that I was one of your captains on the privateering expedition."

"They *should* know," he told her, "but they almost certainly don't. If they had associated you with me they would not have allowed you to go flapping off by yourself all over Liberia. Thanks to my father I'm something of a student of history—and I know that very often Military Intelligence has been a contradiction in terms."

They timed their arrival for the beginning of evening twilight. Raoul took the controls and dropped the boat to a field just off the road running up the hill to the Residence. They disembarked—Sanchez first, then Su Lin, finally Grimes. All of them were armed with weapons supplied by Captain Prinn—laser pistols for the pilot and the girl, a Minetti automatic for Grimes. Only Sanchez was wearing anything approximating a disguise, a uniform (which fitted quite well) borrowed from one of *Agatha's Ark's* junior officers.

"Let me know if I can do anything more, Commodore," said the tramp captain.

"You've done plenty already, Agatha. But if things go too badly wrong you can put in a full report, to Rear Admiral Damien, once you get clear of this world."

"I'll do that."

Surprisingly she took him in her arms and kissed him. He found himself wishing that he could carry on from there but there was no time. Besides, Su Lin was looking in through the open airlock doors, an amused expression on her face.

He broke away.

"Thank you for everything, Agatha."

"It was nothing. And, good luck, John. The very best of luck."

Grimes jumped down to the damp grass.

He stood with the others and watched the boat lift, watched her running lights dim and diminish as she continued her interrupted voyage to the spaceport.

They walked up the road.

They met nobody.

They did not use the front entrance to the Residence but went round to a back door, to what Grimes thought of as the tradesmen's entrance. Surprisingly, there they were met. Wong Lee, the old butler, seemed to have been expecting them. He bowed and said, "It is good that you are back, Excellency."

"I'm pleased to be back," said Grimes. "Too right I am."

He followed the old man through the maze of corridors. They came at last to the Governor's quarters. The sitting room was empty but there were voices coming from the adjoining office. One belonged to Smith, the A.D.C., the other to Jaconelli, the secretary. They seemed to be having a party. There was a clinking of glasses and the speech of each man was slurred.

"Flattery's got his step up to half colonel," Smith was complaining, "but there's no hint that I shall get my captaincy."

"But *you* didn't actually *do* anything," said Jaconelli. "Flattery did do something. He got that bastard Grimes out of our hair for keeps. And that poisonous tart Sue-Ellen or whatever her name was . . ."

"What've you got against *her*?"

"She wouldn't play, that's what. Anyhow, they're all out of our hair. Grimes, the uppity tart and that upstart of a ferry skipper . . ."

"No, they're not," said Grimes, stepping into his office with his Minetti out and ready.

That was just the start.

There were the soldiers of the guard to be disarmed and locked up. They were not so easy to deal with as Smith and Jaconelli had been. There was actually gunfire while Sergeant Martello, holed up in Smith's office, got through on the telephone to Colonel Bardon, quite bravely ignoring Grimes's finally successful attempt to shoot out the lock. (Sanchez's prior attempt, using his hand laser, had succeeded only in fusing this into a mass of metal that held the door as firmly as in its original state.)

Martello got up from his seat at the desk to face the intruders. He was a big, paunchy man, almost bald and with little, porcine eyes in his fat face. His hand went to his holstered weapon, then he thought better of it. He raised his hands reluctantly above his head.

"All right," he growled. "You've won—for the time being. But the Colonel will soon fix your wagon . . ."

"That will do, Sergeant!" snapped a voice from the telephone screen. "You have my permission to surrender to the pirate. You will be released very shortly."

Martello moved to one side, away from the scanner.

Grimes looked into Bardon's angry face.

"Colonel Bardon," he said, "you are to place youself under arrest. Before you do so, however, please see to it that Major—or should I say Lieutenant Colonel?—Flattery is clapped in irons."

"It's you who's under arrest, Grimes. Do you want to hear the charges? Whilst under the influence of drugs or alcohol you, in charge of a dirigible airship, deliberately collided with another such vessel owned by the Terran military establishment on Liberia, causing considerable structural damage. Returning to the Residence, you have threatened officers, noncommissioned officers and enlisted men of the Terran Army with firearms and illegally incarcerated them. A man in your employ, one Raoul Sanchez, attempted to steal a shuttlecraft from the Port Libertad spaceyard. A woman in your employ, one Su Lin, murdered a laborer under the protection of Senor Eduardo Lopez.

"A pirate, sir, is obviously no fit person to be appointed as governor of a civilized planet."

Grimes laughed.

"You must have suspected, Bardon, that I just might get out of the mess that your precious Flattery left me in—otherwise you wouldn't have been so ready with all those charges! But I must correct you on two points. One—I was a privateer, not a pirate. Two—I rather doubt that this is a civilized planet."

"Are you giving yourself up, Grimes?"

"Are you putting yourself under arrest, Bardon?"

"Don't argue with him!" There were two faces in the

screen now; the other one was that of the President. "Send your soldiers to take the Residence. *Now*—or as soon as you can get them out of the whorehouses and grogshops!"

"I'll send Flattery to bomb the bloody place!" growled Bardon.

"You will not. The building—and it cost plenty!—is Liberian property. And what about your own men imprisoned there?"

"They wouldn't be much loss," Bardon said.

"I heard that, Colonel, *sir*," put in Sergeant Martello. "Now, let me tell you that I've never liked working for you and your officers. If the Commodore will have me, I'll fight for him!"

Bardon cursed, then the telephone screen went blank.

Grimes stared at the big sergeant, who was still standing with hands upraised, still covered by the weapons held by Su Lin, Sanchez and Wong Lee.

Was the man sincere?

What was his motivation?

Grimes had . . . glimmerings. A lifetime in the Army, a failure to attain commissioned rank, a growing, festering resentment at having to take orders from officers no better soldiers than himself, quite possibly not even as good. Perhaps harsh treatment by Bardon or officers like him, unjust treatment . . .

Perhaps—it was possible although not probable—the uneasy stirrings of a conscience.

"All right, Sergeant," he said, "I'll believe you—with reservations. I'm not a soldier—so you shall be my advisor. But I'll be obliged if you'll hand your pistol—butt first—to Captain Sanchez. No, cancel that. Keep *very* still while Captain Sanchez takes the gun from its holster . . . Good. Now you can drop your hands. . . ."

They watched him, more than half expecting an explosion of hostile energy. But the sergeant just stood there, grinning.

He said, "You'll not believe this, Commodore, but as a boy I used to read space stories, pirate stories especially. I wanted to be a pirate when I grew up. Now, whatever happens, I'll be able to say that I served under one of the famous pirate captains."

Grimes started to explain, for the thousandth time, the

difference between a privateer and a pirate, then decided that he would be merely wasting his breath.

Out of earshot of the sergeant he had a few words with Wong Lee.

"Get word to the spaceport," he said, "to Captain Agatha Prinn of the ship *Agatha's Ark*. I can't use the telephone; Bardon will be monitoring any calls made from here. See that Captain Prinn is told just what's been happening since I got back. Then, as soon as she's off this world, she can make a full report to Earth."

"Very good, Your Excellency."

"How many of your people can use firearms?"

"Most of them, Your Excellency."

"How . . .? But no matter. Round up all the weapons you can and have men on the roof. That parapet is more than merely ornamental."

Chapter 41

Grimes stood with Su Lin on the small, railed platform that was at the highest point of the low-pitched roof. They had binoculars with them, powerful night glasses that converted infrared radiation into visible wavelengths. They swept the terrain on all sides of the residence. Of one thing they could be certain—nothing big was out and moving, although there were small, glowing sparks representing tiny nocturnal animals.

"How is it," asked Grimes, "that so many of the domestic staff—if Wong Lee is to be believed—are expert in the use of weapons?"

She said, "You must have guessed by now that the Underground—or one of the many Undergrounds—has seen to it that the Governor's personal entourage are capable of defending him should the need arise."

"Mphm. But I thought that only full citizens of this world were allowed to own firearms."

"Ever since firearms were invented they've been falling into the wrong hands. Or—in this case—the right hands. Criminals or freedom fighters have always been able to get arms. When you went a-pirating it wasn't in an unarmed ship, was it?"

"For about the four thousandth time," growled Grimes, "I was a privateer, not a pirate."

"Sorry." The laugh following the word indicated that she wasn't.

Grimes broke the short silence.

"Isn't it time," he asked, "that I was put into the picture? After all, should things come entirely unstuck who'll have to carry the can back? Me, that's who."

"Too right," she said, in an imitation of an Australian accent. "But I agree. You have been kept in the dark—by everybody, from Admiral Damien on down. Liberia is on the point of blowing up. Not only is there the OAP but there are the secret organizations of the various refugees. The aim of PAT is that it shall be a *controlled* explosion. We may be People Against Tyranny—but we are also against Anarchy, using the word in its very worst sense, against mob rule and mindless violence. One of our requirements was a Governor who could stand as a figurehead for the rebels and who would recognize whatever sort of government is formed after the revolution.

"We had our doubts about your predecessor. He was a good man, but rather lacking in glamour. But you are a glamorous figure."

"Who? *Me*?"

"Yes. The people will rally behind a famous pirate, a man who was a pirate for the very best of motives. . . ."

"Mphm. Well, Su Lin, where do we go from here? What happens next?"

"Bardon sends a detachment here to arrest you. That will be the signal for rioting to break out in the city, for risings on many of the big estates and plantations. . . ."

"And if the detachment Bardon sends," said Grimes, "is a really powerful one, with hover-tanks and aircraft, we stand a very good chance of winding up very dead."

"Bardon and O'Higgins want you alive, so that you can stand trial for your crimes. And then they'll crucify you. No, not literally. But you'll be crucified, all right. Deported to Earth in disgrace together with a curt note from the President. 'Please do not send us any more criminals as Governors.' But, of course, they will have to arrest you first. . . ."

Sanchez came up to the lookout point. Grimes handed him his night glasses and then, with Su Lin, went down to his quarters. He sent for Sergeant Martello. The big man soon made his appearance, escorted by two machine-pistol-toting chefs. He drew himself to stiff attention.

"Commodore, sir!"

"Sit down, Sergeant. And that'll do the rest of you. Oh, Su Lin, will you organize tea for us? Good. . . ."

"You sent for me, sir?" said Martello.

"Obviously. I want your expert advice. I know, of course, what forces the good colonel has at his disposal *on paper*. What's the situation in actual practice?"

"If any hostile power from outside tried to invade this world, sir, they could take it with an armed space tug and a platoon of Boy Scouts. One of the things that sickened me was the way in which equipment has been allowed to deteriorate. I was in charge of the maintenance of armored vehicles at the barracks—and I made such a nuisance of myself trying to get people to do their jobs properly that I was shifted to the Residence Guard, just to get me out of the way. It'd take all of a week to get the hover-tanks in order for any sort of real action. The wheeled vehicles, the armored cars, are in slightly better nick, but they're only lightly armed."

"Aircraft?" asked Grimes.

"Flattery's ship was damaged after that collision with yours. I don't think that anybody has gotten around to starting repairs yet. There's another dirigible but, the last I heard, all the helium cells were leaking badly. Three ex-Survey Service pinnaces, I suppose you'd call them. Inertial drive jobs. Light armament. Half a dozen little helicopters. . . ."

And I've a pinnace of my own, thought Grimes. *And a near-wreck of a helicopter. And, of course, Raoul's little flitterbug. . . .*

He asked, "If you were Colonel Bardon, Sergeant, what would you do?"

"Bardon," said Martello, "has always liked making arrests in the middle of the night or in the small hours of the morning. The same applies to the civil—if you can call those bastards civil!—police. But they've been arresting people who weren't expecting it. And they haven't had to be rounded up from the nightspots to go on duty.

"Believe me or don't believe me as you please, Commodore, but I think that the attempted arrest will be in the morning—and not too early in the morning, either. The approach, I think, will be made by road. Bardon was involved in a minor crash once and he's scared of flying. He'll not be expecting any armed resistance except that from you, your pilot and, possibly, Miss Su Lin. . . ." He looked admiringly at the girl, who had just come in with a tea tray. "However did you organize all the Residence Chinks, miss, right under our noses? I can see by the way they're handling their guns that they know how to use them."

She smiled coldly. "I suppose that I should thank you for the implied compliment, Sergeant. But in China, many, many years ago, there used to be a saying. Horseshoes are made from inferior iron—and soldiers from inferior men."

Amazingly Martello did not take offense. He laughed. "That certainly applies to Bardon and most of his officers!"

But not to the enlisted men? wondered Grimes, but said nothing.

He sipped his tea. So did the sergeant and Su Lin.

He said, "Since it doesn't seem that anything is going to happen tonight—what's left of it—I'll get my head down. You know where to find me if you want me."

He got from his chair, walked through to his bedroom.

He heard Martello whisper to the girl, "He's a cool customer, the Commodore. We could do with a few like him in the Army. . . ."

Nonetheless he was a long time getting to sleep. He was hoping that Su Lin would join him. But she, he reproached himself, would be doing all the work while he caught up on his rest.

Chapter 42

Grimes should have given orders that the prisoners be thoroughly searched before they were locked in a storeroom. He was awakened, shortly before sunrise, by the unmistakable clatter of an inertial drive unit. His first thought was that Bardon had mounted an attack by air after all, especially as there was also the rattle of automatic fire. Snatching the borrowed Minetti from his bedside table, pausing briefly to throw a light robe about himself, he ran into his sitting room, stared out through the wide window. He could see people on the lawn, could see the muzzle flashes of the guns that they were firing upwards. The noise of the inertial drive diminished. So the pinnace—as he assumed that it was—had been driven away.

He decided that it would be better if he stayed in one place rather than go running around, making inquiries. He collected his pipe and tobacco from the bedroom, went into his office and sat down behind the big desk. He had succeeded in establishing his personal smokescreen when Su Lin and Sanchez came in.

He grinned at them.

"So you repelled boarders," he said.

They did not grin back.

"We failed," said the girl, "to prevent the prisoners from escaping."

"They were only a liability," said Grimes.

"But they escaped in the pinnace," Sanchez told him. "*Our* pinnace. Worse—before they left they made sure that the two helicopters will never fly again."

"Who let them out?" demanded Grimes. "Martello? I was a fool to have trusted him."

"Come in, Sergeant!" called Su Lin, turning to face the open door into the living room.

Martello entered.

"It was my fault, sir," he admitted.

"So you released your cobbers."

"No cobbers of mine, Commodore. But I should have remembered that Levine was a professional thief before he joined the Army. Yes—and after. Burglar Levine they call him. He used to boast that he could pick any lock ever made. . . ."

"And now you tell me." He turned to Su Lin. "Any of our people hurt?"

"None badly. Two sentries knocked out; but they're recovering."

"So it could have been worse."

"But our aircraft, sir! We don't have any aircraft now!"

"And so what, Raoul?" asked Grimes. "What could we do with them if they were still operational?"

"They'd give us a chance to escape from here."

"*All* of us, Raoul? All the Residence staff? Cooks and gardeners and maids and scullions and . . . and . . . I'm surprised at you. What about the tradition that the captain should be the last to leave the sinking ship?"

Sanchez flushed ashamedly.

"It's just that, even now, I can't think of the refugees as being part of the revolution."

"But they are," said Su Lin. "And they've far more to rebel about than you romantic Original Anarchists."

Grimes got to his feet.

"Since I'm up," he said, "I might as well stay up. I'd like breakfast, Su Lin, in half an hour's time. But let me know if there's any sign of an attack."

After the others left his quarters he went through to his bathroom.

Chapter 43

There was a uniform that he had brought with him in his luggage—his own uniform, that of a Far Traveler Couriers captain. If there was any fighting to be done he would prefer to do it properly attired. So he dressed himself in the slate-gray shorts, shirt and long socks, flicked a few specks of dust off his gold-braided shoulderboards. He contrived a belt from a dressing gown sash, thrust the borrowed automatic pistol into it. He walked into his sitting room just as Su Lin entered with a laden tray.

"No morning paper?" he asked severely.

She looked him up and down with amused approval. She said, "Something seems to have gone wrong with the delivery, Commodore."

"I wonder what?"

He sat down to enjoy his meal. (The condemned man ate a hearty breakfast?) Su Lin sat down to talk to him, sipping coffee from her own cup.

"All quiet," she said. "Too quiet. The telephone's dead. On the credit side, there's no sign of any air activity. Back to the debit side—I'd have been expecting that there'd have been rioting in the city by now."

"How would we know if there was any rioting?"

"There would be fires, explosions. All I can think of is that the various rebel factions are waiting to see which way the cat will jump. And there are so many rebel factions. The OAP and all the planetary organizations. The Texans, for example, would be quite happy to see the New Cantonese pulling the hot chestnuts out of the fire from them."

"And everybody would like to use me as a cat's paw."

"We're here with you, Grimes. Raoul, and all the New Cantonese, and even Sergeant Martello."

"I still can't make him out."

"It's simple. He just hates Bardon, is all. He had his rackets, as do all the Terran troops on Liberia. He was poaching on Bardon's preserves. Bardon became the heavy colonel and put a stop to the sergeant's little games. And then, when Bardon, during that telephone conversation, made it plain that he didn't give a damn about the safety of his own people in the Residence, that was it."

"So all his other talk, about playing at pirates and the rest of it, was just so much bullshit."

"Mm. Maybe. Maybe not. . . ."

Sanchez came in.

He, too, was in his own version of uniform—the faded blue denims, the scarlet neckerchief.

"Armored cars, Commodore," he announced. "Approaching from the city."

"ETA?" asked Grimes.

"Thirty minutes from now, sir."

"Good." Grimes broke another crisp roll, buttered it and then thickly spread the exposed surfaces with marmalade. "Then I've time to finish my breakfast in comfort."

"But we could ambush the armored cars, sir. There're low walls along the road as they approach the Residence."

"Captain Sanchez," Grimes told him severely, "*we* cannot afford to break the law, such as it is. *They* must be seen to fire the first shot. Besides," he went on, "our firearms won't make much impression on their armor."

"We could get the officers," said Raoul, "before they button up. And the kitchen staff has been making Molotov cocktails."

"Their intentions may be peaceful," said Grimes. "Mind you, I shall be surprised if they are. But, until we know for certain. . . ." He bit into his roll. He did not, now, feel much like eating but he had to consider his reputation—Gutsy Grimes, the man who would not miss a meal even though the Universe were crumbling about his ears.

"I'll get back on top, sir," said Sanchez at last. "I'll let you know what develops."

"Do that, Raoul," said Grimes through a mouthful of roll and marmalade.

Eventually he got up, patted his lips with his table napkin, filled and lit his pipe. Accompanied by Su Lin he took the elevator up to the roof. They joined Sanchez on the lookout platform. Grimes took the proffered binoculars, looked at the advancing armored column. There were a half-dozen of the drab-painted six-wheeled vehicles. Their hatches were open; in each one stood the begoggled car commander. It was all very pretty and, thought Grimes, remarkably archaic. From a staff mounted on the leading car flew a large, white flag.

So there was to be a parley first.

Oh, well, thought Grimes, *I might as well hear what the man wants to say.*

He went down to the portico, stopping off in his quarters to collect his cap. He glanced at himself briefly in the wardrobe mirror. In his rather shabby uniform, with his cap at a rakish angle, with that scarlet dressing gown sash into which the pistol was thrust, he looked like the pirate that many supposed him to be. Then, outside the main entrance, he was standing there, Su Lin and Sanchez beside him and behind him the Residence staff, all armed, their colorful liveries making them look like a smartly uniformed army.

The leading car came to a halt about twenty meters from the portico. The officer climbed down from the turret. He was a man whom Grimes did not recognize. He was carrying, on a stick, another white flag, a small one.

He came to attention before Grimes and then, it seemed, thought better of it. He fell into what could be described only as an insolent slouch.

"You are John Grimes?" he asked.

"I have that honor," Grimes replied.

"You are under arrest. I have to inform you that any resistance will make things all the worse for you and your people."

"You've come to the wrong shop this time, Major Johnston," said Grimes.

"My name is not Johnston," said the major, obviously baffled by the historical allusion.

"Maybe not. And this isn't Sydney, New South Wales. And now, sir, I'm ordering you off my premises. And take your mechanized tin cans with you."

"Very well, sir. You have been warned."

The officer turned, marched back to his armored car. Grimes and the others retreated inside the Residence. The big, solid doors slammed shut but they could not keep out the sound of the highly amplified voice that was shouting, over and over gain, "Come out! Come quietly! Come out, or I open fire!"

This ceased when a marksman on the roof scored a hit on the sonic projector. Almost immediately there came the rattle of heavy machine gun fire. The doors shuddered but held. Nothing came through them—but it could not be long before they were literally chewed away. The doors held—but windows shattered. "Down!" Martello was bawling in his sergeant's voice. "Down!"

People were dropping to the floor but none of them was a casualty.

Yet.

Grimes went up to the roof, found his way to the parapet that was little more than a low gutter rim. He crouched behind it, beside one of the chefs who was pouring automatic fire down on the cars. He tapped the man on the shoulder. "Hold your fire until it can do some good," he admonished. "Ammunition doesn't grow on trees. . . ." The man grinned at him cheerfully, inserted a fresh clip into his weapon and blazed away again. But if the defenders were the rankest amateurs the attackers were not much better. Had they continued to concentrate their fire on the main entrance they would have been through it in minutes. But they seemed to be playing at Red Indians attacking a wagon train, circling the Residence. And they were not using their laser cannon. That made sense, Grimes supposed. Lasers could start a disastrous fire and Estrelita O'Higgins had made it clear that she did not want the building too badly damaged. Meanwhile, these circling tactics ensured that nobody escaped. Perhaps the intention was to starve the defenders out.

Then Bardon would have a long wait, thought Grimes wryly. The Residence's larders were very well-stocked. There was a deep freeze that could almost have accommodated a herd of mastodons.

It was a situation approaching stalemate—until one of the armored cars broke down. Martello's tale of slovenly maintenance had been a true one. The defenders on the roof concentrated their fire on the stalled vehicle. There was a chance, just a chance, that a lucky bullet might find a chink in the armor. Eventually the major decided that he had better do something about it. Three cars moved into position to shield the disabled one from the fire from the roof while a fourth one moved into position just in front of it. A tow . . . thought Grimes. A tow. . . . That meant that hatches would have to be opened so that somebody could climb out to fix the towing wires. Where were those Molotov cocktails that he had heard about?

And somehow they were there, ready to hand, ten bottles with rag wicks, not yet ignited, filled with some clear fluid. An aroma more intoxicating than unpleasant was making itself known despite the reek of cordite. And Su Lin was there, her golden lighter in her hand. Grimes got recklessly to his feet, holding one of the bottles. "Light it!" he ordered the girl. She obeyed. The flame blowing back from the flaring wick scorched his arm as he threw.

The missile fell well short, bursting spectacularly but harmlessly.

"I should have played cricket when I was a boy," remarked Grimes glumly. He raised his voice. "Are there any cricketers here? Any fast bowlers?"

(If only the Residence staff were Indian and not Chinese . . .)

"Cricket?" Martello's rough voice was contemptuous. "Baseball was my game, Commodore. Still is. An' I'm a pitcher, not a bowler . . . Gimme!"

He snatched the bottle from Grimes's hand, waited until Su Lin had ignited the wick, then threw. Neither range nor direction could have been bettered. He threw again, and again. From the armored cars there was screaming. At least one of the Molotov cocktails must have found an open hatch.

He let fly with two more bottles.

He was a good target standing there, too good a target. A burst of machine-gunfire caught him, threw him back onto the gentle slope of the roof. Crabwise, Grimes scrambled to him but there was nothing he could do. The entire front of the big man's body was . . . shredded. Shredded and pulped. Even his face was gone.

I shall never know what really made him tick, thought Grimes, gulping back his nausea.

Then he heard the explosions.

Crouching, he made his way back to the parapet. Two of

the armored cars were burst open, literally. Their ammunition must have gone up. A third was on its side, its wheels spinning uselessly. A fourth, its rear wheels gone, looked ludicrously like a circus elephant trying to sit down.

The two survivors had turned and were retreating, fast.

The turret hatch of the down-by-the-stern car opened. From it was poked a rifle barrel to which a white rag of some kind had been tied.

"Hold your fire!" ordered Grimes.

Su Lin repeated the command in a language that the New Cantonese could understand.

Slowly a man clambered out through the hatch, slid down to the ground, stood there with hands upraised. He was joined, after a long interval, by two others.

"We surrender!" shouted the first man, a sergeant.

"We don't want you!" called Grimes. "Just get the hell out of here!" Then, "No! Stop! Look after your mates first!"

They managed, at last, to persuade those in the overturned car to open up. Only two men crawled out.

"Where's the other?" shouted Grimes.

"Dead, sir. His neck's broken."

"I want to see him!"

"Why?" whispered Su Lin.

"Haven't you heard of the Trojan Horse?" he countered.

The corpse was dragged out. The man was obviously dead, his head almost twisted off his body. And, thought Grimes, nothing could possibly be living in the two still-smoking wrecks.

The five men shambled down the road.

"You're too soft-hearted, Grimes," said Su Lin. "You should have made them bury their own dead before you let them go."

"I never thought of it," admitted Grimes.

He was conscious of the smell of burnt meat drifting up from the destroyed cars. He thought ruefully that disposing of the mess left over after a space battle is so much easier than disposing of similar mess on a planetary surface.

Chapter 44

The gardeners formed the burial detail and seemed more annoyed at having to mar the beauty of the Residence lawn than by the true, gruesome nature of their work. Martello was laid to rest a little apart from the others. Some day, thought Grimes, the sergeant would have his monument, a statue depicting him in the uniform of a baseball player, not of a soldier, frozen in stone or metal in the act of pitching.

Grimes, as Governor, conducted a brief service, one that he modeled on that used by the Federation Survey Service, whose personnel observed a wide variety of religions or none at all, that was used for enemies as well as friends.

"These men," he said, "did their duty as they saw it. They will be missed by their friends and relations. Let us not dishonor their remains. May they rest in peace."

Then Sanchez, with a work party, set about salvaging weaponry from the wrecked cars. He hoped to be able to dismount both the heavy machine guns and the laser cannon from the two not too badly damaged vehicles. Su Lin and Grimes went to his sitting room to see what news programs, if any, they could find on the playmaster.

They were lucky.

Almost immediately they found a channel on which a grave-faced newscaster was keeping his listeners up to date on what had been happening.

". . . the criminal John Grimes. According to reports that we have received, Colonel Bardon, as instructed by President O'Higgins, sent a force of six armored cars, under Major Jackson, to arrest the ex-Governor. It seems that Grimes and his criminal associates have barricaded themselves in the Residence and are refusing to give themselves up to justice. Two of the military vehicles have returned to the city, to the barracks, where Major Jackson is making his report to Colonel Bardon. The remaining four are maintaining the siege, ensuring that the notorious ex-pirate and his gang do not escape to terrorize the countryside.

"A statement issued by Colonel Bardon assures us that the situation is well in hand."

There followed a report on a game of soccer. Su Lin switched channels. The commentator whom she found could have been an archbishop in mufti.

". . . must be made to realize that we, as a proud and independent planet, cannot, will not and must not accept as gubernatorial figureheads men of dubious character. . . ."

Su Lin switched channels again.

". . . minor rioting in the Vanzetti Plaza district . . ."

There were shots of police charging demonstrators, of demonstrators pelting police with rocks, bottles and other missiles. There was an explosion, after which the façade of a building crumbled in almost slow motion. A mist of tear gas hung over everything.

And there was the shouting: Grimes! Grimes! Grimes!

"Somebody is acting at last," said Su Lin happily. "I vish I could see who they are. Oh, hell! Here come the water cannon!"

And so that riot, thought Grimes, soon became a washout.

"We shan't get the real blowup," said Su Lin earnestly, "until there's a direct confrontation between you and Bardon, and you win. You've seen how O'Higgins and Bardon have handled the first engagement. Almost certainly there was TV coverage of the action; I shan't be at all surprised if Raoul finds cameras in the armored cars. But those shots will never be shown. Not unless—*until*—we win."

"And I can't see us winning until there's something better than that abortive riot we saw. And I can't see any sort of uprising until we show the people that we can beat Bardon." He thoughtfully filled and lit his pipe. "But why doesn't he use his ground-to-ground missiles? He must have some in his armory. . . ."

"Because he wants you alive. He's not fussy about the rest of us—but he wants *you*. There must be a show trial. And *he* will be on trial as well as you. He must be seen to have acted with moderation despite great provocation. He must present the image of statesman as well as soldier. And then, after you've been found guilty and deported, who will be Governor *de facto*, soon to become Governor *de jure*?

"Bardon, of course."

"I'd never have given him credit for that many brains," said Grimes.

"It's dear Estrelita that has the brains, not him."

"Estrelita may be the statesman, but not the soldier. What Bardon does next is our immediate worry. Mphm. My guess is another attack, by land, tomorrow morning. With full TV coverage—not be released unless things go well. If I were him I'd use a squadron of hover-tanks. . . ."

"Sergeant Martello cast doubts upon their serviceability."

"I hope he was right. I hope most sincerely that he was right. Meanwhile, we'll maintain full watches during the night and have all hands on deck at sunrise."

Chapter 45

Grimes—just in case Bardon did mount a bombing attack, either from aircraft or by rockets—ordered that bedding be shifted down from the ground floor into the basements of the Residence. He decided, however, that he would remain in his palatial quarters. Su Lin had almost convinced him that he would be more use to O'Higgins and Bardon alive than dead. He was willing to take chances with his own life—but not with the lives of others.

The armored cars had yielded two useful heavy machine guns and a good supply of ammunition. Their crews, however, had removed the crystals from the laser cannon before abandoning the vehicles, must have taken these with them. This was annoying, but Grimes felt a grudging respect for the men. They were not altogether devoid of the soldierly virtues.

The night was quiet.

The sentries, with their powerful night glasses, maintained their vigil on the roof. The only thing that they reported was a fire of some kind in the city. Grimes went up to look. It did not seem to be a very big conflagration. He and Su Lin caught a late night TV news session on the playmaster and there was no mention of it. There was no further mention of the riot that they had seen earlier. And, they learned to their amusement, Colonel Bardon's armored cars still had the Residence under siege. It would not be long, said the smug announcer, before the notorious pirate commodore was brought to justice.

Grimes turned in.

Su Lin turned in with him.

They knew, both of them, that no matter what the outcome would be they would not be enjoying much more time together. They had been thrown together by circumstances beyond their control—and other circumstances, inevitably, must soon send them on their separate ways.

They would enjoy what they had while they had it.

When Grimes awoke, in the early morning, Su Lin was no longer with him although her place in the bed was still warm. Had there been some kind of emergency? But had this been so he would have been called.

Then the lights came on as the girl entered the bedroom, bringing with her the tray with the steaming teapot, the cups, the sugar bowl and the lemon slices. They sipped the hot, fragrant drink in companionable silence, their naked bodies in close contact.

She said, at last, "You pirate chiefs do yourself well, don't you?"

"Only when they have pirate molls like you to look after them. . . ."

There was a gentle tapping at the door.

Wong Lee came in. He looked at the couple in the bed with an odd combination of regret and approval; certainly there was no censoriousness.

"Your Excellency," he said, "a body of troops approaches from the city. "

"Hover-tanks?" asked Grimes.

"No, Your Excellency. There are vehicles, but they seem to be personnel carriers."

"See that all weapon posts are manned. Oh—and better get

the galley staff to make plenty of tea and piles of sandwiches. We may have the chance to grab a bite before the shooting starts."

"All that is already in hand, Your Excellency."

"Good man!"

Grimes jumped out of the bed, ran through to the bathroom. He made a hasty toilet, despite the fact that he was joined there by Su Lin. He even found time to depilate, knowing that a scruffy, unshaven commanding officer does not inspire the same confidence as one who looks clean and bright and on top of the Universe. He dressed again in his Far Traveler Couriers uniform, with the pistol thrust under the red sash. Followed by the girl, who was clad in form-fitting black blouse and slacks, he went up to the lookout platform.

The sun was just up.

The column of personnel carriers, led by a command car, was still a long way off, approaching slowly along the winding road from the capital.

Raoul Sanchez came to him.

He said, "I've set up the two heavy MGs to cover the drive."

"What makes you think they'll use the drive, Raoul? Those are foot soldiers. They have almost the same freedom of movement over any sort of terrain as a hover-tank."

"I had to put the guns *somewhere*, sir."

"Sorry, Raoul. And, after all, guests usually try the front door first."

He could see quite clearly now, with the aid of the powerful binoculars, the men sitting in the personnel carriers. They were wearing full battle armor. This would restrict their freedom of movement but would protect them from almost anything short of a direct hit by a heavy artillery shell. Too, a laser cannon would fry them inside their carapaces but Grimes didn't have any laser cannon, only a few pistols.

He absentmindedly munched a ham sandwich that somebody had brought him. There wasn't enough mustard.

"They're stopping," said Sanchez unnecessarily.

They were stopping, had stopped.

Two tall figures got down from the command car.

Bardon, decided Grimes. Bardon, and . . .?

In spite of the all-concealing battle armor he knew that the other one was a woman by the way that she was moving.

So Estrelita O'Higgins was making political capital by being present at the kill.

Soldiers were disembarking from the troop carriers, forming up on the road. How many of them were there? Grimes swore under his breath. There must be at least five hundred of them. Five hundred well-armed (definitely), well-trained (possibly) professional soldiers against less than one fifth that number of rank amateurs. Even Grimes was an amateur in this sort of warfare. The Residence was not a spaceship.

Somebody must still be in the command car, using a sonic projector.

"Surrender! Come out, all of you, with your hands raised! Show a white flag to surrender!"

There was a small flagstaff on the lookout platform; so far as Grimes knew it was rarely used. But the halyards were intact. He went to them, cleared them.

"A flag . . ." he muttered. "A flag . . ."

"Sir, surely not . . ." Sanchez sounded heartbroken. "You're not showing the white flag, sir?"

"Who said anything about a *white* flag? I want something, anything, that's as unlike a white flag as possible!"

"Here!" said Su Lin, thrusting a bundle of some black cloth at him. He took it from her and suddenly realized that she had removed her shirt.

But it would do.

The black flag—the black flag of piracy, Grimes's enemies would say—rose jerkily to the masthead, stirring lazily in the light morning breeze.

Bardon put on a show.

Grimes watched it with grudging respect. There was more to the man than he had thought. He must have made a study of Australian history. Perhaps he had gotten the idea from Major Jackson's report to him on his conversation with Grimes, when Grimes had said, "You've come to the wrong shop this time, Major Johnston . . ." The New South Wales Corps, with rattling drums and squealing fifes, had marched on Bligh's Government House to place him under arrest. A drum and fife band preceded Bardon's Bullies, playing some derisory tune that Grimes could not identify.

And those musicians were unarmed, unarmored. Bardon was trading on Grimes's decency, gambling that he would not open fire on the bandsmen.

Grimes at last recognized the tune. *Lillibullero*. It had never been one of his favorites. Nonetheless, he thought wryly, the bandsmen deserved to be shot for murdering it.

But how would it look, how would it look on TV screens throughout the planet—and, eventually, on Earth—when men whose only weapons were fifes and drums were mown down by a man who had just hoisted, atop his castle, the black flag of piracy?

They were taking their time marching up the drive toward the main entrance of the Residence—the bandsmen in their colorful dress uniforms, Bardon behind them, with Estrelita O'Higgins striding, in step, beside him and, after them, the rank upon rank of robotlike troopers.

Down came the troopers, one, two, three . . .

And four, and five, and six, and . . .

Those drummers couldn't keep a tune. The beat was ragged, becoming more so. Men were having trouble keeping in step. But was that arhythmic throbbing coming from ground level? It was not. It was surging down from the sky in ragged waves.

Whistles shrilled.

The approaching army halted. Men looked upwards. Weapons were deployed to sweep the sky—but not fired. There was a ship there. A civilian ship, not a warship. An *Epsilon* Class star tramp. It would not be the first time in history that neutral onlookers had been present at a battle, as sensation-hungry voyeurs.

The spaceship steadily lost altitude. Was she going to land? Did Captain Agatha Prinn intend to rescue her one-time Commodore? *Keep out of this, you silly bitch!* Grimes was thinking, was saying aloud. *Keep out of it! If you do land you'll get shot up, and Bardon's story will be that you were caught in the crossfire . . .*

But *Agatha's Ark* was not landing. She hovered there, the cacaphony of her inertial drive deafening. And was that a cargo hatch opening in her dull, pitted side? It was. Things were falling out, tumbling earthwards, bursting as they hit the ground. Bardon's men stumbled through the stifling, white cloud, the machinery of their armor clogged by the fine particles. They looked like men caught in a sudden blizzard. Grimes was reminded of pictures he had seen of Napoleon's Retreat from Moscow.

There was a lull in the bombardment.

Grimes, accompanied by Su Lin and a half dozen of the Residence's domestic staff, ran out over the flour-caked lawn and grabbed the dazed Bardon and Estrelita O'Higgins, hustled them inside the building. Sanchez, with another party, captured Bardon's command car without firing a shot. In it was the TV equipment that would be covering the taking of the Residence.

It was covering, now, the ignominious defeat of Bardon's Bullies.

Very shortly afterward other TV units, in the city, were covering the riots that immobilized the remainder of the Terran garrison and drove the members of Estrelita O'Higgins's police into hiding. Those who were lucky.

Chapter 46

"I didn't think of it myself," admitted Agatha Prinn. "It was my agent, actually, Mr. Dennison of Starr, Dunleavy and Bowkett . . ."

"Dennison," said Su Lin, "is one of us. But go on, Captain Prinn."

"Mr. Dennison's idea was that I lift off as scheduled and then just sort of drift over the Residence, make a landing and snatch Grimes to safety. I said that I didn't fancy landing on anybody's lawn, no matter how big. I like to have something solid under my tail vanes when I set down. Why, I asked him, couldn't I, sort of accidentally, drop something on Bardon's boys? 'But you don't have any bombs,' he told me.

'You're just a star tramp, not a warship. And, in any case, if you play any active part in a battle, no matter on whose side, you'll be as big a pirate as your pal Grimes.' "

" 'I've a cargo of flour,' I told him. 'In bags. And, while it was being loaded, some ill-intentioned person planted an incendiary device in the middle of it. Luckily this will be discovered while I'm hovering over the Residence, to play my last respects to my old Commodore. So I will have to jettison cargo . . .' "

"Which you did," said Grimes. "I'm eternally grateful to you."

"Gratitude isn't enough, Commodore. Who's going to pay for the delay while I load a fresh cargo? Who's going to pay for the cargo that's been destroyed?"

"Lloyd's of London," Grimes told her. "I imagine that the jettison will come under the heading of General Average."

"But as the owner of *Agatha's Ark* I shall still be held liable for my share of the expense involved."

"I'm sure that Rear Admiral Damien will see you right.'

"Eventually. But the tide runs very slowly through official channels."

"Then, Agatha, would you accept a job on this world, a sinecure, for a very short time and at a *very* high salary? Terms to be negotiated."

"What is it?" she asked suspiciously.

"I'm the ruler of this world until things get sorted out. A new president has to be elected and approved. Until it's done I'm the only one with legal power. Liberia has no Examiner of Interstellar Masters and Mates. Yet. Do you want the post?"

"What's the catch?"

"There's no catch. All you have to do is supervise just one examination. Mine. As I read the law, a Liberian Master's Certificate of Competency will be good anywhere in the Galaxy. My real Certificate, issued at Port Woomera, was suspended by that Court of Inquiry.

"So . . ."

"You're an opportunistic bastard, Grimes," she said.

"Too right," he agreed smugly.

"So we have a farce of an examination, after which I issue a Certificate of Competency, autographed by myself. Are you sure that you wouldn't like to sign it too, as Governor? And then, just to oblige you still further, I put young Sanchez on my books as Fourth Mate so he can start getting in Deep Space time for *his* certificates. Is there anything else?"

"At the moment, no. But if there is, I'll let you know."

"Do just that." She grinned. "Well, Commodore, it was all an exciting break from the usual tramping routine, just as the privateering expedition was. But I have to get back to the spaceport to see what's happening to the *Ark*. I have a strong suspicion that Lloyd's surveyors will be sniffing around the hold, trying to find evidence of a fire. . . ."

"And will there be?" asked Grimes.

"Surely, Commodore, you would not expect me to defraud an insurance company?"

She finished her drink, got up and strode out of the Governor's sitting room. (Its windows repaired, the Residence was habitable again.) Grimes and Su Lin watched her go.

Agatha Prinn, thought Grimes, was one of the women whom he would always remember with affection. Just as—he looked at her, lounging gracefully in her chair—Su Lin would be.

"What will you do now?" she asked suddenly.

"I . . . I was thinking of resigning. As soon as they can arrange a relief for me. Once I have a valid Certificate of Competency I can take over command of my ship again. But . . . I'm not so sure. Suppose I don't resign. Suppose I stay here, as Governor . . ."

"If they let you."

He ignored this.

"Being Governor's Lady wouldn't be a bad life for a woman, Su Lin. And I'd need somebody like you, who knows the planet better than I do."

"I'm sorry," she told him. "Genuinely sorry. But PAT will be reassigning me. Dennison is arranging for my passage off Liberia now. But cheer up. We'll meet again some time. There's bound to be some complicated mess somewhere that will take the two of us to clear up. And I could never settle down on one world for keeps, any more than you could.

"You're lucky. Admit it. You'll soon be getting your precious *Sister Sue* back."

But I lost Fat Susie, he thought, *and even that lopsided apology for a balloon,* Little Susie. *And it will not be long before I lose Su Lin.*

Somehow, suddenly, his memories of the girl were more vivid, more real than her flesh and blood actuality. Their lovemaking in the wrecked airship . . . She standing beside him, proudly bare-breasted, while he hoisted the piratical black flag on the flagstaff on the roof of the Residence . . .

Damn it all, he would even miss having her lighting his pipe for him.

Was he, after all, so lucky?